FLYGIRL

FLYGIRL

Sherri L. Smith

G. P. PUTNAM'S SONS

PREVIOUS NOVELS BY

Sherri L. Smith:

Lucy the Giant
Sparrow
Hot, Sour, Salty, Sweet

ACKNOWLEDGMENTS

Many thanks to Professor Abe Ravitz for overseeing the seedling version of this novel and to my manager, Garrett Hicks, for recognizing what the story could become. Special thanks to my husband for his input and support. There's no crying in writing!

G. P. PUTNAM'S SONS
A division of Penguin Young Readers Group. Published by The Penguin Group.
Penguin Group (USA) Inc., 375 Hudson Street, New York, NY 10014, U.S.A.
Penguin Group (Canada), 90 Eglinton Avenue East, Suite 700, Toronto, Ontario M4P 2Y3, Canada
(a division of Pearson Penguin Canada Inc.).
Penguin Books Ltd, 80 Strand, London WC2R 0RL, England.
Penguin Ireland, 25 St. Stephen's Green, Dublin 2, Ireland (a division of Penguin Books Ltd.).
Penguin Group (Australia), 250 Camberwell Road, Camberwell, Victoria 3124, Australia
(a division of Pearson Australia Group Pty Ltd).
Penguin Books India Pvt Ltd, 11 Community Centre, Panchsheel Park,
New Delhi – 110 017, India.
Penguin Group (NZ), 67 Apollo Drive, Rosedale, North Shore 0632, New Zealand
(a division of Pearson New Zealand Ltd).
Penguin Books (South Africa) (Pty) Ltd, 24 Sturdee Avenue, Rosebank,
Johannesburg 2196, South Africa.
Penguin Books Ltd, Registered Offices: 80 Strand, London WC2R 0RL, England.

Library of Congress Cataloging-in-Publication Data
Smith, Sherri L.
Flygirl / Sherri L. Smith.
p. cm.
Summary: During World War II, a light-skinned African American girl "passes" for white
to join the Women Airforce Service Pilots. 1. Women Airforce Service Pilots (U.S.)—
Juvenile fiction. 2. World War, 1939–1945—Participation, Female—Juvenile fiction.
[1. Women Airforce Service Pilots (U.S.)—Fiction. 2. World War, 1939–1945—Participation,
Female—Fiction. 3. Pilots—Fiction. 4. African Americans—Fiction.] I. Title.
PZ7.S65932Fl 2009 [Fic]—dc22
2008025407
ISBN 978-0-399-24709-5
5 7 9 10 8 6

For my mother, Joan Marie.
You taught me to soar.

December 1941

Chapter 1

It's Sunday afternoon, and the phonograph player is jumping like a clown in a parade the way Jolene and I are dancing. We're cleaning the Wilson house and Nat King Cole's singing on the record. It sounds fine. This is one of the best places to clean because they have a big yard and no neighbors close enough to hear our ruckus. Otherwise, working on a Sunday would be a real drag. But the Wilsons are gone for the weekend and Mr. Wilson said he'd pay extra for a clean house when he gets back. With Christmas just a few weeks away, the money will come in handy.

I am knee-deep in Murphy Oil Soap, washing Otis Wilson's sticky fingerprints off his mama's fine oak banister, when Jolene comes waltzing down the stairs with the laundry.

"I swear, these people must change their clothes every hour on the hour, every day. I've never seen such a mess of laundry in my life. Ida Mae Jones, hurry up with that polishing and come help me."

"I am hurrying. If they'd stop giving Otis jam for breakfast, I wouldn't be cleaning this railing every week."

"If they stopped giving Otis jam for breakfast, he'd cry for a week," she says.

Otis Wilson is the most spoiled white boy in New Orleans. Just a year younger than Jolene and me, but at seventeen, he's still a slobbering mess. Jolene says it's because he's soft in the head. I think it has more to do with being spoiled.

"You think he'd enlist if we ever join this war?"

Jolene laughs her big horse laugh. "Girl, can you see that little jam jar in a uniform? I mean he's big enough, for a white boy, and not bad looking, either, if you like the pasty type, but taking orders and holding a gun—we'd be better off surrendering than sending him to fight."

"Too true, too true." I laugh, thinking about Otis's broadbellied self in a uniform. "Think they've got maids in the army to wipe the jam off his rifle?"

It's Jolene's turn to chuckle. "Now stop making me laugh and get to work. We're going to have to clean this house a hundred more times if you're going to get the money to go to Chicago."

"Don't I know it." I sigh. At home, we get by running our little berry farm, but getting by is far from getting rich. Even with cleaning houses full-time since Jolene and I graduated high school in June, the saving is coming slow. Sometimes it seems like my purse is nothing but a sieve with money running through it like water. "The way I see it, another month of solid work and I'll be set. Then all I have to do is find a way to get my mother to let me go to Chicago by myself."

"Or work another six months and take her with you."

"Oh, I can see that now," I say, rolling my eyes. "'Mama, you wait right here, I'm gonna go take my pilot's test.' She only lets me fly now because Grandy's with me. She hates to fly."

"Girl, I know better than to tell you to give it up. You've got the flying bug just as sure as your daddy did, but some days I think it's more trouble than it's worth. More money than it's worth, too."

"Bessie Coleman had to go all the way to France to learn

2

how to fly just because she was colored." She was one of my idols—the Negro Amelia Earhart. "She was nothing more than a hairdresser, but she did it. So why can't I? I already know how to fly, Jolene. If I can't get my license in Tuskegee, at least Chicago's closer than Paris."

Jolene shrugs over her armful of dirty shirts. "If you say so."

"I do."

Just remembering my first time in a plane, in my daddy's old Curtiss JN-4 "Jenny," I get goose bumps. Nothing else on God's green earth does that to me. Of course it's worth it.

Last year, just before I turned seventeen, Mama's daddy, Grandy, convinced her to let me go to Tuskegee to take my pilot's test. I'd taken over Daddy's side business of dusting crops, but I needed my license. Daddy would have taken me, had he lived. I'd already flown over forty hours with him, and I had passed the written exam by mail just before he died. All I needed to do was go up in a real plane with a certified instructor. Mama kept Daddy's promise by letting me go.

Grandy and I showed up real early at the airfield. I was so excited I thought I'd have to run to the restroom and pee every five minutes. Grandy was as calm as could be, though, and that helped me a lot. The instructor, a Mr. Anderson, showed up, and he was a white man, with blue eyes and a firm jawline. I'd heard he had passed other colored pilots at the base, and I thought he looked tough, but fair.

Well, I said a little prayer asking Daddy for help, and I took that instructor up in the test plane. It was a Jenny, like Daddy had taught me on, easy as slipping into an old sweater. We did rolls, and loops, and landings, and I could hardly stop smiling because I knew I'd done good.

But when we climbed out of that plane, Mr. Anderson looked at me and said, "You can fly, no doubt about it. But no woman's gonna get a license out of me. Go home, Miss Jones. You've failed."

I stood there, staring at his strong jawline and his blue eyes, and if looks could set a fire, he'd have been a three-alarm blaze by the time I was done. Grandy, who's seen more than his share of wrongness, just took my arm and said, "S'all right, honey. We've got better places to go."

That better place is Chicago, the Coffey School of Aeronautics. Owned and run by colored people, like me. Teaching men and women alike. No matter how long it takes me, that's what I'm working toward.

"Stop daydreaming, Ida," Jolene says, disappearing into the washing room. "Hurry down here so we can talk." Her voice carries from the back of the house. I finish scrubbing the banister, still trying to figure out how to get to Chicago without letting Mama catch on. She doesn't like the idea of me flying. She only lets me dust crops because it pays a little and Grandy comes with me. Daddy is the only person who could convince her that I'd be okay by myself. But since he's gone, I'm on my own. As far as Mama is concerned, going to the big city by myself is crazy enough. She'd call me a damn fool if she knew it was because I wanted to fly.

"Finally," Jolene says as I round the corner to the washing room. "Grab a tub—this is old-fashioned dirt in these socks. It'll take a washboard to clean them."

She pours boiling water from a kettle into the washer and runs those socks through about a hundred times each. Mr. Wilson fancies himself a golfer, but you'd think he was a gopher with all the dirt he brings home with him from the

4

course. The socks are a hopeless cause. Still, I put them in a galvanized tub with bleach to get them white and bluing to get them even whiter. Laundry is my least favorite part of housekeeping. The smell of the soap and chemicals stays in your skin for a week. Sometimes, on a hot day, I feel like I sweat bleach.

"Now, about Chicago," Jolene says, sounding just like her mother. Miss Tara is a math teacher, and whenever she puts herself to any sort of problem, math or otherwise, you just know she'll solve it. Jolene isn't as reliable as her mama, but it is comforting to have her on my side, just the same.

"Here's what to do. Tell your ma that you're visiting my mama's sister in Natchez, with me. I'll even go see my old aunt to keep your story straight."

"You make it sound like a sacrifice," I say, "when everybody knows your aunt lives across the river from the city. And that she falls asleep early every single night, Miss I'll Be Back Before She Knows I'm Gone."

"Why should I suffer for you?" Jolene raises an eyebrow and laughs. "Besides, we can't all fly airplanes. Some of us have got to keep both feet on the ground. New Orleans is a good place to do just that."

"On the ground, Jolene? On the dance floor of a jazz club is more like it."

Jolene grins, the gap showing in her smile. She pats her Marcel curls beneath the gray scarf that is part of our cleaning uniform. "Don't I know it, don't I know it." Jolene has a fantasy of leaving Slidell to sing in a New Orleans nightclub. Trouble is, she has no voice for it. So she spends her days in the city with me, washing clothes and cleaning houses.

"Jolene, you are nothing but trouble." I reach over her head and turn on the radio we have stashed on the laundry room shelf. There's a ball game on, so I fiddle with the knobs.

"Put some music on. *Sammy Kaye's Sunday Serenade* should be on."

"You've already got the record going, and every radio station's starting up with Christmas carols. Besides, I just want to hear the news."

I twist the dial until the news comes in good and strong. The news is much the same as it was last night. The Germans and Russians are fighting in subzero temperatures, and Japan's moving troops in the Far East despite our peace talks. Jolene sighs and goes back to scrubbing the laundry. I turn the volume down so we can talk over the news and the phonograph playing upstairs.

"Did you know the Russians let their women fly military planes?" I say. "In England, too. Ferrying planes for the air force. Isn't that a kick?"

"Loony's more like it. What girl in her right mind wants to be flying around in a war zone?" Jolene rolls her eyes at me and my face goes hot. "Baby, you're not only fly crazy, you're war crazy, too. That's a bad combination."

I cut off the radio to keep the peace, and Jolene starts singing along with the record. It's nearly four o'clock by the time we're finished with the Wilsons'. We yank off our head scarves and shake out our hair on the back steps of the house. We button up our sweaters against the slight December chill. Jolene pulls her copy of the house key from her pocket and locks the place up tight.

"I sure hope Mr. Wilson is grateful for the Sunday cleaning," Jolene says, dropping the key into her bag. "I need a new pair of stockings."

"Why do you waste your money, Jolene? Silk is for show-girls and debutantes."

"And young ladies who hope to catch a man someday. You'd do well to get yourself a pair, or you'll end up an old maid."

"Takes one to know one."

"Speak for yourself," she says. I turn to see her smiling her prettiest little smile at some city road worker across the street. The boy can't be much older than we are, and he sure looks all right in his overalls and cap. It takes me a minute to recognize him as Danny Taylor from our elementary school.

"Danny Taylor, is that you?" I call out.

Jolene frowns and drops the able-Grable sexy act. "Aw, heck, Dan. What you doing, looking all grown up like that?"

We wait for a break in the traffic and jog across the cobblestones. Poydras Street is a leafy place, sheltered by live oaks with crepe myrtle trees growing in between. Danny Taylor smiles at us when we get closer. He's got a nice smile, broad with teeth as white as milk in a strong brown face.

"Ida Mae Jones, I thought you was a white woman walking over there with that fine light skin and pretty brown hair."

My hand goes instantly to my curls, loose and smooth, like my daddy's. The kind of curls Jolene calls "good hair." Not tight and hard to handle, like hers.

"What about my hair?" Jolene asks, eyebrows arched. "And my fine *brown* skin?"

Danny grins, unaware he's offended her or me, for that matter. I'm shy of my fair looks, and Jolene's more than a little jealous. "Well, that's how I knew she wasn't white. You're dressed the same, and Jolene, you're as black as a good cup of coffee."

7

"Best coffee you'll never have," she says, and turns her nose up in the air.

"Well, it was good to see you, Danny," I say, anxious to leave.

"What's your rush? I haven't seen either of you two since the eighth grade."

"Well, some of us stuck around and graduated," Jolene snaps. She's decided not to like Danny Taylor.

"Well, some of us had to work," Danny says right back. At school, I had known Danny mostly through my brother. I remember when Thomas came home one day and told us his friend had to quit school to help his family pay the bills. Jolene knows it, too.

"How's your mama?" I ask.

"Fine, fine. Doctor says she has a sugar problem, but she's doing all right."

"Glad to hear it," I say.

Jolene's folded up her arms now. She looks at me and frowns.

"Well, Danny, like I said, it was nice seeing you, but we've got to get the trolley and all before the buses shut down. Sundays are always awful tight."

"Say hi to your brother for me."

"I will." Jolene is dragging me away now. I stumble on the pavement, catch myself, and wave goodbye.

"You just keep waving goodbye to Joe Corn over there," she says in a clipped voice. "Girl, you can do better than smiling up in his face like that."

"Jolene, I was being polite. You could take a lesson or two. What's wrong with you?"

Jolene stops in her tracks and screws up her face so tight,

8

I think she's going to cry. "I don't know," she says unhappily. "It's just . . . am I pretty at all? He didn't even look at me. Just Little Miss Pretty Hair and Her Creamy White Skin. I love you, Ida, but he just made me so mad."

"Me, too." I put an arm around her. We stand there, half hugging, with nothing left to say. Daddy once told me color didn't matter as much to folks up north. Light-skinned like me and him or dark like Mama and Jolene, up there he said they'd treat all colored folks the same, like we were all white. I'd sure like to see that, 'cause down here, color seems to be the only place it's at.

The trolley down St. Charles Avenue is empty of colored folks. Jolene and I sit to the back and watch the big houses roll by. St. Charles Avenue is the prettiest place on earth, a green tunnel of live oak trees arching across two paved roads, the trolley running down the middle on its cables. Only the richest, whitest folks live up here. We trundle past Audubon Park and the university, same as always, but inside this trolley car something is different. Jolene nudges me with her foot.

"It's like a funeral in here," she says. It's true. Usually, the trolley is buzzing with laughter, chatter, and just plain noise. But now, it's like a storm is coming. The few people on board are deadly quiet.

"Sooner we get home, the better," I tell her. The trip up Carrollton Avenue is just as slow. At the last stop, we hop off and run across the wide street to catch the bus back to Slidell.

There's more folks sitting in the back of the bus. One of them, a dignified-looking, coffee-colored gentleman in a neatly pressed suit, has a newspaper.

"Excuse me, sir. What's the news?" I ask him.

He looks up at me, startled, and starts to stand. There are plenty of seats, though. Jolene has saved me one.

"Ma'am, I'm sorry," he says, rising.

"Oh, no, no. I just noticed you had the paper. Does it say what's going on? Everyone seems so . . ."

He looks at me a moment longer and settles back into his seat, seeing that I'm colored, too.

"Ah, sorry, baby girl. You haven't heard? We've been attacked by the Japanese."

Chapter 2

My mother is standing on the front porch, waiting for me.

"Ida Mae, Ida Mae, get in here, quickly!" As if the war had already reached our front door. I run, my shoulder bag swinging against my ribs, and climb the stairs, into her arms.

"What happened, Mama? What's happened?"

"Come inside, it's on the radio. They'll play it again."

The radio sits on the sideboard in the kitchen, where Mama listens to music while she cooks the family meals, humming and singing the whole day through. Mama's daddy, Grandy, is at the table now, and his big head with its close-cropped white hair is bowed over his clasped farmer's hands, like he's praying. My little brother, Abel, is sitting at the table like it was Sunday school, his seven-year-old face solemn and unsure. He watches me with round eyes as I sit next to him. Mama pulls up a fourth chair. Music is playing, just like any other day. We sit there, hands clasped like Grandy's, until a news bulletin breaks in.

"This is an NBC news bulletin. The Japanese have bombed our naval base at Pearl Harbor, Hawaii, this morning. In an unexpected attack, a squadron of Japanese planes came out of the sky, dropping bombs on the naval base and the island of Oahu. The president is expected to speak tomorrow morning. This can only be taken as an act of war. We now return to our regularly scheduled program."

Grandy sighs, long and low, and raises his head. "They'll be wanting Thomas," he says.

I stare at him. "What do you mean?"

Mama shakes her head. "But there are so many others who will *want* to go. He's not meant to be a soldier. He's going to be a surgeon. Will they really . . ." She trails off, tears settling in the worry lines around her eyes.

"Don't worry, Mama," I say quickly. "Thomas knows we need him here. Besides, Hawaii is a long way off from Louisiana. Europe is, too. They can't touch us here." I stand up and put my arms around her. She holds on to me tight, the way I used to hold on to her when I was little. It scares me, but it's all right. We'll be okay.

Grandy cuts off the radio. "President don't speak until tomorrow."

"Supper's almost ready," Mama says, pulling away from me. She straightens her apron, wipes her eyes on a corner, and smiles at me.

"Ida Mae Jones, what have you done to your hair?"

I feel the thick wave of it and realize I forgot to comb it out after taking my head scarf off. "Oh, we were cleaning. I'll brush it. Does it look bad?"

"Girl, you'd leave your head in the dishwater, if you weren't paying attention," Mama says. She's okay now. "Good thing you got your daddy's hair, else you'd be looking like a feather bed. Now go wash up and help me finish the potatoes. You've got to have an appetite after all the running you must've done to get home today."

"Yes, ma'am," I say. And we move about the house like we have a thousand times before, Grandy in the living room shuffling cards to play Old Maid with Abel, Mama and I side by side at the kitchen sink. Sailors are dying in Hawaii, women are flying overseas. But everything is the same for the Joneses of Slidell, Louisiana.

That night, after dinner, I go into the barn and pull the cover off of my father's airplane. Even in the dark, she's beautiful, with her stacked yellow wings, blue-and-white-striped tail, and red propeller. She shines like new. You take care of a plane, Daddy used to say, and it will take care of you. It's dark in the barn, but I know the Jenny like the back of my hand. I climb into her open cockpit and settle myself inside. The leather seat cups my back and I rest my head, looking at the rafters up above. The war is here, flown in by Japanese fighter planes. I close my eyes and wonder if it will ever be safe for me to fly again.

Monday morning dawns clear and blue. It was probably just as blue over Hawaii when the Japanese bombs started to fall. Mama keeps us busy while we wait for my big brother to come home. Thomas is a medical student at Meharry Medical College in Nashville, Tennessee. But he's taking a leave of absence after what happened yesterday. At a time like this, everyone should be home. I clear away the breakfast dishes, wash them, dry them, put them in the cupboard, and try not to think.

Grandy disappears into the barn and comes back with a piece from his tractor. He turns on the radio, then sits at the kitchen table and begins to dismantle the greasy bits of metal over a piece of newspaper. Abel sits on the living room floor with one of the barn cats and some of Mama's yarn. Mama never lets the cats inside. But today, she doesn't seem to mind.

She's knitting a scarf for Thomas. "Christmas is almost here," she says, and I can hear the choke in her voice. All of us fiddle with our hands and listen to the president speak.

I think of those warplanes, flying over American houses, American families. I listen to the sky over our kitchen and pray. On the radio, Mr. Roosevelt's speech ends. A thousand miles away in Washington, the Congress erupts in applause. For me, there is nothing to clap for.

Thomas reaches the house, dusty and tired. He runs up the stairs and throws the door open as the radio ovation fades. Yesterday, we were a nation at peace. And now we are at war.

Thomas sweeps Mama into a hug.

"Oh, baby, I'm so glad you're home," Mama says, holding him tight. She wrings her hands as my big brother takes off his jacket and hangs up his hat on one of the hooks by the door. "How could all of this have happened on a Sunday?"

"It doesn't seem right," Thomas agrees. We have no answers. None at all.

"Right or wrong, we'll make it through," Grandy says. "Good to see you, son." He and Thomas grip hands. Seeing the two of them together makes me wish my daddy was here.

Thomas clears his throat. "I made a decision on my way over here. I'm enlisting."

The room gets so quiet I can hear the clock ticking on the mantel. I look from Mama to Grandy to Thomas. Mama is the first to speak.

"You'll eat lunch first." Her face is gray, but she keeps her dignity. She pats Thomas on the shoulder, tells Abel to get rid of that cat, and goes into the kitchen, humming.

"How you doing, Clayfoot?" Thomas grins at me. His smile is contagious. I hug my big brother.

14

"Don't be stupid, Tommy," I tell him. "You can't enlist. We need you here." But he doesn't listen.

"It won't be just the Japs," he says into my hair. "The Nazis'll be next. And the Negro doesn't stand a chance in a world run by them."

I nod as though I understand, but I don't. Like those women flying over Europe, it seems like a picture show, far away and unreal. "It's almost Christmas, Tommy. There's a whole ocean between here and the Nazis. Let the ocean do its job."

Thomas pulls back, and he's frowning now. My brother's gotten taller and more handsome since he's been at school. He looks more like Daddy every time I see him. The same strong hands, the same warm eyes. Only the curlier hair and pale coffee skin are different.

"The ocean didn't stop the Japanese," he says.

My heart sinks into my stomach. "Tommy, please."

"Clayfoot." He uses the pet name again. "You sure are just a kid after all. Which makes it harder for me to ask what I need to, but I'll ask it, anyway. I'm going to join up in this war, a lot of young men are, and I'll be leaving you all. Not like for school in Nashville, but far, far away. And Abel is too young to do this for me, and Grandy is too old. So it falls to you, Ida Mae."

My heart pounds; he is serious, serious if he's calling me by my given name.

"Take care of Mama, Ida. Take care of Grandy, of Abel, of yourself, too. There are important things in this world that a man's got to do. But we do it for our families. I'll fight for our country, to keep you all safe. You just make sure everyone's still here when I get back."

15

I want to close my eyes. I don't want to see Thomas standing there, looking so serious, as serious as he did kneeling by that tractor the day Daddy died. I never wanted to see that look on his face again, but it's there. I grab his hand and try to smile.

"You're too serious sometimes," I want to say. But I can't. Instead, I end up giving him another hug.

"I promise. We'll be all right. As long as you are, too."

He laughs then and shakes my hand very formally. "It's a deal."

Neither one of us knows we've made promises we can't keep.

It was a hot day in August when Daddy died. I was sixteen years old. Thomas was nineteen. He and Daddy were working the east field, turning the old husks into the soil, when something went wrong. The tractor flipped over on top of Daddy, and Thomas ran three whole miles to get help. Mama and I came racing out of the house as Thomas flew past us, pointing and hollering, running to get more men to lift the tractor.

He was too late, but not too late to hear Daddy, with his last breath, talking to Mama and me. She was holding his hand like she could keep his soul from leaving his body, but he just squeezed it back and smiled. "Stella, look at that boy run," he said, seeing Thomas come up all sweaty and scared, ten men and the doctor behind him, ready to pull that tractor off of Daddy. "Did you see that?" Daddy said. "Look at old Thomas. He sure can fly."

Thomas flew, all right; he flew right out of Slidell. He was never going to be a dirt farmer, he said, set to die in the tracks of his plow. He got as far as Meharry, where he is learning to be a doctor so he will never have to run three miles for one again.

And now my big brother's running all the way to the war.

After dinner, Grandy is the first one to speak.

"Now, be sure you get posted as an officer," he tells Thomas, jabbing the table with a blunt finger. Grandy fought in the trenches in the Great War. "That'll keep you out of the worst of it, even in a Negro unit."

"Yes, sir." Thomas nods. Grandy's got everyone's attention.

"Shouldn't be too hard," Grandy says. "A half-schooled doctor is better than no doctor at all. That should get you a commission. You'll be all right, as long as you're not in the trenches. A colored man in the trenches is worse than dead."

Mama goes real quiet. She was two years younger than me when Grandy went off to France. She remembers it well enough, I know, but she never talks about it. Thomas puts his hand over hers on the table. I don't know what to say to anybody, so I go get Abel and bring him upstairs for bed.

"Ida, what's gonna happen to Thomas?" Abel asks me when I tuck him in.

"Nothing, Abel. Nothing."

Abel fixes me with those sharp brown eyes of his and frowns. "Don't tell stories, Ida. I been to the picture shows. I seen the war reels. I know what it means when he says he's signing up."

I sit still and look at my little brother. Abel is just a kid. He shouldn't know this stuff. "Yeah, well, Tommy is pretty smart, don't you think? Training to be a doctor and all. I think he'll be helping other soldiers stay strong and not in any real danger himself."

"I guess." Abel lies back beneath the quilted coverlet Mama made for him from Daddy's old sweaters. "You're not going anywhere, are you?"

"Now, where am I supposed to go?" I ask him, laughing. But in the pit of my stomach, I realize I did have someplace to go. Chicago. Chicago, to prove I can fly.

My heart sinks when I didn't think it could get any lower. The dreams of one little colored girl don't matter to a world at war. But they matter to me. I swallow my sorrow and kiss Abel on the forehead.

"Go to bed, silly. And stop asking fool questions."

"Good night, Ida Mae."

"Good night, Abel James." I wrinkle my nose and he giggles.

I cut off the light as I'm leaving, and I hear Abel singing in his seven-year-old voice, real soft, so he thinks I can't hear him. "Shoo, fly, don't bother me. Shoo, fly, don't bother me. Shoo, fly, don't bother me. For I belong to somebody . . ."

I smile in the dark at the top of the stairway. Thomas taught me that song. Used to sing it to me in that same reedy little boy voice whenever something was bothering me or making me sad.

"Troubles are like flies, Ida," he told me. "You just have to brush them away."

"Shoo, fly, don't bother me," I repeat softly in the dark at the top of the stairs, struggling to keep the loss I feel at bay. Chicago will happen someday, maybe after this war. "Shoo,

18

fly, don't bother me. Shoo, fly, don't bother me. For I belong to somebody. I feel, I feel, I feel like a morning star; I feel, I feel, I feel like a morning star. Shoo, fly, don't bother me. Shoo, fly, don't bother me. Shoo, fly, don't bother me. For I belong to somebody."

August 1943

Chapter 3

The war is not going well. Thomas has been gone for more than a year and a half, and his letters are few and far between. It's for the best, I know. Mama couldn't read more of the kind of news he'd been sending. We'd barely started fighting Japan when Germany and Italy jumped on top of us, too. The whole world's gone to war.

Thomas is a field medic for the colored infantry in the South Pacific, where we're fighting the Japanese. I don't know how he gets along. He survived the Battle of Midway just months after enlisting, and we thanked our lucky stars. But our Thomas is still on the other side of the world, where boys are dying like flies in the August heat. This war looks like it's here to stay.

There's more work now that the war effort is on. In addition to the Wilsons, Jolene and I are cleaning for the LaRoches and the Thibodeaux family on Camp Street. The money's good, but I'm not any closer to Chicago. Daddy's Jenny is up on blocks in the barn for the time being. Airplanes and fuel are reserved for the war effort, not for colored girls who dust crops without their licenses. There's not much else for me to do these days except for clean houses and keep my promise to Thomas.

For two whole days, Jolene and I do nothing but collect silk stockings from all the women we work for and turn them in to the army parachute program. Jolene looked like to die when she had to give up her sackful, but it's for a good cause, so she's being stoic about it.

Seems there's a different way to help every day. Mama's been saving up all her bacon grease because the military says they can use it to make ammunition and medicine. I don't know how bacon fat can kill a Nazi unless you feed it to him by the bucketful, but they've got some use for it, anyway. Mama likes to think Thomas has helped some wounded soldiers with the grease she donates at the butcher shop. Even Grandy has gotten into the effort, turning in the spare tires from our tractor. Rubber was one of the first things to be rationed, and any little bit that's nonessential goes into the war machine.

With everything so rare these days, the government has issued ration books through the elementary school. Mama and I got ours from Abel's teacher, Mrs. Marvin. She checked our names off her list and gave us four little books of twenty-eight stamps each, one book for everybody in our family. Every time we buy a rationed item, the cashier rips out a stamp to show we've used up our share. Just before Christmas, they added coffee to the ration list.

Today, Mrs. Wilson gives me and Jolene her ration book to get her some sugar. "I thought about what you said, Ida. I'd better get it now before the well's run dry."

I was actually only repeating what Mama had said to me the week before. Rationing's got her remembering what she learned in the Depression: "Stock up, Ida Mae, or you'll be like that grasshopper come wintertime." I nod at Mrs. Wilson and smile. "That's right, Mrs. Wilson. It'll keep in the cupboard real nice, anyway."

"You girls run along and let me know if you see anything else that might be getting low."

The day is so humid, our dresses stick to our skin the minute we step outside. Jolene and I walk the three blocks to the corner grocery store, swinging our shopping bags over our shoulders.

"Why the long face, Miss Jones?" Jolene asks me in a joking voice.

"Nothing, I guess. We got another letter from Thomas today."

Jolene shakes her head. "I wish I had some fine young Negro writing letters home to me," she says with a cluck of her tongue. I roll my eyes.

"Jolene, we're talking about my *brother* here," I remind her.

She gives me a look, raising her eyebrow. "I know. He's fine."

"Oh, no! You are something else!" I exclaim.

"I know that, too," Jolene replies, shaking her hips. "You can put *that* in your next letter to him for me."

I laugh in spite of myself. "You're terrible."

Jolene smiles. "Don't tell him that part. Besides, you're smiling again, aren't you?"

"Yeah." I sigh. Just pointing it out makes my smile fade. "In his letter, Thomas said things are bad out there. Not in so many words, but I can tell."

"That's war," Jolene says, as if she's lived through more than one. But I know she's right.

"Still, it seems silly. Thomas has men dying on his stretchers every day, and we sit here hoarding sugar and saving rubber, like that's gonna make a difference."

Jolene shrugs. "What else can we do? We don't fight the wars. And I wouldn't want to, anyway."

"Nobody wants to, Jolene. But don't you think we could be doing something more? There are nurses overseas. And there's the Women's Army Corps. Those women must be doing something to help out if the army's using them."

Jolene swings her bag onto her hip and fixes me with a look. "Now, I *know* you're not thinking of joining the WACs. You want to be a secretary, you can do that right here at home."

"They do more than that," I protest. "Like radio operators and such."

Jolene shakes her head. "Ida, those women are either man hungry or funny in the head. No, ma'am, we are exactly where we belong."

"On the corner of St. Charles and Camp Street, loading up on sugar? Jolene Dupree, you sure do aim low."

Jolene harrumphs and keeps walking. "Call it what you will, but I'll be alive and looking good when those boys come home again. Remind them of what they've been fighting for."

We are in front of the grocery store now, but Jolene's not done reprimanding me. We step to the side of the doorway to let an old lady pass us by. Jolene looks up at me and I notice, for the first time, sorrow in her face. "Men do the fighting, Ida Mae. Women take care of the home. You can be proud of that. It's enough. Too much, sometimes, but it's more than enough."

We stare at each other in the afternoon light, the door to the market swinging open and shut as other women, clutching their ration books, go by.

"I'm just worried about Thomas," I say finally.

"I know, sugar, but it doesn't do much good. You remember that Danny Taylor from school?"

"Of course." I nod. "He still doing roadwork for the city?"

"No. I heard he shipped off last month. Headed to France."
A shadow crosses Jolene's face. "I think about the last time
we saw him. I should have been nicer to him."

We stand together a little longer in the thick heat filtering
through the leaves of live oak above us.

"Missus is waiting," Jolene finally says. We go into the store
to stock up on sugar for the Wilsons' morning coffee.

The sorrowful mood from the afternoon is still sitting on me
when I get home. It's too warm to cook inside the house.
Mama and Grandy are keeping cool on the front porch. In
the kitchen, I find the ham sandwich Mama has made for me
from Sunday's supper and eat it quietly with a glass of milk.
The newspaper is lying on the table. I haven't read the front
pages in months. I don't want to read any more about the war.
Instead, I hunt for the recipes page and learn thrifty new
ideas for using Spam and an apple pie recipe that doesn't use
apples.

"Abel's upstairs," Mama calls to me from the front porch.
"Why don't you see him to bed for me, Ida."

"All right, Mama." I fold up the newspaper and clean up the
dishes before trudging up the stairs. The air is warmer at the top
of the landing, but the windows are all open, and the slightest
breeze is pulling through the upper rooms of the house. Abel is
sitting on his bed, already in his pajamas, playing with a wooden
horse the size of a small kitten.

"Hi, Abel. Mama says it's time for bed."

"Hey, Ida Mae." Abel's smile sparkles. He pulls his knees
up to his chin and draws the covers up around him. "It's too
hot for a quilt, but it makes me sleep."

"Sleep makes you sleep," I tell him, and sit on the edge of

his bed. "The quilt is just a good reminder. How was class today?" School starts early in Slidell so kids can be home to help with the spring and summer harvests.

Abel shrugs. "It was all right. It's too hot for school, too. I got you something, though."

"What is it?" I ask him, half afraid it'll be some frog or worm he found in the fields. But Abel surprises me by reaching beneath his pillow and pulling out the front section of today's newspaper.

"Mrs. Marvin read it to us. On the third page. She said it was all part of what we can do for the war effort."

I turn up the lamp beside Abel's bed and search for the article. My eyes widen when I see it. *Free a Man to Fight*, the headline says. *Mrs. Jackie Cochran, the cosmetics mogul and celebrated pilot, has joined forces with the United States Army to train women as ferrying pilots, freeing men to fight in the war effort overseas. The program will be called the Women Airforce Service Pilots, an offshoot of the Women's Auxiliary Ferrying Squadron, begun by Nancy Love.*

I squint at the fine print in the yellow glow of the lamp. I can't believe a word I've just read. I read it again. And a third time. My heart starts to thump a little louder in my chest.

"They're doing it, Ida," Abel says excitedly. "Making women pilots, just like those Russian ladies you're always talking about. Only ours get to fly planes, not brooms."

"Well, I'll be," I say, but my mind is a thousand miles away, at Sweetwater, Texas, where the training is taking place. Sweetwater must be nothing but wide-open sky. I take a deep, calming breath. Don't get ahead of yourself, Ida Mae.

"You could do it, I bet," Abel says, yawning. I look at the clock on the dresser. It's getting late.

"You need to sleep, little man." I kiss Abel on his smooth brown forehead and again on each cheek. "You're something else," I tell him. I kiss him again, until he starts to squirm. "Thank you," I whisper into the shell of his ear. "Good night!"

I run down the stairs as fast as I can. On the front porch, I race by Mama and Grandy.

"I'm going to Jolene's, Mama," I call out as I pass by. "I'll be back before ten."

"Ten?" I hear Mama say. "Ida Mae . . ." But I don't hear any more. I've got to tell Jolene about this. It's what I've been looking for. It's a sign from heaven above.

I don't go to Jolene's, though. I'm halfway through the strawberries when I realize she won't even be awake by the time I get there. Instead, I head out into the fields where my daddy used to work so hard and lie down between the rows of sweet green leaves. I look up at the sky, the same sky my daddy loved.

Daddy had gotten it into his head one day back in 1934 that a crop duster plane was the way to go for farmers. It was the future. Sure, they'd only been around a few years, they were dangerous, and, quite frankly, only a handful of colored people knew how to fly. Yes, there was Bessie Coleman, she was one of the first, and a few people up north, but in Slidell, Louisiana, heck, in all of the South, not a single colored man or woman could fly.

So, Daddy went north. I was only eleven years old, Thomas was fourteen, and Abel was still a bump in Mama's belly. Mama was mad that Daddy was leaving her on some fool's errand, as she put it. That's the year Grandy came to live with us. He looked after us, and the farm, while Daddy was away.

Even with her own daddy there, Mama was lonely. Airplanes were dangerous and she was scared. She dressed in black the whole time he was gone, practicing to be a widow, she said. But Daddy had his ideas and wouldn't let them go. He took the train up to Chicago and enrolled in the aeronautics school, a new flying school set up by two colored men who were also licensed engineers. Daddy worked his tail off, he told us in his letters. At the end of five hundred hours of hard work, he was licensed to fly.

Daddy came back in a whirl of dust and wind with a trailer carrying his "big surprise." I remember that day like yesterday. Daddy was waving his hat like a circus ringmaster, looking tall and handsome. Mama was big as a watermelon with Abel and Thomas was scowling. He was still mad at Daddy for making Mama unhappy. I was so excited I shifted from foot to foot in my gingham dress. It was, Daddy told us with a wink, a solemn occasion.

Once we were all gathered around, he whipped off the tarp and—ta da! There she stood, in all her glory—Daddy's very own plane. Her name was Jenny, actually a Curtiss JN-4. It was the same kind of plane Bessie Coleman had flown in, Daddy told us proudly. It was also the plane she was flying in when it malfunctioned and she died, Mama added.

Daddy didn't mind, though; he was like a sunny day that could not be dimmed by clouds. After much fanfare and a thorough once-over of all of the moving parts, he took us up in that Jenny one by one. Grandy went up first, serious-faced and silent. When he landed, he declared that it would be a good way to spray the crops rather than have to worry away crickets and cicadas by hand. Thomas came back down smiling, and even Mama went up, though she swore that Abel was born early because of the fright that flying gave her.

Me, I went up last. And I never wanted to come down again. First the driveway, then the farm, then all the fields of cotton and alfalfa and all of Slidell dropped away until it looked like the quilt on my bed, big patches of green and brown, stained with shiny swampland here and there. For the first time in my eleven years, I felt like a giant, like I was tall as the sky.

So, whenever Daddy was willing, I flew with him. A few of the farmers in the area saw Daddy flying and, when they weren't asking for rides, they paid him to treat their crops, too. It was at my daddy's knee that I first learned to fly, naturally. As I got older, I read his school manuals and took the same tests he did, and I was good. He told me so. Good enough to get my own license and be a genuine pilot. After he died, I kept up the crop-dusting work. I felt close to Daddy every time I flew.

The war put an end to my flying days.

Until today.

The stars twinkle down like giant fireflies, and the fireflies in the field hover above me like tiny stars. Abel's newspaper story is still in my hands, the ink staining my fingertips. I take a deep breath and smile.

"Daddy, I'm gonna be a pilot in the U.S. Army," I whisper. "Your little girl is gonna fly again. She is gonna fly."

Chapter 4

"It's for white women," Jolene says. Her words are like a club coming down on my head. We are alone at the LaRoche house, washing windows for a big war fund-raising party they are giving. It's a chance for the rich folks around here to feel useful. I have Abel's newspaper article inside my apron pocket, keeping it close to me the way some people keep rosaries. But Jolene is a cold cup of water on my excitement.

"It doesn't say that," I protest.

"It doesn't have to," she explains. "Just say 'Sweetwater, Texas,' and I know it's whites only. Texas is as Jim Crow as it gets. Come to think of it, all you really needed to do was say 'army,' and I could have told you how it would go. Sorry, Ida Mae. It's a pretty little dream, but it's only that." Jolene sighs dramatically. "You should've just become a nurse."

"Maybe," I say. She's right, of course. Thomas is only allowed to treat other coloreds in the army. In fact, it's like Uncle Sam runs two armies at once—one all white and the other colored. Grandy says that's the way it's always been. They've finally decided to let women fly military planes. I don't know why I thought that meant colored women, too.

"Do you ever wish you were white, Jolene?"

Jolene raises an eyebrow and cuts me a sharp look. "There ain't enough wishes in the world to make me white," she says. "Besides, the darker the berry, the sweeter the juice."

I have to smile. "All right, Miss Juicy, but you know what

I mean. Most days it doesn't matter. You go to work, you go home, you've got a family and the sun's still shining . . . you're happy. But then sometimes it's like when I tried to get my license. If you're colored, you get the short end of the stick. If you're a woman, you get the short end of the stick. So what do we get for being colored *and* women?"

Jolene sighs. "Beat hard with both ends of a short stick." She smiles wryly. "Well, honey, like I've said before, I'm Negro for life, but you could always pass."

My skin prickles at the thought. "You remember Stevia Johnson?"

"Hoo, boy, do I," Jolene exclaims. "Stevia was white as milk and had light eyes to boot. Her mama's mama's mama made sure they all married up the light ladder."

"And she married a white man, too," I add. Stevia was a year ahead of us in class. She got married almost right out of high school. When other girls were learning to be teachers or cleaning houses, Stevia married her boss at the department store she worked in. She'd been passing for years. It wasn't unheard of, passing for a job or marrying white so your children could pass into a better life. Daddy's family had done the same, until he married Mama, that is.

"Stevia always was too uppity for me," Jolene says.

"Do you remember Janice?"

Jolene's eyes narrow, and she gets real busy on a window streak.

Janice Johnson was not someone either of us were likely to forget. Two years ago, Stevia's parents threw a graduation party for her, and I was invited because she knew Thomas. Jolene and I showed up just as happy as could be, excited to be invited to a senior class party. But Stevia's cousin, Janice, was standing at the door with a paper bag. Janice was as fair-skinned as Stevia. She could have gone blond if she wanted to without anyone batting an eye.

"Just a moment," she said when Jolene and I tried to walk through the door. She held up the paper bag to my cheek and said, "Go right in, honey," in a sweet drawl that sounded more like a Georgia debutante than a New Orleans farm girl with a little bit of education. I went right on in and turned around to wait for Jolene.

Jolene never got past the front door.

"Uh-uh, sugah, you're black as molasses." Janice held the paper bag up, pale as nutmeg against Jolene's chocolaty skin. "You're back-of-the-church black," she said, referring to the way folks separate by skin tone in some churches. The blackest people sit in the last row, farthest away from God.

"You can't be serious!" I said. I'll never forget the look on Jolene's face, like she could've scratched Janice's eyes out.

"Let's go, Jolene. We don't need this." I grabbed her hand.

She pulled free of me. "This is my business, Ida," she said quietly, and stepped right up in that yellow girl's face and said, "Janice Johnson, everybody knows you got your skin from the milkman and not your mama's husband. He's as black as me. At least I know who my daddy is!"

Janice Johnson's eyes went real wide, and she made a noise like a hiccup. "You—you little tart," she stammered. People were turning to watch. Jolene smiled, liking the audience she had. She looked at Janice sweetly. Janice's beautiful pale face had gone red and blotchy.

"Tell it to your mama," Jolene said, turned on her heel, swished her hips, and left. I had to hurry to keep up with her.

We laughed about it all the way down the block, but it had left a sour taste in my mouth. I never wanted to be like Janice Johnson or her cousin Stevia.

Now I smile in spite of myself. "Look at me. No license, no chance of getting one, and not even allowed to volunteer myself to fly. Thomas was right to call me Clayfoot."

Jolene gives me a hug. "Cheer up, Clayfoot. Something's gotta give."

"Yeah. Something."

Abel is the first to notice the Oriental girl in the photograph. "Is she colored?" he asks me. I'm folding clothes on my bed, still stiff from hanging on the clothesline. Abel thinks he's helping me, but he's really just sitting at my dressing table, fooling around with my combs and things. I turn to see what he's pointing at. It's the article about the WASP. After my little talk with Jolene, I cut the article out and clipped it to my mirror. It just gives me something to think about if I can't join them. Abel is pointing to the article's photograph, a picture of a group of the women in uniform.

"There aren't any colored folk in the WASP," I tell him, barely giving him a second glance. I'm too hurt to want to talk about it anymore.

"No, you're not looking. Her. She's colored or something. Her name is . . ." He leans in real close to read the caption of the photograph.

"Hazel . . . Ah Ying. Ying? What kind of name is that?"

Ying. It's like a bell going off in my head. "Ying? Are you sure?" I drop the blouse I've been fussing with and scramble over to the vanity.

"There," Abel says proudly. It's true, at the end of the row of white faces, one is a little darker than the others. Hazel Ah Ying.

"She's not a Negro, Abel. She's Chinese."

"Chinese? Aren't we at war with the Chinese?"

I kiss my brother on his curly head. "No, silly, we're fighting the Japanese. Two different countries. You'll learn about that in school."

I can't stop smiling. They let a Chinese girl into the WASP program. A real Chinese girl. That means there's hope for me, too.

"You should sign up," Abel says, like he's reading my mind.

"Should I?"

"Yeah, why don't you?"

Why not? I think, but then the other reasons come knocking. "For one, I don't have a license—"

"Daddy does."

"That's not the same thing, Abel. I need my own pilot's license to apply. All the flying and studying in the world won't make up for that."

Abel frowns. "You could borrow Daddy's license. Just like you borrow the truck sometimes, can't you?"

It's my turn to frown. Abel got my hopes up without meaning to, and now I'm feeling hurt all over again.

"No, Abel, you can't. Now, don't you have somewhere to be?" I snap. I don't mean to, and I feel sorry the minute I say it, but I know I'll be better off alone.

Fortunately, Abel is too caught up in his own thoughts to notice me. "See you later, Ida. I'm a help Mama make a pie."

He slides down off of my dressing chair and bounces out of the room.

The next morning, I'm up early, not because I'm eager for work, but because I never really went to sleep. The article Abel gave me is clutched in my fist, the newsprint smeared across my fingers. I head up into the attic and find Daddy's flying box.

It's a cash box, really, metal with a key still stuck in the lock. All of his flight manuals and paperwork are inside. I settle to the floorboards and put the box in my lap, running my fingers over the cool gray edges. This little box was like a treasure chest for me from the minute we landed in Daddy's Jenny. It was a school and a library, too. I must've read everything in here at least a hundred times. And now, my fingers know exactly what they're looking for.

In a small leather portfolio, worn as an old shoe, stuck in a place of honor, is my daddy's pilot's license. The license photo was one of the few pictures we had of him, so Mama took it out a long time ago and put it in the locket around her neck. It's just a blank sheet of yellowish paper now, a little rough where the photo was peeled up. I rub my fingers across the page. Iden Mahé Jones. He was named in English and French by his mother, and I was named after him.

Daddy's license photo was taken with a Brownie camera, just like the one Mama used on vacation in Philadelphia when I was a baby.

I sit up there in the dust and the heat of the attic, Mama's bedroom clock ticking away through the floorboards up to me, and I feel a hand on my shoulder. Daddy's hand. He gives me just a little push, and though I don't believe in ghosts, I believe my daddy is with me, and he's telling me what to do next.

Iden Mahé. Ida Mae. There's a typewriter at the Dupree house, and I know Jolene will help me. I'm down those stairs just as soon as I can close the flying box. "Mama, where's the camera?"

"What, girl? Don't you come running through here like some man, banging your feet down those stairs."

"Sorry, Mama." I round the corner to the kitchen, where she's sitting at the table, balancing the books. "It's just that . . . where's the camera? The Brownie Daddy bought for your trip to the World's Fair?"

"What you want with it?" Mama is way too good at reading when I'm up to something. I think fast.

"I thought I could take some pictures of home to send to Thomas."

Mama's face softens, and I feel terrible for lying. I promise myself that I will take some pictures for him.

Mama sniffs. "Baby girl, you do think of the sweetest things. All right, it's in the closet in my room, on the top shelf. There's some film in there, too, but it might be old. Take some change from the counter and buy some new film at the drug-store."

"Yes, ma'am. And thanks, Mama." I kiss her soft brown cheek. She's the best a mother can be. When I run outside, I try not to slam the screen door, just for her.

Chapter 5

"Girl, that ain't never gonna work," Jolene says, but she takes the picture, anyway. I stand in front of a white sheet hanging on her mother's clothesline, held taut at the bottom corners with clothespins clipped to strings on stakes, like a one-walled tent.

"Do two more, just to be sure." The sun isn't too high in the sky anymore, so the shadows should look all right. I've got my hair done in a little wave, nothing too fancy. This is a serious photograph, after all. "Should I be smiling?" I ask. I don't know why I'm so nervous. It's just a picture.

"Ida Mae, if you don't stop fidgeting, we'll waste the whole roll of film on this nonsense."

"Sorry." I've already used up half the roll on pictures of the farm for Thomas, for Mama's sake. I don't want to spend more money to buy more film just because I'm nervous.

"All right, then, one with a smile, one without."

The next day, on our way home from cleaning houses, I drop the roll off at Katz and Besthoff's and wait for the prints to arrive in the mail. And then I write a letter to the director of the WASP program, at the address printed in the paper, and tell them I'd like to apply.

The pictures are the first to come back, in a thick cardboard envelope in the mail. I send half of them to Thomas, like I told Mama I would, then I go back to my room and try to figure out which picture will work the best on Daddy's license. You can see the grass in the corner of the first photograph, and Jolene's shadow is covering half my face in the second. The third shot is good, but I'm smiling and I don't know if I should be. Daddy's not smiling in his picture, except for his eyes. The last photo will have to do. I look serious, but not too serious, and the sheet looks like a real photo backdrop.

I lick an eraser and use it to carefully remove the *n* and the *hé* in my father's name and year of birth. It will be best to put the picture in and then run the whole thing through the Wilsons' typewriter to make the changes. That way, the photo might curl a bit and look less new. With a jar of paste borrowed from Abel's school supplies, I carefully paste my picture into the booklet, over the place Daddy's picture used to be.

It looks good there, side by side with the official pilot's license. I'll bring it to the Wilsons' day after tomorrow, when Jolene and I do our next cleaning. And then, well, we'll just have to see.

The day I get the letter telling me to come to the Armory Building on Canal Street for an interview, I almost swallow my tongue to keep from letting Mama hear me squeal. Now my paste job on Daddy's license gets put to the test and so do I. Jolene lets me borrow some of her best nylons—a rare treat since the war rationing began. I pack them in my cleaning bag, along with my best navy blue skirt suit, the one Mama bought me for high school graduation. It's a fine Tuesday morning when we go to clean at the Wilsons'. But instead of cleaning, Jolene helps me get dressed for my interview. We put my hair back in a bun so it looks neat and out of the way. I pull on those nylons and put on a low pair of heels. I feel like an army girl already.

"Girl, that suit's all you got? You'd best borrow something from Mrs. Wilson's closet. No point in looking podunk if you can help it."

I look at my suit in the Wilsons' bedroom mirror. "There's nothing wrong with this suit. Besides, Mrs. Wilson would fire us both if she caught us playing dress up in her closet."

Before the last word is out of my mouth, Jolene's dropping a stole around my shoulders. Silver gray fox fur. It makes the blue of my suit look richer somehow.

"Now, Jolene, listen to me. I'm not wearing a fur in the middle of this heat."

"Girl, you'd better hush and let Jolene do her magic."

I huff but bite my tongue. The fur does look good. The little hat Jolene puts on me next looks even better. Black felt with a blue grosgrain ribbon, a couple of dyed blue pheasant feathers, and a short blue birdcage veil. I look at my reflection in the mirror. I look like a movie star.

"That's fine, fine," Jolene says approvingly.

I hesitate, but my reflection makes the decision for me. I really do look like a different person, not a housemaid in her graduation suit, but a lady with confidence.

"I suppose . . . as long as I return it before she gets back into town."

"That's what I'm saying," Jolene agrees with a self-satisfied smile. "Now remember, walk tall, say 'yes' instead of 'yeah,' and for heaven's sake, don't talk to anybody you know. You're white now. Act like it."

I laugh, until I realize she's not kidding. "Jolene," I say, butterflies crowding my belly, "I wasn't gonna try to pass. If they took an Oriental girl, I think they'll accept me."

Jolene scowls at me, and I can't tell if it's because she's

41

angry at me or at what I'm doing. "Sugar, do you or don't you want to fly?" she asks me.

"Of course I do."

"Then you'd better be safe over sorry. The more you sound like a country cousin, the less they'll want you, Negro or not. So, stop saying 'gonna' and get yourself downtown before you chicken out. And every time you think of turning back, remember this is your war effort. Do it for your brother. Just go."

She sends me off with a kiss on the cheek and not another word. I look at her in the doorway of the Wilsons' house and she doesn't wave. Neither do I. I turn my back on Jolene and walk to the trolley car that will take me downtown. I'll be able to do something more than collect bacon fat and iron scraps if they'll let me fly. Light skin and good hair could put me in a military plane. Lord knows I don't want to stand by the door waiting for Thomas to come home. I want to help him. And I guess if that means playing white, that's what I'll do.

When my trolley comes, I have to remind myself to take a seat in the front. My skin gets all prickly just walking up the aisle. I start to feel hot when I sit down and fan myself with my gloved hand. No one says anything, though, and before I know it, I'm downtown, walking through a doorway where nobody stops me. The man operating the elevator is colored, but he doesn't look twice at me, avoiding my eyes. That same shyness we all learn down here might work in my favor today.

On the third floor, a secretary takes my name and asks me to sit in a small wooden chair outside of the representative's office. Only one other woman is in the hallway, standing a

42

few yards away. She's colored, the same shade of mahogany as my mother. I smile at her. She smiles back, shyly, and looks away. I have never seen another colored female pilot before, but I know that is what I'm looking at the minute I see her. There's something straight in the way she stands that says she's seen what the world looks like from the clouds. I open my mouth to say something, anything, to her, when I remember my new place. Jolene was right. White women don't ask colored women if they can fly.

It's my turn to drop my eyes shyly. My stomach turns over and my skin prickles as a blush of shame spreads over me. I don't feel white, but I do feel less like Ida Mae. I wait in the hall in the hard wooden chair and wonder if I've made a mistake. After all, if she's here, maybe they would take me as I am, too. And then I could talk to this woman. My palms start to sweat. This is going to be harder than I thought.

A minute later, the office door opens and a girl with a milkmaid complexion and light brown hair comes out of her interview smiling in her Sunday best. She turns her broad smile on me. "Good luck!" she says, and she hurries toward the elevator.

"Janet Weakes," the secretary calls. Janet Weakes is the colored woman. She nods and goes into the office, shutting the door behind her.

Her interview does not take long. Three minutes later she emerges, her head held high, but her face holds the opposite of the smile the milkmaid wore. She does not look at me or at the secretary, just shakes her head and waits for the elevator to arrive.

I watch her back, her shoulders, the chestnut brown legs beneath her charcoal gray dress suit. And I know that she's been turned away because of that deep brown skin. I take a tissue from my purse and fiddle with it, trying to dry my palms and stop the feeling that ants are marching up and down my spine. I wish Jolene was here. But she's not. I guess that's what it means to pass for white—suddenly, you're all alone.

"Ida Mae Jones," the secretary calls out.

My knees go weak, but I stand. I clutch my purse, my makeshift pilot's license a good luck charm in my hands. You do want to fly, don't you? The voice is Jolene's, or maybe it's my father. I can't tell. All I know is the answer is yes.

The interviewer has a real serious look on her face, like Mama when I'd bring home a not-so-good grade. I hesitate inside the doorway, drop a small curtsy, then bring it up short, realizing I'll look like the help that way instead of a white lady pilot.

The woman sitting behind the desk is fair-skinned, with dark hair cut into an efficient if unfashionable bob and a sprinkling of freckles. She looks more like a flapper than a military officer. In fact, she's not wearing a uniform, just a skirt suit of navy blue wool.

"You know," she says abruptly, "I've met more than a few good women pilots out there . . . but good flying isn't the only qualification. It's a shame." She looks past me into the hallway. I follow her gaze and let the door shut behind me. The colored woman has come and gone, but it looks like she's on both of our minds.

"Ma'am," I say, and tug my gloves off my hands.

She looks up at me. "Say, nice hat." I feel myself blush and mutter a thank-you. So much for my newfound confidence.

"Elisabeth Murphy," the interviewer introduces herself,

44

standing up behind the desk. I come forward to take her out-stretched hand and curse myself for taking off my gloves. What if her skin is fairer against mine? I smile and shake her hand, hoping to distract her.

"Ida Mae Jones." I don't know if it's my smile or the fact that I'm a hundred shades lighter than the lady who just left, but Elisabeth Murphy doesn't seem to realize she's shaking hands with a colored housemaid.

"Pleasure, Miss Jones. It is 'miss,' I take it? Few husbands allow their wives the freedom to fly, let alone join the armed services."

I laugh in nervous relief and take the offered chair. "Oh, it's 'miss,' all right. Much to my mother's dismay."

Elisabeth Murphy laughs. "Ah, yes, the single woman's burden, a lovingly over-involved mother. What does she say about you being here today?"

I take a deep breath. I don't know what I expected Uncle Sam to ask me today, but this is not it.

"Actually, ma'am, she doesn't know. I mean, she knows about the program. I couldn't help but tell her, but I don't want her to know about this until it's for sure. She's . . . well, it'd take some doing for her to see another child off to war as a good thing. So she doesn't really know."

I study my shoes, embarrassed by how young I must sound. I blush and my skin gets even darker when I think about the truth. How angry my mother would be at me for using Dad-dy's license to be somebody I'm not. How she'd just die in-side if she knew I was playing white.

"You know, maybe this was a mistake." I start to rise, clutching at my purse, trying to pull back on my gloves. My face is hot, my skin prickling. Whatever confidence made me think I could do this is gone. That feeling of certainty I felt in the attic, holding Daddy's pilot's license, has left me, replaced with a cold, stinging sureness that I am about to get into more trouble than I can possibly handle.

"I can't say I don't understand, Miss Jones, but the type of pilots we need are getting hard to come by. Lots of eager girls, but not ones with the right attitude. You came in here and you curtsied, first thing. That's something I don't see every day, except on the base, where we salute our superiors. It shows a humility a lot of kids don't have today. A humility our boys are learning every day we fight overseas. It'd be a shame if we didn't at least finish the interview and see where it goes. Who knows, maybe your mother will come around if she knows that you are special enough to make it into the WASP."

I can't believe my ears. Here's this white lady, smiling encouragingly at me. She's come all the way from Washington, D.C. And she wants me. Ida Mae Jones.

Elisabeth Murphy nods at the chair.

I close my eyes. *Mama, forgive me.*

I follow Mrs. Murphy's lead. She sits down. I slowly, slowly follow.

"Good. Now, that was the hard part. Being sure you want to be here. So, convince me. What makes this worthwhile to you? It's a hard life; you might not make it through training. Most girls don't. And people in your hometown will not understand. But I know you know that already. So why, Miss Ida Mae Jones? Why do you want to be a WASP?"

I swallow hard, but the answer is easy. "Because, Miss Murphy. I want to fly again. I want to fly."

Elisabeth Murphy nods slowly. "That's not good enough."

I feel myself start to blush again. Stop it, Ida Mae, don't

show this woman who you are, don't give it away now, now that you've decided to stay. And then I realize, that's it, show her *who* I am, not what I am. I am Ida Mae Jones of Slidell, Louisiana. Even if I'm playing at being white, even if I paint myself blue, I am still the child of my parents, still that little girl who loves her brother and loves to fly.

"My daddy brought home a Curtiss JN-4 when I was eleven years old. He taught me how to fly her, and that plane was my first real friend, aside from my brother Thomas. Daddy used to say the only time we are free is when our feet are off the ground."

"Well, a lot of people don't think women can fly," Elisabeth Murphy says. "Certainly not military planes. But that's what the WASP are here to do—prove them wrong."

"Yes, ma'am." I smile self-consciously. Pay attention, Ida Mae. Don't forget what line you're walking. I take a deep breath and start again.

"So, when the war started, and the Japanese bombed our own ships and our own soil, my brother went off to fight to keep us free in his way. He's doing his part, and I want to do mine. Now, I can stay at home stretching flour rations and collecting nylons, or I can do what God and my daddy taught me to do. I can fly. I can fly straight and far or however the army needs me to. I learn quick and well. And I just know, if you give me a chance, I can do as good a job or better than any—" I have to stop myself from saying "white woman."

Elisabeth Murphy smiles. "Go ahead, finish your sentence. 'Better than any man.'" She grins more broadly. "Good. You need that kind of spirit. The army is a hard place for a woman, Miss Jones. And the Women Airforce Service Pilot program is even harder. We have a lot to prove. The men don't think we have it in us to fly, let alone fly for the government. We'll show them otherwise, but it takes determination and skill. We can teach you the skills. But you have to bring the rest."

She looks at me for a long moment, and I can hear my heart pounding in my ears. Slowly, my shoulders relax. What am I first, I wonder, a woman or colored?

"Don't look so concerned, Miss Jones. Tell your mother there's a good chance you'll wash out in the first month, and you'll be home with your tail between your legs ready to listen to all of her 'told you so's' and settle down to make fat, happy babies."

Elisabeth Murphy flips through the files on her desk. I resist the urge to mop my forehead with the handkerchief tucked into my handbag.

She eyes me. "But I don't think so. Now, did you bring your license?"

My heart skips a beat. "Yes, ma'am." I feel like I'm moving in molasses when I hand Daddy's license over to her. I hope the glue stays stuck, I hope the typing looks official. I hope a lifetime's worth of hoping. And then she's nodding and handing it back to me.

"Congratulations. This is only the first step." She thrusts out her hand. I take it, bewildered.

"Expect papers to arrive in about a week. If they give you the final go-ahead, training for the next class starts in one month. Texas. Ever been?"

I shake my head slowly, dazed. She shrugs and hands me her card. "Well, you'll get enough of it soon. You can reach me at that address if you, or that mother of yours, have any questions."

I rise to my feet for the second time, light-headed with

disbelief. I forget myself and curtsy again. "Thank you, ma'am. Thank you very much."

I want to whoop for joy. A grin slides across my face. Jolene will never believe this. Not until there is a letter in my hand signed by President Roosevelt himself. And even then, she'll think I'm fooling.

"There's that curtsy again. Good luck, Miss Jones." Elisabeth Murphy opens the door. "You'll need it."

Chapter 6

"Mama, there's a white lady coming up the walk." I can hear Abel's voice ring out, calling to Mama in another part of the house. Sound travels farther than I ever thought, out here in the strawberry fields. I turn around to see who's been following me from the turn off the road. It takes a second for me to realize who he's talking about. Me.

I walk down the little road that becomes our driveway, gloves on my hands and Mrs. Wilson's hat still perched on top of my head, my face half hidden behind the blue veil . . . I forgot to change, I wanted to get home so bad. Well, there's nothing to do about it now. I can bring the hat and stole back tomorrow morning. The stockings feel silky against my legs. No wonder Jolene loves them so much. I'll have to wash them and give them back to her scented with lavender perfume to say thank you.

The farmhouse door opens up and Mama steps out on the porch. The minute she looks at me, I know she doesn't see a white lady. She sees something else. Her face goes blank.

"Hi, Mama," I say, and close the last few feet between me and the front steps. She lets me get halfway up, her hands resting lightly clasped in front of her apron. I smile up at her and she slaps me. Hard. Tears fill my eyes.

"Mama!"

"Don't you 'mama' me, Ida Mae Jones. One look and I can tell what you've been doing. Playing at that same mess as your daddy's people. Do you think white folks don't know? Do you think they can't tell what you are? A high yellow putting on airs and a borrowed hat."

She comes toward me, all the way to the last step, and holds on to the banister, as if she is on a ship and I have gone overboard, lost at sea.

"You take back that hat and those stockings and whatever ideas have gotten into your head, girl. You are part of *this* family. All the clothes in the world can't change that."

I blink back my tears. My mouth opens, but I don't know what to say. "I didn't think . . ."

And then I see the tears in my mother's eyes.

The porch door swings open and Abel peeks out. "Ida?"

The look Mama gives him sends him scampering away. I hear the side door slam open and shut and I know he's gone to find Grandy. I drop to my knees in the dust of the driveway, the gravel scraping the tender stockings on my legs. I can't look at anything but the gloves on my hands. Mama's Sunday gloves.

I hear Mama go back up the stairs. The front door creaks and she's gone.

"Go clean yourself up, Ida," Grandy says as he comes around the side of the house, his work boots crunching on the gravel. "Then you can explain yourself." I look up and Abel is hiding, scared, behind Grandy's legs. Neither of them reaches to help me as I pull myself up to my feet. No one holds the door for me when I follow them inside.

In the bathroom, I wash my face twice. The red rims around my eyes won't go away and neither will the tender bruising where my mother slapped me for the first time in my life. I give up and finish getting dressed. There is a tiny hole

51

in Jolene's nylons, right on the knee. Maybe it won't run. Maybe I can buy her a new pair.

The girl in the mirror looks hollow. Big dark eyes like empty wells. I look unnaturally pale, sickly, almost green.

I turn away from my reflection and hang Jolene's hose up to dry. Adjusting the straps on my overalls, I go downstairs to pay the piper.

Grandy and Abel are sitting at the kitchen table. I wish Abel wasn't here for this. There are things he shouldn't have to worry about until he's older. But Mama's always made us sit through each other's talking-tos so we both learn the lesson with only one of us having made the mistake. Mama jumps up from her chair the minute I come in and goes to the window. She won't look at me. I stand in front of all of them, unsure if I should sit down. Unsure if I'm welcome.

"I knew one day you'd go to see her," Mama says, her voice strained and quiet.

I blink in confusion. "Mama?"

She turns around and her eyes are as red as mine. "Don't 'mama' me, girl. You know who I'm talking about. Was this for her?"

I swallow hard, all the pieces falling into place. "No. This wasn't about Grandmère Boudreaux."

My father's mother, French-speaking, Creole, light-skinned Grandmère Boudreaux, has money and status that goes with her maiden name. She's my daddy's only immediate family and we've never even met. I know where her house is, on one of those streets uptown in the Garden District of New Orleans, one of the old houses built for the free people of color before the Civil War. A fashionable neighborhood for the almost white. The rest of my family would never dare set foot

52

there—Thomas's hair's too kinky, Abel's skin too brown. But I've got the right complexion, the right texture to my hair. I'd fit right in.

She could take me to Paris if she wanted to, to where colored women can learn to fly. Just like Bessie Coleman, the first colored woman pilot. Of course, with my father's mother, I wouldn't need to be colored if I didn't want to be.

I never knew my mother was afraid of that fact until now.

My father's people were town people, city folks who followed opportunity the way a compass follows north. Sometime back, one of them found herself with child by a white man. They steered that half-colored girl down a path that made each generation lighter than light, having children by white men and marrying those children to other mixed coloreds, lighter and whiter until my father was born.

Daddy was destined to marry a white woman, to be a *passé blanc* and give his family a better lot in life. But Daddy wasn't an opportunist. He was a romantic, and his heart chose Mama. Grandmère Boudreaux never forgave Daddy for his choice of a brown-skinned bride or his career as a strawberry farmer, which he learned from Grandy and mixed with his college learning. Grandmère drove out to our house only once, when I was nine years old, to have a look at us, as Daddy said. A look was all it was, too.

She drove up in a brand-new Studebaker caked with country dust. Our dust. The back window rolled down slowly as the car came to a stop at the end of our driveway. It never turned to come up to the house.

From the front steps, itching in my Sunday best, between a stiff-jawed Thomas and an unusually quiet Mama, I caught my only glimpse of Grandmère Boudreaux through that open window. She was fair. Not like milk, but cream, the good kind you pour into coffee on special occasions, the same shade as the paper flowers in Mama's old Easter hat. Her hair fell in soft, graying finger waves, like a movie star. Her powdered skin was set in an expression so severe it looked like it hurt. Her mouth was a firm red slash in that pale, pale face.

One of her gloved fingers went up in the air, like she was pointing at a bird. The window rolled back up and the Studebaker drove away.

Mama harrumphed, the way she does when she knows I'm lying, and marched us back inside to put on our regular play clothes. Daddy just sat down on the front steps, his hat in his hands, and hung his head. I'd never seen him like that before. Later that night, when Mama gave me my bath, I asked her how I could be like Grandmère. Her jaw clenched real tight and she said, "Marry a white man."

Mama seems to deflate when she hears I haven't been to see Grandmère Boudreaux, a sigh of relief that loosens her shoulders and makes her seem like my mother again. Grandy sighs and gets up from the table. My eyes follow his back as he starts to make a pot of coffee.

"Young woman, you'd best not be setting after a fella like that," he says without turning around.

I blush, but it's a feeling of relief. "Only one fella, Grandy. Thomas." That gets everyone's attention, even Abel. Grandy comes back to the table but doesn't sit down. Mama sits real still, her eyes on me.

"I had an interview. To join the Women Airforce Service Pilots. And it looks like I might have a shot." I smile in spite of myself and drop it just as fast. No one's saying anything. I swallow hard. "Remember that article Abel gave me?"

Abel ducks his head so Mama can't see his smile.

"Oh, Lord," Grandy says under his breath.

"What are you talking about, girl?" Mama asks. "You might be able to fake white, but even you can't fake being a pilot."

I didn't think I could feel more ashamed than I already did, but leave it to Mama to get me there.

"I used Daddy's license," I say quietly. Now I'm the one ducking my head.

My mother gets up and walks away. I can't let it happen like this.

"Just listen to me. Listen to me!" I all but shout, and Mama stops in her tracks. I've never raised my voice to her and gotten away with it. But I'm not a little girl anymore.

"Somebody has got to do something. So I went. I put my name on Daddy's license and I went and got an interview. And you know what? I wasn't hiding anything when I went into that room and sat face-to-face with an actual woman Army Air Forces pilot. And do you know what she saw? Not a Negro woman, not a white woman, not a high yellow. But a pilot, Mama. A good pilot that they need. Don't you see? This is what Daddy used to fly for. The chance to be everything other than the color of his skin."

No one says anything and I realize I'm on my feet and my heart is beating fast.

"Maybe Uncle Sam doesn't care about Thomas. Maybe a colored soldier doesn't have a chance in the world. But I do, Mama. So what if they think I'm white? Let them see what they want to see. I'm still me."

Mama laughs then, a low chuckle. She leans up against the

doorjamb and for a minute she doesn't look like my mama anymore. She looks like the woman in my parents' wedding picture—young and full of pride. The picture ran in the paper, the only time Daddy's mother ever saw her new daughter-in-law up close.

"Baby, you don't know what you are getting into. You do not know. But your daddy did. He knew what his mother was asking of him, every day to turn his head away from his people but never really hold his head up with white folks, either. Always looking in the mirror, making sure his hair stayed straight, his skin stayed light. Do you know there's a whole side to his family he wasn't allowed to see? Didn't want to be marked 'colored' by association. Are you prepared for that? Are you willing to give up your brothers? Grandy? Me?"

I don't say anything. We are "that" side of the family, because Daddy married Mama. My jaw tightens, but I don't back down. I've gotten this far. I'm not going to let anything stop me now. Besides, plenty of folks have passed for a better job, like Stevia Johnson. What I'm doing is no different, except it can help my brother win the war.

Mama must see the determination in my face because she leans in close and jabs a finger into the tabletop. "Listen to me, girl. Because you are young and you don't know, I'm here to tell you: you cross that line, you cannot cross back just as you please. Look at her, at Mrs. Geneviève Boudreaux, too proud to even visit her own grandchildren or go to her son's funeral! And now this . . ."

Mama shakes her head. "I hope to God you don't get in. I hope to God you never have to learn what your daddy already knew."

She looks at me with such sorrow, I think my heart will break.

"Ida Mae." Every fear, every hope, a dozen slaps, and a thousand hugs are in those two words, my name. She repeats it: "Ida Mae."

On the stove, Grandy's coffee comes to a boil.

"Abel, want a sugar lump of coffee?" Grandy has stayed quiet through all of this. I'm Mama's child to raise, not his. If he has something to say, he'll take it up with her later.

Abel happily scrambles off his chair to get a saucer for his little sip of coffee. Grandy puts a half spoon of sugar on the saucer and adds two spoonfuls of coffee. Thomas and I used to do the same thing when we were his age.

The house feels stuffy all of a sudden. "I'm gonna get some air," I say.

Grandy nods and pours a cup of coffee for himself and for Mama. I hear them out on the porch rocking and murmuring low as I find a place to sit down in the fields. The stars are coming out. I count them, and my blessings, and wonder if Mama is right.

Chapter 7

It's an ordinary Wednesday. Jolene and I work our fingers to the quick, rubbing beeswax into the wood floors at the Wilson place.

"If ever there was a reason to fly," I tell Jolene, "it would be to save me from having to wax floors."

"Shoot, fly all you want," she replies. "I'd rather be rich."

By the time we leave for the day, we are worn down to the bone, but the floors shine like honey in the late-afternoon light. Otis Wilson has shipped off for basic training. He looked like a sad puppy in his best travel suit, ready to face the Nazis head-on. Mrs. Wilson was so proud, but his daddy knew better. Otis Wilson is not cut out for war. Jolene and I baked him some thumbprint cookies with his favorite jam, just to keep him company on the bus.

"Ida Mae, ain't that the mailman?" Jolene asks as we turn the last corner toward home. Jolene lives less than a mile from my place, and we usually walk a ways together. But today, when we step off the bus, the mailman is waving at me. We break into a run.

"Here you go, Miss Ida Mae. I knew you was looking for something in the mail, but I didn't know what. Says United States Armed Forces right on the envelope, so I figured it was something important."

"Are you gonna open it or what?"

The letter feels like a weight in my hand. "Of course," I say, but my fingers don't comply.

"Give it here." Jolene takes the envelope from me and rips it open with one dark brown finger. She reads the letter, and I try reading her face, but her brown eyes and her smooth forehead tell me nothing.

"Jolene," I finally manage to say.

She raises an eyebrow and looks at me.

"Texas? You're really gonna go to Texas?" She stuffs the letter back in its envelope. "Shoot, girl, you're crazy." She hands the letter back to me. "Go on, tell your mama. I'll watch the fireworks from my front porch."

She saunters away, leaving me standing in my cleaning uniform in the dust. I drop my bags and tear into the envelope, devouring the letter as it unfolds in my hands. *Pleased to offer . . . Report to training . . .* My heart starts beating faster and faster, like the train that will carry me off to Sweetwater, Texas.

"Jolene!" I holler at her. "I'm going to be a WASP."

She's grinning at me from a few yards down the road. I take a picture of her with my mind. That's how I'll see her, I tell myself, whenever I get to missing her. But I'm on my way to flying.

Mama's walking the fields with Grandy when I reach the house. My acceptance letter is tucked into my pocket. I think about hiding it, but there is no point. Grandy sees me coming and waves. He and Mama cut across the strawberry plants and meet me in the driveway.

"Hey, baby girl, back from work late, huh."

"We did a lot of extra work. The Wilsons are having folks over for dinner," I explain. I hold up the envelope. "This just came. The WASP accepted me."

Mama doesn't say anything. She just stares at me. Grandy takes off his hat and wipes the sweat from his forehead.

"We've had such a long day," he says, and shakes his head. "Come on, we'll talk about it over dinner."

They head into the house. I stand outside just a moment longer, the evening wind rising around my ankles, tossing the hem of my dress.

There's ham casserole for dinner, the last of the meat from Sunday's big meal, with noodles and bread crumbs and mayonnaise in the sauce. Usually, everyone likes ham casserole. It's hot and tasty and sticks to your ribs. Tonight, I push it around on my plate, and I'm not alone.

Mama stares at her plate.

Abel pokes at his food. He's always either hungry as a wolf or finicky as a cat. Tonight's got him jumpy.

Only Grandy seems to have an appetite. He chases forkfuls of meat and noodles around with a slice of bread. Grandy has been a farmer his whole life. He won't waste a meal, no matter what else is going on.

"Now," he says when he's satisfied. He sits back and takes a sip of black coffee. "How do you think this is going to work, Ida Mae?"

I blink. "Well, I'm due at the training camp in two weeks, and then I either make it or I don't and I come home again."

"Are they paying for you to go?" Mama asks. Those are the first words she's said on the subject since the fight in the kitchen over a week ago.

I glance down at the table, the letter memorized already. "No, Mama. They say I've got to pay my own way. But it makes sense, right? I mean, I haven't actually become a WASP yet."

Mama sighs and stirs some molasses into her coffee cup. Sugar is too hard to come by to use it every day.

"But I've got my Chicago money I've been saving. I can pay my own way."

"Chicago," Mama says with a shake of her head. "I should never have let you carry on about that." She looks so tired it makes my heart ache.

"Come to that," Grandy says, "what about rest of your pay, Ida? We all work together in this family. With you gone, that's another bit of money that's not coming in for us," he points out. I swallow and nod.

"I can set some aside for you and Mama and Abel from my savings. Then there's a stipend during training, $150 a month. I can send some of it to you. And when I get assigned, I'll be making a real paycheck. I can send money then." It suddenly feels possible and real. I can do this, I know I can make it work.

Grandy doesn't sound convinced. "So, you have to buy a train ticket and be gone for who knows how long . . ." He shakes his head and turns to Mama. "Well, Stella, she wouldn't be the first colored girl who passed for an opportunity. And flying for the military—that's a big one."

Mama's face stays carefully blank. "How many of those girls ever come back?" she asks Grandy quietly.

Grandy nods and rubs a big hand slowly over his cropped white hair. "Sure, there's that. But if they keep the men and women anywhere near as separate as they keep the Negroes and whites, ain't no convent gonna be safer, despite what they say about them WACs."

Mama stays silent. Grandy shrugs. "Besides, what are we gonna do for her here? The girl's got the bug, just like her daddy. It's the army or Chicago one of these days, and no-body's watching out for her in Chicago."

Mama looks at her hands in her lap. When she looks up at Grandy again, I can tell a decision's been made.

Grandy shakes his head. "I've got to tell you, Ida Mae, this is one for the record books," he says. "I mean, a little colored girl flying for old Uncle Sam."

"Does that mean I can go?"

Grandy shrugs. "Your mama and I have been talking. And you're not a baby anymore. An adult has to make adult decisions."

I look at Mama. All the planning in the world won't matter if she says no to me. I can't stand to break her heart.

"If it'll help Thomas," Mama says at last. I can hear the resignation in her voice and it pains me. But a yes is still a yes.

I slump back into my chair, glad to have Grandy's blessing, stunned to have Mama's, no matter how begrudging.

I start to ask if they're sure, but it's not worth having them change their minds, so I hold my tongue.

"Show me that letter," Grandy says. I pull it out of my pocket and place it on the table. Grandy takes it and gives a low whistle.

"Texas. Uh-uh. Texas is hard, baby girl, hard for the col-ored man. You've got to be extra careful not to slip up. They won't take kindly to it in Texas. And if anybody asks or even suspects something, tell them you've got Spanish blood on your mother's side. More than a few folks around here claiming Spanish Creole blood." He gives me a look of concern that turns into concentration. "I got a few friends out by Sweetwater. It's not much to look at, from what I hear."

I can't help but smile. "I'll be looking at the clouds."

Grandy grins. He pats me on the arm. Abel gives me the thumbs-up. Mama gets up and gathers the dishes. I start to help and she waves me away.

"Just sit down. I've got to get used to doing this by myself," she says. There's nothing I can do but watch as she carries the plates to the kitchen sink and begins washing them one by one. She's humming "Amazing Grace" as she washes. The same song we sing every Sunday in church, but tonight I can only remember it as the hymn we sang over my father's grave.

Chapter 8

"Shoo, fly, don't bother me. For I belong to somebody . . ." I hum to myself like the words can keep away the fear gnawing at my insides. Those two weeks have flown by and here I am, itchy in my travel suit, a wool skirt and matching jacket, white gloves. I wish Abel was here to sing with me, to hold my hand. The only brown faces I've seen are on the side of the road, working in prison gangs. This is the last leg of my journey, the bus from Sweetwater to the WASP base at Avenger Field.

The bus was waiting for us outside the Blue Bonnet Hotel in town. I even had a room for a night at the hotel without anyone sending me across the tracks to the Negro neighborhood. The night was cool enough for me to smooth out my hair with an iron, and it stayed straight all the way up until we got on this bus. That's when I learned that Texas is hot. Hot enough to make even my good hair go frizzy from sweat. I check to make sure I have enough setting cream to keep it tame, even if my curls get wet. In the summer in Slidell, it can get so you wish you could take off your own skin. Stripping down to your bloomers just isn't enough. Some days are so humid, you can't tell where the air ends and your sweat begins. Like being in a wet oven, that's what Slidell summers are like. But this Texas heat is like desert heat. It's drier than dry, but you sweat in it just the same.

I resist the urge to put a hand to my hair, because it'll only make it worse. Instead, I end up fidgeting with my handbag. I'm like to tear the handle off before we get to our destination.

Pretending to be white is like holding your stomach in at the lake when the boys walk by. You know they're looking, but you don't want to be seen the way you really are, tummy all soft and babyish, with a too-small chest and behind. So you stand up tall, suck it in, tilt it forward, and try to do the best you can. Jolene was always better at posing. A regular Jean Harlow. Not me. I suck it up, stick it out, and I'm surer than sure I'll never get to the end of this bus ride without being found out.

I look around, trying not to show that I'm moving my eyes. I'm not the only one in gloves. I sigh, relieved. Now that I've made it this far, I'll do anything not to stand out. I close my eyes and remember the last time I felt this scared. Right before my flight test in Alabama, when I didn't get my license. Not a good sign.

There are twenty-five of us. There are supposed to be a hundred girls in all, but I guess the rest have cars or came out yesterday. At eight o'clock this morning, the bus pulled up to take us to Avenger Field. It's a queer one. They call it a cattle truck, but it looks more like a long horse trailer, a big metal box with rectangles cut out for the windows, although there isn't even any glass. And the hard seats seem like an afterthought. It makes me wonder what kind of planes they've given us. But I don't care what they look like. I just want to get there.

For the first time since leaving New Orleans, I don't need to think about sitting in the back or the front. I'm squeezed square into the middle of all the other girls. I say girls, but some of them are women, all right. In age, they look to be anywhere from my age to a little younger than Mama. There

65

are brunettes, blondes, redheads, and even a few people going gray early. And every single one of them is white.

I wipe the sweat from my forehead with a folded handkerchief. I feel sick.

"Are you all right, sister?" The girl across from me is looking at me with concern. She looks like Snow White, all black curls, ruby lips, and creamy skin, eyes like blue forget-me-nots. I wave her away.

"I'm fine, thank you," I say. I fight the urge to add "ma'am" or bow my head. Jolene warned me not to be a maid. I twist my fingers in the fabric of my skirt.

The woman smiles. "The hell you are. None of us are. How could we be, with this damn heat, this damn bus, and—" She pauses. "Well, I ran out of *damn*s. How old are you, honey?"

"Twenty last month," I tell her. I really do think I might be sick. "I need some water."

"Hold on. Driver?" Snow White is up and walking down the bouncing bus aisle with perfect balance. I would have tripped over myself with all of this jouncing, but Snow White is cool as November, a real beauty queen.

"Hey, Mack," she says to the driver. "We've got a sick girl back here. Do you have something she can drink?"

The driver fumbles around for a canteen under his seat. I put my head down on my knees, dizzy. My hands shake and my stomach turns sour. Drinking from a "whites-only" water fountain would earn me a beating back home. Sharing this man's canteen could be a hanging offense in Texas for all I know. But then I steel myself. You wanted to fly, Ida Mae. This is what it takes.

A moment later, Snow White's lifting my head up with a cool, dry hand. "Here, honey, take a sip. It'll help."

66

I sit up and put my lips to the metal rim of the canteen. A split second before it touches my lips, I realize it's not water. The rich, fiery smell of whiskey hits my nostrils. I push it away, eyes burning from the fumes. The liquor has splashed my mouth. I wipe it away with my handkerchief. Some of the other girls around me laugh and whisper. And all I wanted to do was lie low.

"Better?" Snow White asks.

"That's not water," I say hoarsely.

"Oh, I know, honey. But this rotgut is almost as good as smelling salts. You'll be all right now, at least until we get to the base."

I sit up straight and stare at Snow White. My cheeks get hot, but I don't say anything. I don't feel anywhere near "all right." My hands are still trembling, but now it's as much from embarrassment as it is from fear.

Snow White smiles. "Oh, honey, I'm not messing with you. I was trying to help, really. I was afraid you'd pass out before we got to the base, and then they'd send you right back home."

I can feel my face go from red to gray. "Of course. Thank you." I cover my eyes with my hand and sigh. "This is going to be harder than I thought."

"Don't worry," Snow White says. "We'll get through it somehow." I give her a wry smile. I hope she's right.

Snow White sticks out her hand. "The name's Patsy, Patsy Kake. You can call me Cakewalk."

"Ida Mae Jones." I shake her hand. This time, I can't help but bob my head, like a seated curtsy. She doesn't seem to notice.

"Pleased to meet you, Jonesy." I start to correct her and

decide against it. The less I am Ida Mae, the better off I'll be. Patsy's hand is cool in mine. We give each other a tentative smile.

The other women are whispering excitedly and looking out the window at the flat, unending plains. I want to be home in Slidell. I want to sit at the edge of the berry fields and spread my toes in the grass and never hear another word about the war again.

Then the bus driver lets out a shout. All of the girls on the bus stand up at once. Airplanes are flying overhead.

"That sounds like an AT-6," one of the girls says. I don't recognize the name from the spotter cards Thomas sent me and Abel: like a playing deck but with pictures of both U.S. and enemy planes so we could identify them in case of an air raid. "That's an Advanced Trainer," another girl says, which explains why I don't know it. I've got every plane on that card deck memorized, but they're the real deal, not teaching planes. Some of these girls must have family in the air force to know what a military trainer plane looks like.

Like a bunch of tourists, the other girls scramble to see the AT-6, racing to the left side of the bus. Me, I sit real still and let the sound of the buzzing engines wash over me. My stomach settles right down, like a perfect three-point landing. I'm here, I tell myself. Daddy would be proud.

Outside the window, the sky is peppered with airplanes, taking off, landing, circling the field.

"There it is," Patsy Kake says, grinning. "Avenger Field."

I tear my eyes away from the sky long enough to look at my new home. At first, I don't see much. Just an old split-rail fence, followed by more pancake-flat dirt, going on for miles.

But then in front of us is a gate, an archway, really, like the ones in front of cowboy ranches in the movies. The wooden sign looks exactly the way I've seen it in the newspapers. A long dark rectangle with white letters that read AVIATION EN-TERPRISES, LTD. In the center, above the words, a globe of the earth sits, wrapped with a small banner that says AVENGER FIELD. And flying above that globe, like she's coming in for a landing, is the mascot of the WASP, Fifinella. I smile up at the girl gremlin. She's a sight to see, with little horns and curling eyelashes. Her outfit is like nothing I've ever laid eyes on— blue flight goggles, an orange bomber jacket, glamorous elbow-length gloves, and yellow jodhpurs with a matching helmet. Her blue wings are spread out behind her, like she's coming in fast.

"That's a Walt Disney original," Patsy tells me.

I smile. "What a looker." Gremlins are supposed to be nasty little devils. The flyboys in the Pacific say that the Japanese send these little troublemakers to tear up their airplanes and make flying harder. Fifinella is the exact opposite. She's one of the good guys, here to help us women fly.

The guard at the little gatehouse waves us through. My butterflies return, but now they're from excitement instead of nausea. After months of newspaper clippings and daydreams, I am finally going to fly in this man's army.

I take a deep breath and step off the cattle truck onto the dry, powdered soil at Avenger Field. The noise of the planes overhead has my heart thumping. My fingers are itching to pull me inside a cockpit, but first things first.

We are greeted by an Army Air Forces officer with a stiff khaki uniform and an even stiffer frown.

"Welcome to Avenger Field," he says. The way he says it reminds me that this man's army has been "men only" for a very long time. Not everyone is so happy to see us here.

They march us past the administrative building to what they call the training theater, where we will be processed. It's an old white building that sits like a box on the flat earth. The low roof doesn't make it any cooler in here. A small, kind-faced woman enters the room, a clipboard stacked with papers in her hands. She's in uniform, a tailored blue skirt and matching jacket, with her dark brown hair cut into a neat bob.

"Welcome to Avenger Field, ladies," she says. Her voice has a no-nonsense kind of gentleness to it that reminds me right away of Mama. "My name is Leni Leoti Clark Deaton. I am the establishment officer here. Anything you need, anything concerning any WASP trainee, come to me and we will take care of you. For the next five months, you will be in training for the Women Airforce Service Pilots. Some of you will succeed, but most of you won't. Take a look at the girl to the left of you."

Dutifully, we all turn and look at the turned heads of our fellows. Some look like kids. Some look like movie stars. I can only guess how I must look to them.

"Now," Mrs. Deaton says, "look at the girl to the right. Say goodbye to both of them today, because two out of every three of you will wash out before training is over. We want only the best, ladies. We keep only the best. Remember that."

There's some nervous shuffling, the kind you hear before a pop quiz in school. Everyone's wondering who will be left standing in five months. I feel my stomach roll again and this time not from the heat. I clench my teeth and take a deep breath. *I will be here,* I tell myself. *I will be here.*

I catch Patsy Kake smiling at me from the corner of my eye. Maybe she'll be here, too. She's got the attitude for it.

Mrs. Deaton passes around copies of a list of rules for living at the base. I glance down the sheet. No smoking, no drinking, no fraternizing with the instructors . . . the list goes on.

"All right, listen up, ladies," she says. "You'll be bunking in the barracks, six girls to a bay, two bays to a barrack. There's a Jack and Jill bathroom accessible from both rooms, or Jill and Jill, if you like. No men are allowed in the barracks. The twelve of you will share this bathroom for the next five months. Make friends. It'll go a lot easier that way."

Mrs. Deaton's voice is clear and mellow. It seems to carry from her small frame like a church bell, despite her size. We all listen attentively. "Barracks are broken up by alphabet. When I call your name, come stand beside me, and we'll take you to the laundry, where you'll pick up your sheets, and then on to your quarters. We are on a military clock here. The hands go from oh-one-hundred to twenty-four-hundred hours. It is now twelve o'clock, or twelve hundred hours. You have the afternoon to settle in. Supper is at eighteen hundred hours, or six o'clock. Get used to the hours, ladies. It will also make life easier.

"Now, Anderson, Attley, Boxer, Bradford, Cunningham, DeAngelo," she begins calling off names. One by one, girls pull away from the crowd to stand by her side. They look nervous, every one of them. Me, I can hear the blood pounding in my ears. This is it. Anyone I room with could be my best friend or the person who turns me in. It's all the luck of the draw.

"Howard,"Mrs. Deaton calls out. "Jennings. Jones." I almost

71

jump. A chill crawls up my spine and I step forward to join my new bunkmates. We don't look at each other, just our feet, and wait for the rest of our group. I don't know what to do with my hands, so I hold my purse with both of them. I don't know what to do with my feet, so I stand there, heels close together, and wait.

"Kake," Mrs. Deaton calls. Patsy Kake smiles and sashays over to stand between Jennings and me. "Laidlaw. Lowenstein." The last of the girls, Lowenstein, looks like a little bird, delicate bones and fine, chestnut-colored hair. She carries a heavy carpetbag with her in addition to her purse. The rest of us left our luggage on top of the bus, and I know I saw at least two steamer trunks up there with her name on it. I wonder what Lowenstein's carrying that's so important.

She carries the bag over to our little group. "Want some help, sister?" Patsy Kake offers her a hand. Lowenstein shakes her head politely. "No, thank you. I'm all right."

We fall silent until the rest of the girls are put into groups. Then, like we're going to our own funeral, we silently fall into line as upperclassman trainees in khaki pants and white blouses lead us to our new homes.

Chapter 9

"Would you look at this place?" the girl named Jennings gasps
as we enter our side of the barracks. She sticks her head in the
bathroom door at the center of the middle wall. "Two mirrors
and two showers. For twelve women? No wonder they say war
is hell." Seeing the close quarters, I thank my lucky stars I
brought a new shower cap with me. The last thing I need is an
audience of eleven catching me with my hair kinking up from
the steam. It looks like I'll be wearing braids most days.

Jennings leads the way into the bunkroom. Whitewashed
cinder-block walls with one window at either end greet me.
It's not pretty, but everything on this trip is still something to
write home about. Jolene would hate the decor, but it certainly looks easy to clean.

"Home, sweet home," Patsy Kake says, dropping her sheets
and her suitcase onto the last bed in the room, just beneath
the far window. The six cots lined up remind me of a hospital
room, except for the narrow metal lockers at the foot of
each bed.

"Everything we own is supposed to go in here?" someone
asks. Nobody answers. I drop my little suitcase by one of the
beds. I didn't bring much to begin with, but Lowenstein's
going to need a team of muscle-bound men to help her with
those trunks.

I take the bed next to Patsy because I'm standing in front
of it. Lowenstein takes the bed to my right.

"Howdy, folks," Patsy says, turning to face us. "I'm Patsy Kake. You can call me Patsy or Cakewalk, whichever you like."

"'Cakewalk'? That's a funny name," Lowenstein says. "What does it mean?"

Lowenstein has the most beautiful auburn hair I've ever seen, two shades darker than sunset. It sits in soft waves about her shoulders. Her voice is like women in the movies. It sounds rich. Patsy Kake talks like a barmaid by comparison.

"It means I'm a wing walker in a barnstorming act," Patsy says. "But I can fly, too. With this war and the gas rationing, air shows are all washed up, so I'm here to be a WASP. I'm gonna learn how the big boys do it."

"A wing walker? Isn't that interesting," Lowenstein says. "And dangerous, too. Oh, I'm Lily Lowenstein." She shakes Patsy's hand, then turns to me. "Hello!"

"Hi. I'm, um, Ida Mae Jones," I introduce myself. Lily's handshake is friendly, but she must be as nervous as I am. Her hands are ice cold and three shades lighter than mine. "I'm Spanish," I blurt out Grandy's lie for no reason. "On my mother's side."

"Oh, Spain's wonderful," Lily exclaims.

"Uh, I've never been." I could kick myself. This girl doesn't suspect me. I shouldn't have jumped the gun like that.

"Jonesy and I have already met," Patsy says.

Down the row of cots, the other girls are making their own introductions. I turn to Patsy and try to change the subject before I say something else stupid. "Wing walking, you say? I saw a wing walker once at a county fair. It looked pretty scary, even if you like to fly."

"No, it's easy. I was practically weaned on an airplane

wing. They make you wear a chute, so it's perfectly safe, but the crowd loves to see a pretty girl risking her neck for a dollar. I do acrobatics, too, with and without a safety rope. More thrills for your bills that way. Cartwheels and such."

Patsy Kake is a fire engine of a girl. I'm guessing she's only a couple of years older than me, twenty-three at most, and she sounds like she's already seen the whole world. I feel my country roots showing, but at least it's only that.

"What about you, Lowenstein, what's your deal?" Patsy asks.

"Oh, I don't know," she says. She blushes at the sudden attention. A tiny sprinkling of freckles stands out against her flushed skin. "Well, my . . . my fiancé enlisted as a doctor, but he's also a pilot. He taught me how to fly when we were dating. And now that he's been shipped overseas . . . Well, I couldn't just sit home and do nothing."

Nobody says anything. We all understand. You can only watch so many newsreels before it drives you crazy.

"What about you, Jonesy? What's your story?"

I'm starting to like the nickname. "Not much of a story, I'm afraid."

"Everybody has a story. And it's always a doozy. Come on, we're all friends here, or at least we will be by the time all of this is over." She waves her hand to include the barracks, WASP training, the war. "I bet I'll know your favorite brand of toothpaste inside a week. So we might as well hear the rest of it."

"I'm just a farm girl. We grow berries, down in Louisiana. I got my start on my daddy's crop duster," I add, glad to be able to tell the truth.

"And why are you here?"

I blink. "Well, to fly."

Patsy laughs, and so does Lily. I find myself laughing with them. When all is said and done, war or no war, patriots or not, it looks like every single girl on this base would drive a thousand miles to nowhere just for the chance to fly.

Two cots over, closest to the door, the blonde who answered to Howard nudges the girl settling into the next bunk. "There goes the neighborhood," she says, loud enough for us to hear.

The other girl, Laidlaw, I think, smiles politely and finishes making her bed. Howard catches my eye and won't let it go. "Carnies and hicks and Jews, oh my!" She smirks, imitating Dorothy's little chant from *The Wizard of Oz*. We've all seen the movie. No one else laughs and I ignore the jab. I've met plenty like her before. Lily must've, too, because she smiles at me a little weakly and starts fussing with her suitcase.

Patsy, on the other hand, crosses the floorboards in three quick strides. "And what have we here? Howard, wasn't it?"

The girl blanches, almost as pale as her hair. She's a strawberry blonde with dramatic red lipstick and blue eye shadow. She probably thinks she looks like Bette Davis. I think it makes her look like Fifinella.

"Nancy Howard," she says, trying not to stammer. She stands up, a little too late to hold her ground. Patsy towers over her.

"Nancy Howard." Patsy says the name like she's biting it in two. I find myself rising to stand at Patsy's elbow. A second later, Lily is next to me.

"Pleased to met ya, Nancy." Patsy holds out her hand. It's the strangest showdown I've ever seen, polite on the surface, but like a snakebite underneath. Nancy actually gulps and looks around. Laidlaw watches from the far side of the bed. No one goes to stand next to Nancy.

Patsy's hand is still thrust in front of her. Gingerly, Nancy takes it. Her handshake looks like one of those soft, fingertip shakes that the debutantes use in New Orleans. Like holding on to a wet sock. Patsy shakes back, but she shakes like a man, swallowing Nancy's little hand whole. Nancy winces and laughs nervously.

"Just a joke," she says, pulling her hand away. "I'm sure we'll all be great friends. Right?" She looks around with a wildly cheerful smile, then skitters back to her bed against the wall.

Laidlaw speaks up. "I'm Mary. Pleased to meet you."

"And I'm Jeanette," the girl named Jennings adds.

We smile and exchange genuine pleasantries this time. The tension all but dissipates, and we return to our side of the room. Just like that, the lines are drawn. These two are my new best friends.

"Like dogs in a kennel," I mutter.

Lily giggles a little nervously. Patsy snorts. "You've got that right, sister. And every one of them female."

"Well, we'd better get these beds made," Patsy continues. "We all need our beauty sleep."

I snap my sheets in the air and let them float down over the mattress. Grandy always liked a crisply made bed, and I'm glad that it looks almost, if not quite, military when it's done.

Patsy finishes her bed when I do, but Lily is a different story.

"How the heck are you supposed to do this?" she cries into her sheets. She looks like a ghost, covered in linens, and none of them on the bed.

"Just toss it over the mattress," I say.

"Haven't you ever made a bed before?" Patsy asks.

Lily falls forward onto the bed, a sheet stretched across her front. "In case you couldn't guess, no, I haven't. Greta usually makes my bed. She's our housekeeper. I asked her to show me how once, but she refused. She said a proper lady didn't have to make her own bed."

"More likely she was afraid she'd lose her job if you knew how easy it was," I say. "Here, separate your sheets. This is the top, this is the bottom. Just toss it out lightly like this." I stand at the foot of the bed and snap the sheet out. It floats down like a blanket of snow.

"You make it look so easy." Lily blushes. "I'm useless."

"Don't be so hard on yourself, honey." Patsy puts an arm around her shoulders.

"If military life was easy, everybody would do it," I add.

Lily laughs, even though she looks like she's about to cry.

"Besides," I say. "I'm practically a professional."

I shake my head. Lily's the kind of girl I'd be cleaning up after back in New Orleans. But now, she's giving me a hug for the same kind of work that I usually get paid a dime for. If only Jolene could see me now.

"Thank you so much," Lily says. "Here, I know I can do the top sheet if you let me."

"Give it a go. And tomorrow we'll teach you how to dust and do the wash."

Patsy and I laugh, but Lily takes us seriously. "Do you think you could? Won't training take up all of our time?"

"I should hope so, sister," Patsy says.

"Why would you want to learn to dust when you can fly?" I ask her.

"Oh, girls, you know we won't be in the army forever. When this war is over, Harry and I are getting married. Shouldn't a wife know how to cook and clean for her husband?"

"I never said anything about cooking," Patsy says, turning away in mock disgust.

"Well, Mother's never taught me a thing about keeping house, but you seem to know what you're doing. Ida here can probably even handle an iron. Isn't that right, Ida? What if I scorch his shirts?"

"Oh, brother!" Patsy exclaims.

I sit down on my own bed, suddenly tired. The image of Jolene and me up to our elbows in Otis Wilson's dirty socks is hard to swallow. "Lily's right. This war won't last forever," I say. "I'm just hoping that the WASP will."

"Amen," Patsy says.

Lily looks at both of us, a little puzzled, and pulls the sheets tighter on her bed.

"Harry will love this," she says at last, and pulls a Brownie camera out of her purse to take a picture of the first bed she's ever made.

Reveille is at 6 A.M. A bugle plays over the base loudspeakers, cracking the morning silence. I wake up with my eyes sore and dry from the hot Texas air. Still, I'm up and halfway to the showers before my eyes are even all the way open. Growing up with two brothers and one bathroom, I know sharing two showers with eleven women isn't going to be a picnic. I'm the second person in line, behind Lily Lowenstein.

"It's hard to get up early," she tells me over the hiss of the water. "But it's worth it for all the hot water. I love long showers and baths."

I smile in spite of myself. "Breakfast is in twenty-five minutes. A short shower will have to do."

Lily sticks her head out of the shower stall. Her eyes have gone round. "Oh, of course you're right. I'd better hurry."

I tuck my hair into my shower cap and jump in as soon as she's done. We don't even cut off the water. It's like an assembly line, the ones you see Rosie the Riveter working on in all of the war ads. The thought makes me laugh.

"Fifteen minutes!" someone shouts into the bathroom. I drop my soap, I'm trying to move so fast.

I come out of the shower with my robe already on and race barefoot to my footlocker. The clothes they've given us make us look like we're in a chain gang: giant overalls with long sleeves that drag even on the tallest of the girls.

"We call them zoot suits," the supply officer who handed them out to us explained yesterday. "You'll see why."

It isn't until this morning, pulling the darn thing on, that I get it. Zoot suits, those baggy, wide-legged, tight-ankled outfits all of the hepcats wear in the movies and in some of the dance halls downtown in New Orleans, have nothing on my new jumpsuit. Real zoot suits are all about being oversized, but at least they don't drag the ground. I look at the label inside the collar. It's too big even for Thomas, and the army says they're one size fits all. I shrug and roll up the legs and sleeves, glad that my brothers aren't here to laugh at me. Lord only knows what Mama would say. A belt might help keep the crotch above my knees, but it's clear I'm not winning any beauty contests in this getup.

"Charming, aren't they?" Patsy says to me. Patsy's at least four inches taller than my five-foot five. Somehow she makes the rolled sleeves look smart, and the cuffs are cute instead of utilitarian. I frown and shrug.

"If they'll stick me in a plane in this thing, I'll wear it," I tell her. "But I hope nobody's taking pictures."

Patsy laughs and helps adjust my cuffs.

Just then, a woman walks in, ash blond and tanned. She winks at us with green eyes. "Morning, girls. I'm your senior squadron leader. I'm just dropping by to say hello. After breakfast have your group meet me outside of the barracks. I'll be talking to the entire class."

"Sure thing," Patsy tells her. I nod silently.

"Senior squadron leader." I shake my head.

"Haven't you heard?" Patsy asks. "You're in the army now."

We smile at each other and head off to the mess hall. Lily, practically draped in her zoot suit, follows us, one foot barely in each shoe.

After a breakfast of scrambled eggs and oatmeal, we line up outside of the mess hall. Patsy, Lily, and I stick together automatically. It reminds me of the first day of school. The ash-blonde upperclassman is already there waiting.

"Listen up, girls. My name is Audrey Hill. I'm part of class 43-W-6, and you'll be known as 44-W-3. With any luck, we'll all graduate before the end of the year. Now, I'm going to need you to divide into two groups, which we call flights. So, anybody with a last name starting with A through L, move to the left. M to Z, over to the right."

She waves her hands and the cluster of girls parts like the Red Sea. Lily, Patsy, and I stay to the left, and we split up, approximately fifty girls on either side. Audrey counts us and makes a note on her clipboard, moving her lips and pointing at each girl as she goes.

"Fine, then. *A* through *L*s, you'll be Flight One, and you others will be Flight Two. Now, I want you all to pick a squadron commander, someone good at organization. She'll be in charge of the paperwork and administrative duties for the flight. Then each flight should pick a lieutenant, who will be responsible for getting you into formation after breakfast and marching you properly from class to class.

"Keep in mind, this is the military, even if we are civilians. We're expected to march and salute just like the rest of the army." She smiles mischievously. "You'll learn to love it, girls. We've made it fun."

"I'll bet they have," Patsy says with a smirk.

"Patsy, I nominate you for squadron commander," Lily says brightly. "You've got stage . . . or, I guess, wing experience, and you're tall, so people will notice you."

"Oh, no, sister, I'm not leadership material," Patsy says, putting a defensive hand in the air. "I'm just here to fly."

"Then you do it, Red," another girl says to Lily. Lily blushes instantly, living up to the nickname originally aimed at her auburn hair.

"Oh, I couldn't possibly."

"I bet you could," I chime in. "Think of how proud Harry would be."

Lily beams in spite of herself. "All right, I'll do it . . . that is, if nobody has any objections."

"Anybody got a problem with Lowenstein doing the paperwork?" Patsy asks.

"Not at all," somebody says. "If I wanted to be a secretary, I'd have stayed at home."

Lily flushes. "Is it really just secretarial work?" she asks Audrey.

"No, dear. It's an important position. And just the fact that you've stepped up to the plate when these other ladies think they're too good for the job means you've got a better shot at becoming a WASP than any of them."

Lily beams all over again. "Did you hear that? I've got a shot!"

"I'll be flight lieutenant," I say quickly. Anything to give me a leg up is a good thing. I wish I'd thought of it sooner.

"Fine," Audrey says. "And the other flight?" A girl named Janet Raines takes the other position. Patsy smiles at me, apparently satisfied at dodging the leadership bullet.

"Well, then, lieutenants, gather your girls into line, marching two abreast, and I'll show you around."

Janet and I step forward, next to Audrey. "What do we do?" I ask softly, so the others won't hear.

"Oh, just say, 'Attention!' and they should fall into place."

"Do they know that?" Janet asks.

"Oh, for heaven's sake!" Audrey shakes her head at us. "Ladies, when they say 'attention,' line up like I asked."

"Atten-shun!" I shout as loud as I can. Lily jumps, startled. Patsy fights to keep from laughing. But it works, and my flight lines up, two women abreast, twenty-four rows deep.

Janet follows suit, and soon we look like the real thing, lined up and ready to march.

"Come on, girls. I'll teach you a few of the camp songs along the way," Audrey says. She turns on her heel and heads off across the base yard.

"Uh, forward, march!" I say, remembering the line from a

movie. It works as well as "attention" did, and we tramp after Audrey in the yellow Texas dust.

"Sing after me," Audrey calls out.

> *"Once we wore scanties, now we're in zoots.*
> *They are our issue GI flying suits.*
> *They come in all sizes, large, Large, and LARGE.*
> *We look like a great big barge."*

We're all still laughing at the song when we pass the hangars and come to the low building where our classes will be held.

"In addition to the classrooms, the pilot ready room is here. That's where you'll suit up and wait your turn to fly."

I break into a grin. "That's the first time anybody's actually said we're going to fly," I whisper to Patsy. "Don't pinch me, I don't want to wake up."

"No kidding," Patsy agrees. We follow Lily and the rest of the flight behind Audrey, across the yard to the actual landing field. The field itself reminds me of Airline Highway in Slidell, fifty miles of straight, unbending pavement, but instead of pickup trucks and fruit wagons, Avenger Field is dotted with airplanes, primary trainers, and advanced trainers, open and closed cockpit. I stop in my tracks, watching as girls like me take off and land. My chest feels so full I think I'm going to explode. I want to run down the middle of that airfield and jump right up into the air myself.

"Hill, what are you bringing out on my tarmac?" a man's voice asks. There's that Texas twang, so different from my own slow New Orleans brogue. I pull my eyes off the runway long enough to see who interrupted our voyeuristic bliss.

"Ladies, I'd like you to meet Sergeant Middleton. He's the head engineer who works on all of our planes."

Middleton gives us a dubious once-over. He's youngish, probably not even thirty, but the way he squints at us, and with his short-cropped strawberry blond hair making him look almost bald, from a distance I'd have probably guessed he was a lot older. He reminds me of that cartoon fellow, Popeye, but in an army uniform instead of a sailor suit.

"Forty-four double-U three?" he says with as much doubt as his hard squint implies. He shakes his head, and I half expect him to spit, he looks so disappointed.

"Well, just keep them off my airfield until they're properly suited and trained. I don't want to see none of you out heres without an instructor," he says, pointing a thick finger. "This ain't no beauty parlor. And it ain't the movies, neither, so quit gawking. You'll get your turns soon enough."

He shakes his head again and runs a hand over his crew cut. "Ma'am." He nods toward Audrey and shuffles off toward the hangars.

Audrey smiles and shrugs. "Damn fine engineer, but not much for the niceties. It's best to stay on his good side, though, ladies. He keeps us up in the air. Our lives depend on Sergeant Middleton."

"Aye aye," Lily says with a sharp salute.

"Aye aye is the navy," I whisper from behind.

"Oh, cripes." She lowers her hand quickly. Audrey Hill just smiles and continues the tour.

"Just a few more things. When you fly, or anytime you're near the planes, you'll have to wear those turbans they gave you with your flight suits. You know, the thing that looks like a towel? Despite Sergeant Middleton's insistence that this 'ain't no beauty parlor,' we have to keep our hair from getting caught in any machinery. We have our commanding officer, Major Urban, to thank for that, so we call them 'Urban's turbans.' Kinda catchy, huh?"

Most of the girls laugh, but a few sigh and primp their perfectly coiffed tresses. I for one would much rather slap my hair into braids and stick it in a towel than have to worry that it's getting too kinky. Thank you, Major Urban, I think.

"So, that's about it. You'll figure out the rest as you go along. Once again, as your squadron leader, if you have any questions, just come to me. I'm over in Barrack Seven."

Audrey leads us back to our barracks. "At thirteen hundred hours, you should all report to the medical unit. Doc Monserud needs to perform a complete physical workup for each of you and get your dental records in order in case they're needed for identification later."

"Identification?" one of the girls asks.

"Yes, identification."

There's a moment of confused silence. Patsy scowls at the girl. "In case we get burned up in a crash. They'll know you by your overbite."

The girl's eyes go round as moons. "Oh."

Audrey frowns at Patsy, who smiles back pleasantly.

"Patsy," I whisper, more than a little shocked myself.

Patsy just shrugs. Audrey smiles at the poor girl. "Don't worry, honey, we hardly ever need them. Hardly ever."

With that, she salutes and walks away.

"That didn't sound enough like 'never' to me," Patsy says, and winks.

It's my turn to shrug. "We'll worry about it when we have

to. But now, I'm going to get five more minutes of shut-eye before we have to go see the doctor."

"Hear, hear." Patsy yawns. "Getting up at dawn wouldn't be so bad if it meant we were flying. But today's a bust."

Fact is, I need the time to try to relax. In the South, folks think skin color shows up in the blood. If that's true, Doctor Monserud will have me on the next bus out of town. My big brother, Thomas, swore to me after his first year of medical school that it just wasn't true. Skin color is only in the skin, he said. I believe him, but today's physical had better prove him right. I don't know if they can tell the difference between Spanish and Negro when it comes to blood tests, so Grandy's advice might not work.

The day goes from bust to worse, but not in any way I feared. By the time Doctor Monserud is done with us, we've been poked and prodded with so many different needles and vaccines, I feel like a sick porcupine. But I passed the test, in more ways than one. Good old Thomas really is learning something in medical school.

At last, it's suppertime. I don't think I can keep anything down, but I know I won't get another chance until morning.

"Jumpin' Jehoshaphat," I say the minute we walk into the mess hall. Most of the other classes are already there, women sitting on one side of the room, male officers and instructors on the other side. But it's not the people that stop me in my tracks.

It's the food on the first plate in front of me. A man is sitting there, eating a steak, casual as day, and a baked potato heaped with pure, sweet, pale creamery butter.

"Pinch me, Patsy. I haven't seen butter in eight months."

Patsy slaps me on the arm lightly. "What, don't you have cows on that farm of yours?"

"It's a berry farm. No. We've got all the jams and jellies you can eat, but not a single stick of real butter."

Lily remains conspicuously silent for a whole half a minute. "Okay, okay. We had butter at my parents' place in the Adirondacks. The caretakers brought in a cow specially for us to have butter, milk, and cheese."

"Well, for those of us born without a silver butter knife in our mouths, make way," Patsy says, and shoves herself through to the food line.

It's like some kind of Hansel and Gretel fairy tale in here. Nothing at breakfast prepared me for this sort of spread. Steak, real sugar, even ice cream, and not a ration stamp in sight. If Mama and Jolene had known what the food was like, they might have signed up, too. I find my appetite quickly enough when it comes to dessert. I go to bed that night happier than I've been in a long time, with a stomach full of food and my head full of tomorrow's first flight.

Chapter 10

I am not the first one in line today at the showers. All twelve of us are up early. Today is the day we fly. Lily times us, five-minute showers each. Even so, the last girl out has no time to worry about makeup or hair; she just yanks her zoot suit on and races outside with the rest of us. Fortunately, Uncle Sam doesn't care about lipstick or perfectly curled hair. Only the first few girls out of the shower can afford to primp. Dolled up or not, our whole bay makes it through the showers and outside in time for formation and roll call. Patsy and I make sure our classmates line up outside the barracks into our separate flights. I stand next to Patsy and watch Lily call out the roll in a high, nervous voice. She catches my eye and I give her a thumbs-up. She smiles and leads us to the mess hall for breakfast.

An hour later, we are back in the barracks, trying to finish what we started in the bathrooms before breakfast. At eight forty-five, Lily leads our flight, zoot suited and Urban turbaned, out to the cattle trucks that will take us to our first day of flying.

The trucks are what they call stake beds, large, flatbed trucks with wooden slats, almost like a fence, to keep the animals in. We stand in back and get towed three miles to one of the auxiliary fields where new classes begin their training. The ready room at this field is nothing more than a Quonset hut, a low-slung arch of a building with a tin roof that touches the ground on both sides. It looks more like a tunnel than a building. Inside, benches are lined up against a blackboard, scribbled with the flight calculations of other pilots. Lily, Patsy, and I stick together. We take seats and wait, like a bunch of first graders on the first day of school. I almost wish I had an apple for the teacher.

At oh-nine-hundred precisely, our instructor arrives. He's a civilian, and his name is Happy Martin. "You may call me 'sir,' 'Instructor Martin,' or 'Mr. Martin.' Neither I nor the majority of your flight instructors are enlisted. That, however, does not mean we do not deserve your respect.

"You've left husbands and children at home to be here, and while I can't approve of that choice, I can make sure that you still know your place in this man's army."

A murmur of disapproval sweeps across the room, not so much sounds of protest as a shifting of bodies in seats. I am reminded of the flight instructor back in Tuskegee. There are no steel blue eyes here, no strong, disapproving jawline. On the contrary, Instructor Martin is a very prim-looking fellow, black hair carefully combed back, not a strand out of place. He is wearing a khaki shirt and matching slacks, despite his insistence that he is not military. His black-rimmed glasses are the only square thing on his round face. He looks like an insurance salesman. It takes me a full minute to believe this man has ever flown in his life. Anybody whose feet have ever left this green earth should have something wild about them, something free. One look at Instructor Martin and I'm pretty sure that military or no, he spit-shines his shoes and his wife presses the crease into his pants precisely the same way every single day.

The moment of tension passes, ignored by the teacher but

well noted by the students. I look at Patsy, fully expecting her to stand up to Martin the way she did Nancy Howard. Instead, she's examining her fingernails as if it's a casual day at the beach. To my right, Lily clenches her jaw in defiance. We'll show him, she seems to say. I raise my own chin a little higher.

"Now, because you'll be sharing parachutes, I'll need you to split up into groups according to height. Anyone below five-foot five over here, five-foot sixes and sevens to this side, eights to nines, and so forth. Although I doubt we'll be getting anyone taller than that." He laughs at his own humor. A few of the girls feel obliged to join in.

"See you on the ground," I say to Patsy. She's definitely in the five-eight, five-nine range, while Lily and I are firmly in the five-two to five-foot five.

"Good luck, flygirl," she tells me.

"Good luck."

The parachutes they give us attach to our torsos with thick olive drab harnesses that go over the shoulders and around the legs. Our zoot suits bag out over them unmercifully, but you could have told me I had to wear iron shoes and I'd still be smiling. I'm about to fly.

Instructor Martin walks us through the use of the chutes— how to pull the rip cord, how to fold up the silks afterward. Feeling the smooth cloth under my fingers makes me think of Jolene's prized silk stockings, reluctantly turned over to the army back home. I guess she did help the war effort after all.

Parachutes in place, Instructor Martin leads the first group of girls, those of us in the five-foot-five-and-under crowd, out to the tarmac. The rest of the girls are supposed to wait in the ready room for their turn, but they rush to the door to watch us.

The plane waiting for us on the tarmac is an absolute beauty. To my farm-raised eyes, those silver wings and open cockpit are like a dream, but some of the girls groan slightly.

"Ladies, this is the PT-19A, a primary trainer. By the time this course is done, you will have completed fifty-five hours in this plane. You will be able to fuel her, repair her, and land her in the event of an accident. I know this all sounds routine to such an accomplished lot of pilots"—he makes no attempt to hide his sarcasm—"but Sunday flying with your beau and actually flying the military way are two different things. These planes are heavier than the Jennys and Pipers you flew at home, and there will be no one here to hold your hand. Having said that, do we have a volunteer?"

Every hand in the group goes up, mine included. Instructor Martin smirks, as if he knew this would happen. "Not a cautious one of you in the lot," he notes. "Very well, we'll make this easy. You, what is your name?"

Lily, the first in line to his left, steps forward, face pale, with two red spots on her cheeks. I can't tell if she's excited or terrified, but I'm guessing it's both.

"Lily Lowenstein, sir." Martin raises an eyebrow at the name. And I thought I'd have it hard.

"Well, Lily Lowenstein." He makes the name sound long and round. "You have your flight suit, your parachute, and your goggles?"

"Yes, sir," she says nervously.

"Well, then, put the goggles on and get in."

Lily hesitates. I want to whisper to her, tell her it's a trap, but I don't need to.

"We haven't run a flight check yet, sir. We should go over the plane first."

Happy Martin doesn't look happy. She's just robbed him of a chance to make her look like a fool. I try not to smile too broadly. Lily knows her stuff. After watching her try to make a bed, I hadn't been so sure.

"Ah, so someone actually did pay attention in flight school," he says. "Miss Lowenstein, lead the way."

Only after giving the plane a thorough once-over does Lily climb in, with Instructor Martin behind her. The PT-19A has an open cockpit with two controls, one in the front, the other in back. Instructor Martin takes the rear seat. He radios the tower for clearance and, without warning, starts down the runway. Lily gives me a quick thumbs-up, and they take off, Martin at the controls. We won't be allowed to take off or land until he's confident we can handle the plane through all the basic maneuvers every pilot here should know.

All of the girls, even the ones in the ready room, line up on the tarmac to watch Lily's first flight. The plane banks and turns. It's a beautiful sight to see in the clear blue Texas sky. Then, suddenly, the plane does a loop in the air, and something awful happens. Lily falls out of the plane! A tiny figure, still visible in her oversized zoot suit, slips from the backseat and plummets toward the earth.

We all cry out. My legs start moving before I can think. Patsy, the entire class starts to run, our eyes on the sky. A second later, the parachute balloons out behind her, and we all heave a sigh of relief.

"Thank you, Jesus, Mary, and Joseph," Patsy mutters.

"Amen," I add. Silently, I say thank you to Jolene, too. We jog the rest of the way across the fields to the spot where Lily has drifted gently to earth. When we get there, she is crying.

"Honey, are you hurt?" Patsy kneels beside her.

"No," she sobs.

"Are you sure? Can you stand?" I give her a hand and we help pull her to her feet.

"Is she all right?" the other girls ask, running toward us, breathless.

Lily's face, already red from crying, turns an even deeper red. "Oh, no, I'm fine. I'm okay." She gives them a weak thumbs-up. A cheer goes up. But Lily turns away.

"I'm so embarrassed, I could die." She begins to pace in little circles.

I put my arm around her shoulders. Patsy begins to gather her parachute. "Well, what happened?"

Lily stops her pacing and gives me an anguished look. "Oh, Ida, I swear I fastened my seat belt, but this darn suit is so big, it got in the way and I guess the belt didn't lock properly. I should've double-checked it, but it felt right, and we took off so fast, and he was saying, 'Look at this,' and, 'Don't forget that,' and then he says, "Do a loop," like he doesn't think I can, and next thing I know, I'm pulling my rip cord. And I'd been so careful, too!"

"It's all right, Lily. It's just the first day. And that's one mistake you'll never make again."

"Aw, honey, it's a rite of passage," Patsy says. "You've joined the Caterpillar Club!"

"Caterpillar Club?" Lily asks.

"That's what they call it when you use your parachute. It opens like a silk cocoon. You've just spread your wings, little butterfly."

We sent the warning to all the girls in Flight One. Don't forget to double-check your seat belt. No one else wants to be a member of the club today.

By the time we get back to the flight line, Instructor Martin has landed. "Any broken limbs?" he calls out to Lily.

"No, sir." Lily blushes three shades of pink and I feel just awful for her, but at least he's not giving her a demerit.

"Fortunately, Miss Lowenstein remembered her parachute, if not her seat belt," he says to the class. Lily starts to protest, but I put a hand on her arm to stop her. Falling out of your plane doesn't earn you a demerit today, but arguing with the instructor just might.

Martin clasps his little hands together with a smug look and says, "The kitchen is safer than the sky, ladies. Let that be a lesson to you. Next?"

Lily bristles, but I have no time to commiserate. I'm up.

My hands start to sweat. This is the first time I've done more than sit in a plane since Tuskegee, three years ago, and it looks like Instructor Martin is determined to make it hard. Then again, this is what I've come here for.

I give the plane a once-over and climb on board. This plane is not too different from my daddy's plane. The same sort of open cockpit, tandem seats for pilot and co-pilot. It's just like going up on a dusting run with Grandy sitting ahead of me. With that thought, all of the butterflies fade away. It's like a cool wind is blowing through my mind. I smile. Settling into the frontseat, I make doubly sure I fasten my seat belt before I look over the instruments and put my hand on the throttle.

"Hands off until we're in the air," Martin shouts at me. His voice comes through the gosport, a speaking tube that runs from his dashboard to my helmet like a one-way telephone.

I nod. "I'll tell you what to do and when." I nod again and sit back. Martin can do what he will; I aim to enjoy myself.

"This is Flight One PT-19A signaling for takeoff," Martin says into the radio.

After a brief moment, the radio crackles to life. "This is the tower," a man's voice says. "PT-19A, you are cleared for takeoff."

"Miss Jones, note the clearance light on the tower and the pattern of the flight and to your left, the wind sock on the hangar. Note the direction of the wind." And the sun and the moon and the cows in the fields, I think. I will not be distracted. I checked the wind and the clouds the minute we got into the plane. Nothing to get in our way. With a hum of engine and tires, we roll up the runway and leap into flight.

The wind snaps around my ears, tugging at my turban and my goggles, burning my face with its speed. I want to laugh. I want to spread my arms into the clear blue sky and soar toward the sun. We climb higher and higher, and suddenly, the plane dips.

"You have the controls, Miss Jones."

My hand falls onto the stick easily, and I pull us level. The instructor told the truth: this plane does not respond as easily as my father's JN-4. But it does respond. We ride the air and I think of Daddy. This is exactly where I want to be.

"Let's begin with an easy turn. Bank right."

I follow his orders and guide the plane into a smooth turn, first right, then left, up and down as he commands. The wind flows over her wings like ice cream, smooth and sweet.

"Release," he says through the tube, and I reluctantly let go of the stick. I can feel him take over and realize a second before he does it that he is throwing us into a loop. I can't help myself, I throw my hands into the air with complete and utter glee. Upside down, I can see Avenger and the other auxiliary fields dotting the flat, sandy landscape like raisins in a piece of bread.

"Parachute!" Instructor Martin yells at me. He thinks I'm falling out of the plane. And then it sinks in—the old codger is trying to dump me! Lily didn't have an accident after all. "The kitchen is safer than the sky," my foot. I snort and bring my hands back in. Martin pulls the plane level and brings us in for a landing.

"That's not proper decorum for a military pilot, Miss Jones," he warns me. I can hear the disappointment in his voice. "Or for a young lady," he adds.

Or for an instructor, I think. Regardless, when we come in for a landing, part of me is still flying high.

"How many girls is he going to try to dump before he realizes we've learned our lesson?" I ask Patsy as she steps up the flight line. "He should be court-martialed for this. Trying to scare us into quitting. It's practically attempted murder!"

She shakes her head. "Like any of the girls here would turn him in on the first day of flight school. Nobody'd take the word of a brand new trainee over an instructor's, and don't think he doesn't know it." She scowls at Martin, who stands smugly beside the plane, waiting for his next victim. "But don't you worry, I've got a fix for Mr. Happy," she says, "and he'll swallow it, or I'll turn him in myself." She throws me a wink and strides toward the plane with a smirk to match the instructor's.

"Lily, come watch this." I call her away from her parachute, which she has been worrying over ever since her awkward landing. Of the bunch, she's the only one Martin managed to actually dump, especially since she was the one doing the flying. Sure, he tried to surprise the rest of us by taking the controls over himself, but you've only got to see a girl fall out of a plane once to make sure it doesn't happen to you. Poor Lily. I hope Patsy pays Martin back a hundredfold. She is the last one to go up today, and everyone comes out to watch her.

Happy sends her into the usual banks and turns, but on the loop, something remarkable happens. At the top of the loop, upside down, Patsy drops out of the plane—but she does not fall. She holds on to the plane with both hands, doing what looks like a handstand, only she's standing right-side up with the plane over her. My heart skips a beat.

"She'll be killed!" Lily screams.

"No, she's a wing walker, remember? Cakewalk Kake?"

"But she doesn't even have a . . . rope or anything!"

One of the other girls steps forward, shielding her eyes for a better view. "Way I hear it, they didn't even wear parachutes until '38." She grins. "Hotdog. She's just out there. Look at her go."

Lily falls silent, but she doesn't relax until Patsy flips herself back into the plane just as it comes level again. When Patsy pays somebody back, she sure does it with style.

"Can't you just hear him screaming at her?" I ask, a broad grin spreading across my face. "Miss Kake, that is not proper decorum for a lady!" I mimic the instructor's prim voice.

The other girls laugh, even Lily, reluctantly. "I suppose, though, I'll have to give her a demerit for that." She looks suddenly crestfallen. "What if she washes out for this?" Everyone else sobers up fast.

"Oh no, she won't," I tell her quickly. "He deserved a scare for what he did to you. And he won't dare punish her—she'll turn him in if he does, even if it's a trainee's word against his. I'll back her up if it comes to that. But for now, we didn't see anything. Let's get back to the ready room. I doubt he'll even mention it. He'll be too embarrassed."

We bustle back to the ready room as quickly as we can. No one stays outside to see Patsy's triumphant return to earth.

She walks into the room a few minutes later, eyes shining. She gives us a curious look. I wink at her. She smiles. "The old buzzard gave me two demerits, but it was worth it," she announces. "He'll never pull that stunt again."

"Oh, Patsy, that's terrible!" Lily exclaims. "Maybe we should report him."

Patsy shrugs. "Do you want to go to court, or do you want to fly?"

The rest of us remain silent. We're pilots and we want to stay, no matter what. I squeeze Patsy's hand. A second later, a very flustered Instructor Martin enters the room.

"Well, ladies, that will be all for today. This afternoon you have physical instruction back at the base. And I'll see you in the morning." He doesn't so much as look at us once. We all stare daggers at him, except for Patsy, who demurely lowers her eyes, trying not to smile.

Instructor Martin clears his throat and busies himself with his papers.

"Dismissed."

Chapter 11

When I was seven, my father took me to Lake Pontchartrain to go swimming with my brother Thomas and his friends. The lake was a dangerous place to be, with an undertow that grabbed on tight and pulled you down. More than a few children have drowned there. Grown-ups, too. But it's where colored people go to swim. The safer beaches are "whites only." Of the five of us there, only Daddy really knew how to handle the water. He knew to stay near the shore, away from the worst of the currents. Me, I had never been in anything deeper than a bathtub, and that not even full to the top. I stared at that dark blue water so long that it wasn't blue anymore, but black. And cold. It must've been August for us to want to go swimming, but I wasn't having any of it. While the boys ran toward the water, I hung back, hugging myself with skinny, goose-pimpled arms.

Thomas was the one to push me in, or one of his friends. Afterward, none of them would say who'd done it. Who had shoved me screaming to cut through the black skin of the lake like a knife. I didn't float, didn't paddle. I simply sank, dragged down by the undercurrent. Daddy pulled me free with one hand and smacked my back until I coughed up half a cup of water, and that was it. I never wanted to swim again.

"Old Clayfoot, sunk like a ton of bricks," Daddy said. But he hugged me close. "Don't worry, Little Bit. You're all right. When you're ready, we'll go in again. This time, without help

from those rascals." He scowled at Thomas and his two bud-
dies. All three looked about ready to cry.

I pressed into my daddy's chest and shook my head. "Uh-
uh," was all I said. And that was that. Daddy didn't push me.
Later, he'd say it was the look on my face that told him not
to. Said I looked like I'd seen the devil under the water, waving
at me. Maybe I had. All I know is I didn't go back to Pontchartrain until high school, and from then on, I stayed on the
shore. That was fine. All the girls did. It was more about
swimsuits than swimming, anyway.

Not like today. Today, we're having a swim test. We're
lined up, two by two, like Noah's Ark at the Sweetwater Mu-
nicipal pool. It's closed to looky-loos, thank goodness, and
I'm at the back of the line. I made sure of that. My hair
is braided tight against frizzing, but that's the least of my
worries.

"One lap, ladies, one lap fully clothed in your flight suits,"
Doc Monserud shouts across the pool to our flight. "Something you should get used to. In case of a water landing."

"Right, water landing," Patsy says, two girls ahead of me.
"In case the plane decides to float."

"Don't jinx it," someone else says. Patsy looks over her
shoulder at me and winks. I don't wink back. I can barely
take my eyes off the pool.

"It doesn't look too bad," Lily says. "Why, the pool in my
apartment building is twice this size. A real Olympic regulation swimming pool."

"Fancy," Patsy drawls. She turns to me. "What's a matter,
honey?"

I grit my teeth. "Nothing. I'm fine."

"Like heck. What is it?"

I stare at my feet. I can't believe I'm going to wash out before basic training has even really begun. I can feel Patsy looking at me. I return the look with watery eyes.

"I can't swim."

The girls near us start to cluck their tongues and shake their heads. "Poor kid." "That's a shame."

"Stop your gobbling," Patsy says to them. "Look, Jonesy. You handle yourself pretty well in the sky. We'll figure something out."

"I could swim for her," Lily whispers.

"What? How?" I stare at her, hating to hope there is a way.

"Sorry, sister, but you two don't look a thing alike, aside from height, that is."

"Not with my hair down," Lily says. "But look at them in there." She points with her chin to the first of the swimmers. They struggle through the water in their overgrown man suits, hair wrapped up in Urban's ugly old turbans. If I didn't know better, I'd say they just want to drown us all.

"She's right," Patsy says. "Bundled up in that mess, you couldn't tell if it was a man or a woman, let alone which woman."

"You'd do this for me?" I take Lily by the arm. If she's caught, we'll both get thrown out. Lily's eyes waver, but only for a second. She sets her jaw and nods at me.

"For the woman that taught me how to make a bed, I'd do anything."

We're at the front of the line now. I hang back and let the other women pass me. Lily jumps in, alongside Patsy.

They sink a little, then float back up to the top of the pool.

Their clothes are another matter. The zoot suits are like an-chors. My heart flutters in my throat just watching them, and I know that I could never do what Lily is doing for me. There are a lot of things I can handle, but water isn't one of them.

After what seems like a dog's age, Lily makes it to the other side of the pool. Doc Monserud is so busy with the other girls, I break free from the group and meet up with Lily and a towel. Patsy climbs out of the pool, grabs another towel, and holds it up as a curtain for both of us. The other girls are too busy with their zoot suits and turbans and pure exhaustion to even notice Lily and me changing suits.

"Are you sure you can do this?" I whisper.

Lily gasps. "Don't ask me again, Ida. I don't have the breath to say yes."

She dresses more quickly than I do, thanks to my dry suit. But a wet zoot suit is a horse of a different color. I struggle halfway into it before Patsy stops me.

"Hey, kiddo, look around," she says softly. Every girl that's finished the swim is half out of her suit and half into a towel. Patsy smiles. "As far as they know, you're done. Just wrap up in a towel now and watch Johnny Weissmuller over there strut her stuff."

I have to laugh at that. Buster Crabbe may be a matinee idol now, but once upon a time he was an Olympic swim champion. I pull the towel around me gratefully and turn to watch Lily catch up with the end of the line. When the doc blows the whistle, she jumps right in without looking at him.

"She sure can swim," Patsy says.

"She's a regular Tarzan," I say, referring to Johnny Weiss-muller's most famous role.

"Heck, no," Patsy says. "Tarzan never had to wear a zoot suit. Our Lily is a Jane all the way."

Lily climbs out of the pool for the second time. She looks tiny in the waterlogged suit but elated.

"I think we did it," she says, waving her hands excitedly.

"Keep it down," Patsy tells her, and tosses a dry towel over her head.

"Thank you, Lily. You saved my skin."

Lily grins back happily. "If it weren't for all this dead-weight, it would've almost been fun."

After the swim test is complete, we're bussed back to the base where Doc Monserud dismisses us. Not all of Flight One has passed. Two girls, Anderson and Shaw, are told to report to Deatie Deaton's office after they shower. The girls head to the showers, chattering about the difficulty of swimming in clothes or, worse, what a wet turban feels like in the Texas heat. It's hot enough to make our clothes steam, but not to dry them.

"Aren't you going to clean up?" Patsy asks me. "We're due at the mess hall in fifteen minutes."

I'm slumped against the wall outside the showers in Lily's wet zoot suit. I feel ashamed. Two of us have already washed out. I'm still here only because I cheated. I've already lied about my license and my race. What else will I do before this training is done?

"I'm fine," I finally say. "But I guess I should report to Mrs. Deaton as a washout."

Patsy stops toweling her hair and gives me a look. "Now, Jonesy, don't let this eat at you. You think those kids overseas get along all by their lonesome in this war? Of course not.

We're a team. We shoulder each other. Anderson and Shaw should've been half as clever as you to figure that out."

I give her a weak smile, but I still feel wrong.

"Ida Mae, hurry up," Lily calls out from the dormitory. She's already back in her khakis, lacing up her shoes. "I'll save you two a seat at the mess."

"Thanks, Lily," Patsy says for both of us. After Lily leaves, Patsy takes me by the wrist. "Listen, Jones. Lily went out on a limb for you. The least you could do is be grateful. Happy, even."

I don't meet her eyes. "The thing is, I'm more grateful than I can say."

Patsy smiles and lets go of my wrist. "Then don't say anything. And repay the favor when you can."

At last I smile. Lily and Patsy aren't just my classmates, they are real friends. Maybe it's not the same as it is with me and Jolene—they don't know everything about Ida Mae Jones. But they know Jonesy, and that's who I really am. For the first time since leaving home, I've got friends, and that tells me I belong.

Dinner is a somber affair as everyone says goodbye to Anderson and Shaw. We've been together only a short while, but seeing two of our own wash out brings everyone down. I hang back, feeling guilty that I'm not leaving, too, but more desperate than ever to stay. After the two girls say their goodbyes, the mood changes and the pressure of training takes over. We linger after dinner comparing class notes, especially in navigation. Reading maps is second nature for some but not all of the WASP. I chatter along with the rest of the girls, and we stay up until lights-out studying flight maps and practicing plotting courses. But afterward, when the lights go off, I lie awake and think of Lake Pontchartrain and how fear, any fear, can be my enemy.

"Shoo, fly, don't bother me. Shoo, fly, don't bother me," I tell myself. I'll get over my fear one day. I have to. Anything else and I'd be less than a WASP.

"Lily." I am across the room and standing by her bed before I can stop myself. "Lily, are you awake?"

Lily moans. Her head is completely under the covers.

"Yes, Mother. I'll be right there," she says sleepily.

"Lily."

Her head pops out of the blankets, red hair wrapped in a sleeping turban, like the high-society version of Urban's finest.

"Ida, what is it? Is everything okay?" Her brown eyes are wide.

"Sorry to wake you. It's just . . ." I sit on the edge of her bed and reach for the right words. "Well, it's like making a bed. I mean, I'm really grateful and all. It was a huge, gorgeous thing you did for me. But I want to be able to do it myself."

"What do you mean?" Lily asks. She's wide awake now, sitting up in her bed. Our whispers add a sense of urgency that shakes away all fogginess.

"I mean, I want to learn how to swim. We come to Avenger Field all big and brave, like we can do anything. And I know that's impossible. We're not superheroes or anything. But I'd at least like to try. To say I gave it a try . . . Will you teach me?"

Lily smiles at me, a kind, happy smile. She puts her hand on mine. "I'd love to. Although we'd best be careful, since everyone thinks you can swim already." Her eyes grow distant. When she looks at me again, they sparkle.

"Oh, this will be fun! It'll be our little secret." She grabs the covers in a gleefully conspiratorial way.

"Mine, too, if you don't keep it down," Patsy grumbles from her bed. Patsy sleeps with a satin mask covering her eyes. She has earplugs, too, from her days working air shows, but she says she doesn't like to sleep with them in because she might miss reveille.

"Sorry," Lily and I whisper simultaneously, and then grin.

"Tell you what, I'll sleep on it," Lily says. "And I'll let you know what I come up with in the morning."

I glance at the clock in the dark, but it's too dark to read. I know it must be late. "Of course. Go back to sleep. I'm sorry to wake you. And thanks, Lily. I owe you one."

"That's two, Jonesy." She smiles and is asleep again almost before she can get the blanket over her head. Poor kid. All that swimming really took its toll. Somehow, I'll find a way to repay her for the test and for the lessons, too.

It only takes me a moment longer to crawl back into bed and fall asleep. This time, I sleep without tossing. I sleep without dreams.

Chapter 12

"Just hold on to the edge," Lily tells me. It's Sunday afternoon and Lily and I are clinging to the edge of the town swimming pool like two shipwreck victims on a piece of flotsam. Well, at least I am. Lily looks as happy as a mermaid in the water. She bobs beside me, legs kicking in a soft froglike movement while she uses both hands to slide my death grip of forearms and elbows off the rim of the pool. If anyone asks, we're just swimming for fun and a little exercise. Never mind the fact that I'm fighting it every step of the way.

The rest of the girls are back at the barracks sunning themselves or writing letters home. Better to be in the water, though, than out in the sun, where my skin will only get darker. Light as I am, I tan deeper than any white girl I've ever seen, and then claiming Spanish blood might not keep everyone from figuring me out.

Eventually I'm holding on just by my very tense fingertips. "See, Ida, that's not so bad."

"If you say so." She's right, of course. It's almost soothing, rocking in the cool water, but that's until I look down the pool to the shadowy deep end. Then it's Lake Pontchartrain all over again, and I can see my doom staring back at me.

"Really, Ida, if you're going to be so melodramatic, maybe we should skip this altogether."

I blush. "Am I that bad?"

"Yes, you are," she tells me. "You don't have to do this."

I consider it for a minute. She's right. I could climb out of the water right now and never get back in again and it won't matter. If I crash at sea, I'm dead, anyway.

Right?

I take a deep breath. "What's next?"

"Well, you put your face in, of course. And I'll teach you how to breathe."

I grin in spite of myself, in spite of the dread I feel. "Shoot, Lily, I thought that was the one thing I already knew."

Swim lessons are soon eclipsed by homework from our navigation class. Every single one of us knows how to fly places we've been before, and we're getting good at plotting our course on maps, but up until now, we've only flown maneuvers over the auxiliary landing fields. Next week, we'll be flying by the map, from Sweetwater to Baker's Pond, a town about thirty miles away, and back. We're expected to make the round trip in under an hour. Getting lost won't exactly look good with the instructor in the backseat.

If we do well, we're up for our first solo flights. That means an end to basic training, a test by an army pilot, and on to bigger and better planes. Audrey says a few girls usually wash out on the solo. I, for one, plan to pass.

Today, Instructor Martin teaches us about railroads. "They are simply the easiest guides to set your course by." He hands out the train schedule for the region. We pass the little paper pamphlets around the room.

"Study these, ladies. Notice the maps you plot on indicate train tracks with little hatch markings, like crisscrossed sticks. You may think you know where you are headed, and that's fine. But remember, landmarks like barns and water towers are a dime a dozen out here. Train tracks, on the other hand, are always the same and they're always there. Unlike a barn or a water tower, train tracks don't burn down, and they don't pull them up too often. They're as permanent as it gets.

"If you get lost in the clouds, bad weather, what have you, drop below cloud level and look for the tracks. Use your eyes. Understand? Use. Your. Eyes."

"Yessir," we say as one. Instructor Martin is a real pain in the neck most of the time, but he's an instructor for a reason. He's got plenty to teach us, besides which, I think he sees the light at the end of the tunnel. He never forgot or forgave Patsy for her stunt that first day. If he can pass us on the basic test, we'll be out of his hair for good. No more antics from Patsy and no more griping from the rest of us. The day we leave his class will be a red-letter day for Mr. Martin.

"Now, today is Wednesday. On Friday, you'll be quizzed on what you've learned. Walter Jenkins, who instructs the intermediates, will join me in testing you. Each of you will have the honor of ferrying either Mr. Jenkins or myself out to Baker's Pond and back again. It's a lovely little hamlet out in the middle of nowhere. I'm sure you'll have no trouble finding it. I expect to see plotted courses tomorrow and weather charts the morning of the flight."

He looks down at his papers and busies himself with shuffling them about. We wait, sitting at attention. This has become a routine with us. The only way he can exert a little power over our rowdy bunch. He stands there behind his desk, humming some old Al Jolson tune, then with a huge sigh that would do a martyr proud, he says, "Class dismissed."

We grab our maps and charts in both arms and race out of there like Friday is a mean old dog that's right on our heels.

"I still can't find Baker's Pond on my map," Patsy groans. "Heck, for all I know, we might've done an air show there, but I wasn't exactly doing the driving."

We're sitting in the ready room, trying to finish our homework in peace. There's a study lounge we could use, but right now it's full of intermediates getting ready for their first instrument-only test. And the cots are full of everyone who's too exhausted to keep studying. Patsy came up with the idea of the ready room as being the perfect place to chart our flights.

Lily has spread her map out on the floor and is standing on it. "A bird's-eye view always helps me," she explains. Then she frowns. "But not today. Maybe it's like that mystical place Shangri-La, and it only shows up to those who are worthy."

"So that means every WASP before us was worthy, but we're trash?" Patsy asks, raising an eyebrow.

"That sounds about right, ladies." We all look up. It's Audrey Hill, our squadron leader. She walks in with the kind of confidence I'm starting to wish I could buy at the dime store. She breaks into a big grin. "Poor kids. From the sound of it, I'd say old Hap's got you flying to Baker's Pond."

"Leave it to Hap," Patsy says with a sarcastic smile. "All these lakes and reservoirs to choose from, and he has to pick the one that doesn't exist."

I'm stretched out on a table, scanning my map with a magnifying glass. "We've been here a whole month and you still haven't gotten a taste for small-town irony?"

Patsy looks at me, befuddled. I sigh. "You got one thing right—it's likely it doesn't exist. Not the way we've been thinking of it, that is. Look at your map. These lakes are huge. The reservoirs, too. But we're looking for something smaller.

As dry as it's been out here, Baker's Pond is probably nothing but a shriveled up watering hole."

Audrey nods at me. "Listen to her, girls. She's on to something."

"But then why's it called Baker's Pond?" Lily asks.

"Why is it called 'Sweetwater'?" I counter. "We're thirteen miles from the nearest lake."

Patsy frowns. "Hey, I think she's right. This place has been drier than Prohibition."

"It's like wishful thinking, isn't it?" Lily says. Her cheeks flush with excitement. "Like when you meet a big man nick-named Tiny. Or Greenland, which is really icy, and Iceland, which is actually quite green."

Patsy and I exchange smiles. "Okay. Now I think *she's* crazy, but you might be right, Ida."

Audrey gives us a little nod and waves goodbye. We turn back to our charts. My smile breaks into a grin.

"Ladies, remember the last thing Martin said to us about navigation?"

"Follow the train tracks," Lily chimes in.

"Precisely." I open my train schedule and search the list of destinations.

"Now, we know the flight has to be less than an hour, so . . ." I take a compass and draw a circle with a forty-minute flight radius around Avenger Field, in case headwinds adjust the travel time. "Baker's Pond isn't on the list of train stops, but it must be near a track somewhere. These are the towns with train stations no more than an hour away." I circle the towns on my list.

Lily and Patsy have come to stand beside me now. I feel

like I'm the instructor and I like it. This must be what Patsy meant by a chance to pay Lily back.

"Now, scan the chart. We're looking for train tracks and a smooth blank spot on the map, near these towns. No hills, no lines. That'll be our dry lake bed." The topographical pictures on our own maps show lakes as blue puddles against crinkled pale green backgrounds. I scan my circle for the hatchmarks indicating train tracks. There. I put my finger down and follow it toward the north. No puddles, no towns. I go in the other direction, and head south. The train tracks stop in a town called Buckhorn and curve around to the east. Just about that curve, just east of Buckhorn, sits a plain brown dot. Below, printed for some unknown reason in green ink that is only slightly darker than the surrounding fields, is *Baker's Pond.*

"Bingo."

"Where?" Lily and Patsy lean forward, squinting.

"Son of a—" Patsy breaks off.

"Ida Mae, you're a genius!" Lily exclaims.

"Way to go, Jonesy." Patsy grins at me. "One for all and all for one. You're a regular musketeer."

She pats my shoulder and it feels good. Lily sighs. "Well, now the rest of the work begins," she says. We all turn back to our own maps and begin working on our flight and weather charts. But I can still feel the glow from their congratulations, and it keeps me working hard all night.

Friday morning dawns with a few fat clouds high in the sky. Cumulus clouds, the kind that look like scoops of mashed potatoes or ice cream, so white they almost hurt to look at.

Everyone in our barracks is ready before roll call. There are some nervous grins, but mostly we're just excited. Lily smiles at me as she calls roll.

"Good luck, Flight One. I'll see you in intermediates," she ends the morning announcements. We all march to breakfast singing "Zoot Suits and Parachutes." I eat a slice of toast, but I'm too excited to eat anything else. Patsy, on the other hand, has two sunny-side-up eggs and a ham steak.

"You've got an iron stomach," I tell her.

Patsy just smiles and mops up the broken yolks with a corner of toast. "Girl's got to keep her energy up," she says.

Next to me, Lily drinks a cup of warm milk. She takes a sip, puts her mug down carefully, and counts backward from ten.

"Are you okay, Lily?"

"Fine." She smiles nervously, her face turning a little green, and takes another sip of her milk. "I just . . . I just need to remember to breathe."

I put a hand on her back. "You'll do fine."

Patsy speaks around a mouthful of ham. "Just don't forget how to fly."

We all laugh, but I can hear Lily's counting turn into something that sounds more like a prayer. The words are foreign, but the tone is familiar. Patsy and I share a look.

"I guess we could all use some of that," I say.

Lily looks up, cheeks red. "Sorry. I was just . . ."

"No," I say, and take her hand. Patsy puts down her fork and toast to pick up Lily's other hand in her own.

"Rabbi," she says with a smile.

Lily blushes and fumbles for a moment. I squeeze her hand. She squeezes back.

114

"Oh, Lord," she says in a trembling voice. "Lord God, hear our prayer. Give us strength . . ." She falters.

"Protect us," I add.

"Pass us, Jesus," Patsy says.

"Bless our flight."

We sit there over our warm milk and toast, Patsy's cooling eggs, and think our own thoughts.

"Amen," we say almost in unison. I feel good. I feel better. When we leave the mess hall, every single one of us is ready to fly.

✈

"Fuel line."

"Check."

"Wing?"

"Check."

"Propeller."

"Check."

It's windy at the auxiliary landing airstrip. Those fat cumulus clouds are skidding lazily across the sky. I stop in the middle of my flight checklist to look at the wind sock floating atop the hangar that serves as storage, classroom, and control tower in one. The orange cone of fabric wafts to the southeast. Good. I'll have a tailwind into Baker's Pond. Every extra minute I gain is more time to fix any flubs in my navigation.

Instructor Martin is off and flying with Lily. I'm going up with Inspector Jenkins, the flight instructor for intermediate WASP. He's a big man, the kind that played football in high school and never lost the broad shoulders or the wide neck. His hair is prematurely turning silver, and his eyes are bright and warm. As Jolene would say, "Not bad, for a white man." I chuckle just thinking about her.

Inspector Jenkins reads out the preflight checklist to me, steadily ticking off each item. He has a nice voice to boot. I smile at him when he finishes the list, and he smiles right back. "All systems go," I announce, and climb into the plane.

I strap my map to my leg with surgical tape. The course I've plotted is charted in red. Instructor Jenkins has a copy in the backseat of the plane. He looks it over silently, determined not to give me a hint whether or not I've done it all right.

We get the all clear over the radio, and I taxi out onto the runway. After that first week of flying with Martin, we've been allowed to handle takeoff and landing by ourselves. I start to grin as we head down the tarmac.

"Watch yourself, Jones," Jenkins says to me through the speaking tube by the throttle. I hesitate and do a mental check, but I'm not doing anything wrong.

"Pardon, sir?" I shout into the tube.

"That grin of yours, you don't want to get any bugs in your teeth."

I laugh. I think I'm going to like intermediate training. I just have to pass basic first. We lift off into the blue sky and I smile even wider, but this time with my lips closed tight.

Being a WASP is all about being in the air. When we graduate from here, we will be assigned to bases across the country to do everything from ferrying newly made planes from factories to the coast—where they will be shipped off to our boys overseas—to towing targets for artillery practice. Some of the first WASP have already logged over a thousand flight hours. There's even a story going around that Nancy Love and her Women's Auxiliary Ferrying Squadron, the original twenty-eight women that eventually became the WASP, once ferried a shipment of planes all the way across country in less than three days.

As Inspector Jenkins and I fly over the train tracks toward Buckhorn, I can't imagine anything finer than seeing the whole country this way. We reach Buckhorn, and I tilt the wings to search for the riverbed I know will take us to Baker's Pond.

It's not there.

Overgrown with brush or just blown away in these darn Texas winds, my landmark has gone AWOL.

Don't panic, I tell myself. We made good time. I just need to be patient. I circle Buckhorn and get my bearings. Baker's Pond should be dead east from here. I look at the sun, at the town, the tracks, the map and say a little prayer.

"Everything okay, Jones?" Instructor Jenkins asks over the tube.

"Roger wilco," I say. "A-OK." I just hope I'm right.

We fly for twenty minutes straight and I'm starting to feel those old butterflies again, slapping against my stomach, when the most beautiful sight in the world comes into view. Three buildings are huddled dead ahead of me, on the edge of a big brown sinkhole. I let out a whoop that would do a Hollywood Indian proud.

"Welcome to Baker's Pond, sir," I shout into the speaking tube.

"Well done, Jones. And not a moment too soon," Jenkins says.

We fly over what passes for a town and I can see the fifteen residents of Baker's Pond sitting at the edge of their dried-up swimming hole, on top of their old cars and pickup trucks. Watching the WASP fly overhead is cause for a picnic in this town.

Some of the kids stand in the truck beds and wave.

"Permission to waggle the wings, sir." I can't see Jenkins's face, but I can tell he's smiling. I like this man.

"Permission granted."

We fly low over the pond bed and I tip my wings left, then right in salute to the fine people of Baker's Pond. With another Hollywood whoop, I change course and we head back to Sweetwater.

Chapter 13

"Howdja do?" Lily asks as I climb out of the plane. I take my time undoing my turban and wait for the instructor to join us.

"Well, Mr. Jenkins?"

Jenkins smiles and waves his clipboard. "A-plus, Miss Jones. You've passed. I look forward to seeing you in Intermediates."

"Thank you, sir." I shake his hand, cool as November, and leave him to his next test subject. At least I think I'm cool. Lily nudges me as we head back to the ready room.

"Ida Mae Jones, you're blushing!"

"I am not," I insist. "It must be windburn."

"Right," she says. "It must be Instructor 'Windburn.' I don't blame you, though. He's a thousand times better looking than old mealymouthed Martin!"

"Lily!"

"It's true!" We've reached the reading room. Lily drops down onto a bench. "Thank goodness that's over!" she exclaims. "I thought for sure Martin was going to fail me, or demerit me, or I don't know what."

I slap my thigh where the course map is still strapped to my pant leg. "Trust your map. No matter what old Martin says."

"Amen to that!" Lily grabs my hand. "And thank you, Ida, so very much, for figuring it all out. If it weren't for you, I'd

119

have flown that plane straight home to New York before I knew I was off course."

I smile and sit down beside her. "What was it Patsy said? One for all and all for one."

"Hear, hear."

I look around the ready room. "Where is Patsy, anyway? I thought she was due to go up with Martin right after you." We look at the clock simultaneously. It's already half-past fourteen hundred hours.

"Oh, I'm sure she'll be here any minute," Lily says, but she doesn't sound so sure.

We sit together in nervous silence. Most of the other girls who've passed their flight tests have gone back to the barracks or the mess hall. Lily and I are dismissed for the day, but we promised to wait for Patsy.

"Maybe we should check with the tower," I say after a minute.

Lily smiles hopefully. "Of course. But you know Patsy. She's probably just pranking on old Martin again."

I smile back, but I don't feel it on the inside. "That's probably it," I say doubtfully. We stand up. "She never could resist putting him in his place."

"And on test day, too," Lily adds.

But our bravado rings false. We break into a run outside the ready room. Sergeant Middleton is at the control tower.

"Keep your pants on, ladies. They were spotted over Baker's Pond about ten minutes ago. They should be here in about half an hour."

"Thank God," Lily gasps. I want to hug the sergeant, but the look he gives me makes me step back and simply nod at him.

"Sorry to bother you, sir."

He snorts and waves us away, but I notice he's searching the skies himself. "Damn radio's probably on the fritz," he mutters as we leave the tower. "Don't want to lose another plane."

Outside, Lily looks furious. "Another *plane*, did he say? Why, I ought to give him a piece of my mind!" She turns in her tracks, but I stop her.

"Let's go, Lily. He's just as worried as we are, but he's an army sergeant. He can't afford to show it."

Lily adjusts her shirt and nods. She lets out a deep breath from somewhere inside that petite body. "Well, thank God we're not army."

I smile. "Come on. Let's go wait for Patsy." I pat my pockets as we walk back to the ready room. "Got any nickels?"

Lily shakes her head. "I never fly with coins in my pocket. I once heard about a pilot who lost his loose change doing a loop. It killed a man on the ground. Can you believe it? They say a dime can do the same amount of damage as a Mack truck if you drop it from high enough up."

"Oh, I think a Mack truck dropped from a plane would hurt a whole lot more than a bitty old dime," I tell her. She rewards me with a poke in the ribs.

"You know what I mean. What's the nickel for, anyway?"

"The wishing well, of course." The well was actually more of a small fountain outside of the ready room. It's WASP tradition to toss coins into it for luck or toss WASP into it when they've done their first solo flight. "Today's a big day," I add. "I think it deserves more than a penny, don't you?"

Lily agrees, but we don't go to the ready room to ask the other girls for change. We don't leave the field until we see Patsy's plane on the horizon.

121

The sky is turning pale purple when she finally appears over the far end of the airstrip, signaling the tower.

"She'd better hurry up or she'll qualify for a night landing," Lily says.

"Yeah." I keep my eyes on Patsy's plane. She's been gone too long. Way too long for it to be good news. Neither one of us has mentioned it, but Lily and I both know that this could be a washout offense.

Patsy lands beautifully and pulls to a stop just a few yards from where we are waiting. But she doesn't get out of the plane. Even when old Martin hops down with his fussy little goggles clamped tightly to his head, a white scarf—far too romantic for a fellow as tight as Martin—thrown twice around his neck against the late-afternoon chill. Patsy just sits in the cockpit and stares straight ahead.

Martin walks past us without a word. His face is red, but whether from wind or something Patsy did, I can't tell.

"You don't suppose she really did do a wing walk on him again, do you?" Lily asks.

"Oh, no, she's smarter than that." And then I think of that crowd of people sitting on their trucks and cars, watching us fly overhead. "At least, I think she is."

We wait for Instructor Martin to disappear into the ready room before we rush up to Patsy's plane.

Patsy doesn't see us at first. She's too busy crying. Not sobbing hysterically, the way I would be if I had failed. Not angry, like we've seen her before. Just slow, quiet tears streaming down her pale cheeks.

"Oh, no!" Lily cries.

I climb up onto the side of the plane. "What is it, Patsy? Did he fail you?"

Patsy jumps, startled to see me so close. She wipes her eyes, embarrassed. When she speaks, she sounds like her old self.

"Well, he tried to, the old goose. Made me run through all the paces, basic training, first-week stuff, all the way to Baker's Pond and back."

"That's why you're late?" I ask hopefully.

She nods. "He was looking for a reason to flunk me. But I showed him. I was like you, Lily." She tips her head toward the other girl. "A perfect student. He said do a loop, I did it perfectly. Do a roll, and I did one, a beautiful one, too. And we come up on Baker's Pond, and there are all these farmers out there, standing on the hoods of their cars and the backs of their trucks, cheering, like we were the circus and the president rolled into one . . ." Patsy looks at us. The sunset catches her face in its glow.

"This was the best flight of my life, Jonesy. The best damn flight, ever."

"Then why are you crying?" Lily asks, brow furrowed.

Patsy smiles slowly, but her smile is big and wide. "Tears of joy, hon. Tears of absolute joy." She laughs. "He passed me. With flying colors, or almost. I had enough demerits for a one-way trip back to nowhere, but even old Martin thinks I've got the stuff."

She pulls herself out of the plane real slow, like she doesn't want to leave it.

"Come on, girls. It's Friday night. We're going to town to celebrate."

"Town" means the Avengerette Club. Here in Texas they call it a honky-tonk hall. Back home, it's a juke joint—the kind of place Mama would never let me go. But tonight I'll walk in with the rest of my friends, not as a teenager, but as a WASP. The brass consider the place an officers' club of sorts, suitable for WASP and military gentlemen. Nothing special on the inside, just a redecorated room above a store in town, donated by the good people of Sweetwater. Still, tonight is a celebration night. Patsy, Lily, and I indulge in extra-long showers, and we take the time to apply long-discarded makeup and curlers.

"I'd forgotten how much better I look with curled lashes," Lily mutters, clamping down on her lash curler in front of the bathroom mirror. Thanks to Patsy's delayed flight, the rest of our classmates are already at the club. The place should be in full swing by the time we get there.

This will be our first trip to the Avengerette. I guess part of me feels like I'm here to fly, not dance. And the other part of me knows Mama just wouldn't approve. Socializing with white men will only get me into the kind of trouble she was worried about. And dancing with soldiers? That's even worse. But tonight is special. I wish Jolene was here with me. She's a regular social butterfly, and boy, can she dance.

The thought makes me sad enough to leave the mirror and take a breather at the foot of my bed. I haven't written home but once or twice in the month since I got here, and that was just to send home some money and say I was okay. Nobody back home would be interested in basic training, or in my white classmates, or anything I'm doing right now. And besides, I've been waiting for something good to tell them. Something that would make Mama and Grandy proud. Today is finally one of those days.

I pull out the little stack of stationery I bought at the five-

and-dime in town last month and put it in my purse. I've never been much for dancing. That's Jolene's specialty. But with luck, there'll be a quiet corner where I can get my letter written.

A sneeze from the other side of the room makes me look up. "God bless you," I say automatically.

"Thank you." It's Melanie Michaels, one of the girls from the other side of the barracks. She's pale and yellow-haired, but her face is even paler than usual.

"Sorry," she says. "I thought everybody had gone out."

"Almost," I say. I close my purse. Melanie is wearing civilian clothes. So am I, but I'm in a party dress, black with tiny polka dots and fluted skirt. Melanie is wearing a tweed travel suit.

"Melanie? Are you leaving?"

She ignores the question and squats in front of a footlocker. "This is Nancy's, right? She borrowed some shoes of mine. I want them back."

I put down my purse and go to her side. Melanie and I don't know each other well, even if we do share a bathroom. She's from Philadelphia, I think, or Connecticut. I kneel next to her.

"Yes, that's Nancy's locker. But what's going on?"

Melanie looks at me and her face crumples like a newspaper, only all the headlines are sad. "Oh, Ida Mae, they flunked me."

"What?" I feel a chill all of a sudden, like angels passing overhead.

"Baker's Pond. I flunked the test."

I scowl. "Martin is a fool. We can appeal it. Go to Jenkins. He's fair."

Melanie wails, "No, I can't! He's the one who failed me. Said I was indecisive and it could cost me my life, or my plane."

She sniffs through her tears and imitates Jenkins's warm voice, but with a sneer to it that I don't remember hearing. "'Miss Michaels, I'm sorry, but I won't have your death on my hands. Or this airplane in yours.' He flew us back. It was so humiliating."

She throws her arms around my neck. I hug her, but there is nothing to say. If Hap Martin had flunked her, it would be one thing, but Walt Jenkins . . . I wish I had paid more attention, seen what she could do. All I can think is Jenkins must be right.

Melanie is the sixth girl to wash out of our flight, the first in our barracks. I try to remember who she was standing next to that first day, when Deatie Deaton said the girl to either side of each of us would fail. Whoever it was must be breathing a sigh of relief. Or feeling the same chill I've got right now.

"It'll be okay, Melanie." I say it, but I know it doesn't help. How could it?

After a minute, Melanie pulls herself together. "There they are." She pulls a pair of black pumps out of the locker. "Apologize to Nancy for me. I just . . ." She wipes her eyes. "I just didn't want to have to tell all the girls."

We stand up. "I understand. I'll let them know."

"Oh, tomorrow. Wait until tomorrow. They should be able to celebrate without pitying me tonight."

"Sure." We hug quickly, and she is suddenly all business.

"Good luck, Ida. You've always seemed like a swell girl. If you're ever in Connecticut, look me up."

"I will."

I walk with her to the door and watch her walk out into the night, her suitcase dragging along beside her, the pumps she lent Nancy still in her hand. I stare into the darkness after she is gone, glad not to be in her shoes.

"Leaving without us?" Patsy asks. I jump at the sound of her voice.

"No, no. I was just . . . looking at the stars." I shut the door and turn around. I give a low whistle. "Boy, you two sure got dolled up."

Patsy is in a sky blue dress with a silk flower on one shoulder. Her straight black hair is curled into waves. Lily's trapped her own natural curls into a bun with brown netting. A chocolate brown dress picks up the red of her hair and her creamy skin.

"Thanks, you're a peach," Lily says with a shake of her shoulder. She giggles. "Patsy's been giving me lessons in sass."

"She learns quick." Patsy winks. "Let's get the show on the road, ladies. Last carload leaves the base in five minutes."

I grab my purse and follow them out into the warm Texas night. I don't feel like celebrating anymore. Melanie Michaels has washed out. Any one of us could be next.

Chapter 14

We hit the Avengerette at a slow moment. The building's certainly seen better days, but you could hardly tell with the music streaming from the doorway and the lights shining so bright.

"Ready, girls?" Patsy asks, straightening her skirt and primping her hair.

"As I'll ever be," Lily says.

My eye falls on the WHITES ONLY sign pasted in the window. My stomach fills with butterflies. "Lead on," I say, setting my jaw and swallowing my nerves. The back of my neck itches when we enter the door, but I don't let it stop me. I'm a white girl tonight. I'm a WASP.

No dogs come running and no one throws me out. My teeth unclench and I pause a moment to take it all in. The Andrews Sisters are crooning in three-part harmony on a record player set up on a corner table next to a small soda pop machine. Somebody must flip the records when they end. But it's smack-dab in the middle of "Dream a Little Dream" right now, and six or seven couples are swaying on the dance floor. I scan the little café tables hemming the dance area. Patsy does the same.

"My, my. Look at all the pretty boys," she says with a predatory smile that reminds me of Jolene. I've never been to a dance hall before, or a bar. From the drab paint job to the scuffed tables, it's a lot less glamorous than I expected.

"Whites only" isn't exactly a sign of quality, I guess. Jolene will get a kick out of that.

"They come in from all over, I hear," Lily says. "Every base within a forty-mile radius. The WASP are very popular girls."

"Not too popular, I hope." It's our squadron leader, Audrey Hill, sitting at a nearby table with a group of senior girls. "Mrs. Deaton frowns on fraternizing too often with the enemy."

"She means men," one of the other upperclassmen says. She's a redhead with high-arched eyebrows. By the way she's decked out like a regular Rita Hayworth, I'd say she's looking to engage "the enemy" head-on.

"Girls, this is Randi, and this is Charlotte." Audrey introduces us to her friends. Charlotte, who looks a little bored with the whole evening, nods and goes back to nursing her Coca-Cola.

"What's that?" Patsy asks.

"Rum and Coke," Charlotte says with a drawl that sounds too soft for Texas. She taps a flask peeking out of her purse.

"Barkeep, three thirsty women with heavy tipping hands!" Patsy calls down to a fella standing by the Coke machine, flipping him some change. Before I know it, there's a bottle of Coke in my hand. "Don't worry, it's a virgin," Patsy assures me. "See you on the dance floor, ladies," Patsy tells Audrey and her pals. Lily and I share a look, but we both know Patsy is the leader tonight. She finds us a table with two servicemen, one with big teeth and the other so short that when they stand up to greet us, he looks like he's still sitting down.

"I'm Hank!" the big-toothed fellow says, and shakes our hands. "And this is Danny! We fly gunnery at Waco! We ship out next month!" Everything he says sounds like an exclamation. It makes me smile.

"I'm Lily," she says, making her own introduction.

"And I'm Ida."

Hank eagerly shakes our hands. "And who's your friend?" He offers his giant hand to Patsy. Patsy shakes his fingertips delicately.

"I'm just here to dance, flyboy. Can you shake it?"

"Boy, can I!" Big-toothed Hank hops up and whirls Patsy out onto the dance floor just as the record flips to some music that really swings.

Benny Goodman starts heating up his band. Lily looks at the dance floor the way I used to look at the clouds in the sky. "Harry and I used to dance at the Palladium every Friday night." Even with her legs crossed, Lily's toe is dipping to the music.

I catch her eye and nod toward Danny, who is politely watching nothing in particular. Lily takes a deep breath.

"Excuse me, Danny. I know we've just met and it isn't proper for a lady to ask a gentleman first . . ." She pauses and we both glance at Patsy, whirling around the dance floor, not in the least bit worried about being a proper lady. Lily takes another big breath. "And I know you're shipping out soon and most likely are looking for some sort of romance, but—" She holds up her diamond engagement ring. "I'm engaged, you see, but I'd like it awfully much if you'd care to dance with me."

Danny's eyes seem to refocus. He looks at Lily like he's seeing her for the first time.

"I'm married, just last week," he says excitedly. "As long as we're both taken, I guess it's okay." He stands up and he's exactly Lily's height.

"Hank dragged me here looking for a little fling, but I told him I'm not interested. Not when I have my Annie. But it would be swell to dance before the night is over."

"Really?" Lily's eyes sparkle. "Let's go!"

I can almost feel myself fade into the background as they hit the dance floor. I thought Patsy could cut a rug, but Lily's a regular Ginger Rogers out there. Danny's no slouch, either. The whole dance floor makes room as he flips Lily over his back and around again into a cuddle and a series of half-moons so quick I think she'll break her neck.

I have to admit, it looks like a blast. Lily could give Jolene a run for her money. With the whole shack watching the dance floor, I realize Melanie was right. Tonight is about celebrating. If I'd wanted to tell anybody about her washing out, now I simply don't have the heart.

Instead, I pull my stationery out of my purse and start my letter home. *Dear Mama,* I begin. *It's been too long since I've last written, but I do have good news. I navigated my first flight today, and I passed. If all goes well, I'll move on to intermediate training next month. With any luck, I'll be home after Christmas, and then I'll be assigned to a base . . .*

My thoughts trail off. Someone is standing over me. Nancy Howard, from my barracks.

We've never been friends, not since that first day, but at least we're civil.

"Hey, Jones. Have you seen Michaels? She was supposed to meet up with us tonight."

I open my mouth and close it again. "Uh, no." I shrug. "Sorry."

Nancy gives me a funny look, then smiles. "Okay. See you out there." She jitterbugs back to the dance floor. I finish my letter home, then one to Jolene, telling her about the Avengerette. By the time I'm done, the lights are flickering on and off, announcing one more dance before the club closes.

It's only then that I realize Patsy and Lily never left the dance floor. They don't even look tired out there, although I see Patsy is no longer dancing with Hank. She's got her arms around the shoulders of some corn-fed redhead. He's smiling like he's struck gold, but Patsy only has eyes for the dance floor as she moves, dreamy-eyed, to the music.

"Excuse me. May I have this dance?"

I almost spill the last of my Coke. Instructor Jenkins is standing in front of me with his hand out.

"Instructor Jenkins, I didn't know you were here."

He laughs. "How could you? You've had your head buried in that letter all night."

I blush and fold my letters back into my purse.

"What do you say? Last chance to really celebrate."

"I'm not allowed to dance with a—" I stop myself from saying "white man." Jenkins raises an eyebrow.

"With an instructor?" Jenkins asks. I blush and remember Deatie Deaton's bylaws. Something about fraternizing with the instructors . . . I hesitate. The rules of the South don't apply to Jonesy, I remind myself, but Mrs. Deaton's bylaws do.

"Don't worry, Miss Jones, I'm off duty."

I don't move. He might be an off-duty instructor, but am I off duty as a colored girl? His hand is still outstretched, reaching for mine. I think of my mother's warnings—is this the line she told me I might cross?

The moment's stretched so long I feel awkward saying no,

even if it's the wrong answer. Besides, it's just one dance. If I stick to my charade, what harm can there be in it?

"Well, all right." His warm hand closes over mine. I follow him to the dance floor. I've never held hands with a white man before. In the South, even in the U.S. Army, this dance is all but illegal. There's a strange thrill in knowing it. Is this how Stevia Johnson felt when she went on the first date with her white boss?

"Cold hands," Instructor Jenkins says. "Warm heart."

I laugh, and I know it sounds nervous for too many reasons. You're white now, Ida. And never mind Stevia Johnson. It's just one dance. "I'm afraid I'm better at flying than dating—I mean, dancing." I blush at my mistake. I'm not looking him in the eye, but he doesn't seem to notice. They never play fast songs when you need them.

"I see what you mean." He laughs. "You like to lead."

"Is that it? I thought I just had two left feet." I look over his shoulder to find Lily and Patsy staring back at me over the shoulders of their own partners. I start to feel sick, like the whole world can see what's going on. Instructor Jenkins is a nice fella, but he's a teacher. And he's twice my age. Even if he wasn't white, which he is, I don't even know his first name.

"Walter," he says.

I practically jump out of my skin. On top of all of it, he's a mind reader, too. "What did you say?"

"My name. You said you didn't know my first name. It's Walter. Walt."

"Oh." I flush hot and tingly. What else did I say out loud? I wonder. I keep my mouth shut for the rest of the dance,

133

concentrating on ignoring the gawking faces of my friends and every other flygirl in the place. Why, oh why did he have to ask me to dance? He's an instructor, soon to be *our* instructor. I'm never going to live this down.

Mercifully, the song finally ends and everyone claps, as if the record player was a real live band. MPs did not come crashing through the door. The local lynch mob hasn't come to take me away, and I'm not dead yet from pure embarrassment.

"Miss Jones." Instructor Jenkins shakes my hand. "Get home safely."

"Thank you, Mr. Jenkins . . . Walt . . . Jenkins."

He's smiling, laughing at me, but he nods and lets me scurry back to my table. I grab my purse and stand there with my back to the room.

"What was that?" Patsy asks me as she disengages from her redheaded dance partner. He waves goodbye and leaves her alone with me.

"Nothing. Just a celebration dance."

"I think it's illegal to dance with teachers." Lily comes up to us, her forehead wrinkled with worry. "I heard they never even come here."

"Illegal?" I repeat. My stomach sinks. "But I didn't do anything wrong."

"Sure, honey." Patsy's droll voice cuts through my thoughts. "You haven't done anything wrong. Yet." She winks at me. "No wonder you scored so well on your test. He was grading you on your curves."

My face flushes and I'm washed in a wave of guilt, over the dance, over passing, over the swim test I should have failed. I go from embarrassed to defensive in five seconds flat to hide my shame. "What do you know, anyhow? You're the one dancing with every man in the place. And we both know you'd still be flying over Buckhorn if it weren't for me, or worse, you'd be washed up and sent home like Melanie Michaels, so get off my case."

As soon as the words are out of my mouth, I wish I could turn them off, make the whole room go deaf. Patsy and Lily stare at me.

"What did you say?"

I close my eyes, but when I open them, they're still there, and a few other girls besides, Nancy among them.

"I thought you said you hadn't seen her," Nancy says accusingly.

"I . . . I lied." I sit down at the table. It's too late to put the cat back in the bag. "I'm sorry. She asked me not to say anything tonight. She wanted us all to have fun. Jenkins failed her, and she must've had more demerits than we knew about. She went home right before we came here."

I look up at the girls around me. The look on their faces makes me sorrier than ever that I opened my mouth. Patsy sits down next to me, but her eyes are far away. "We were just teasing you, Jonesy."

"I know. I'm just . . . It's a long story."

Patsy takes my hand. "Hey, kid. Tell it to us sometime. It might help."

I shrug. Any story I give them will only be part of the truth, unless I tell them everything. And even then they could never understand what it felt like, being a colored girl in the arms of a white man who could destroy me if he knew what I was. Overhead, the lights flicker on and off.

"Closing, ladies," a man by the door announces. He jingles a ring of keys.

Not a single WASP moves.

"One for the road, buddy?" Patsy asks.

The poor man looks about to say no. It's been a long night. I imagine he's got a home and a family to get back to. But then, with the same expression of dutiful patriotism with which Jolene and I used to collect bacon grease and silk stockings, he plugs the vending machine back in. "It's just soda, ladies. You still have to get back to base."

"Sir, yes, sir," Patsy says. We pass out one last round of fizzing colas and sit together for a moment in silence. I look at the faces around me, every last girl from my flight and a few from other barracks. We all look so different, short, tall, dark, light. But the expression on every face is the same.

Lily raises her Coke. "To Melanie."

"To Melanie." We toast with a click of our glasses.

In the small hours of the morning, I sit in the bathroom between our sleeping bays and add a page to my mother's letter. I tell her nothing about Instructor Jenkins, how the weight of his arm feels like a brand around my waist, or my fear, or anything that would give away my secret. Instead, I tell her about Melanie, how her failure clings to me like unwanted perfume, how hard training can be sometimes. Then I tell my mother that I will not fail. And I find myself wishing she were here to convince me that I am right.

Chapter 15

Flight Two lost a few more girls on our first solo tests. I think Melanie Michaels's departure screwed my flight's courage to the sticking place. All of us passed and began our intermediate training with little fanfare and a lot of hard work. Instructor Jenkins is a complete professional in the classroom. Since that night at the Avengerette, no one has mentioned our slow dance, not even him.

"Ladies, when you leave these fine flying fields, you will be stationed from California to Delaware. Some of you will be towing targets for artillery practice. Some of you will fly test planes or weather-checking missions. Many of you will ferry airplanes from the factory to the coast. All of you will need to trust your instruments to fly."

I bounce my pen on my notebook, waiting for him to tell me something I'll need to remember. Up to now, most of our classes have been about theory. Today, we try our hand at the Link trainer.

We follow Jenkins to the training room and stand nervously while he shows us the equipment. The room itself looks just like the beginner classroom, except the student desks are on a platform and the lower third of the floor is taken up by the Link.

The Link trainer is a simulator. It looks like an airplane cockpit, black metal and bullet-shaped, but unlike a plane, the top of the cockpit is dark. Once inside, you're "flying" blind, with only the dials and gauges on the control panel to tell you which way is up. I'm so anxious to get started, I volunteer to go first. The cockpit closes over me with a sharp click. Climbing into the Link is a little like going underwater. Shut inside that warm darkness, suddenly I'm drowning in Lake Pontchartrain all over again.

"Miss Jones, can you hear me?" Jenkins's voice comes over a radio speaker, loud and clear. It's hard to believe that just a few feet away, Lily and Patsy are standing with the rest of my class. Jenkins himself sits at a control panel that mirrors my own. He'll know every move I make.

I take a deep breath. "Affirmative," I say. My voice is strained. I'm sweating, even though the box isn't hot. It's just like a cockpit, same size and shape, but it feels smaller, like my knees are tucked into my chest.

Breathe, Ida Mae. Breathe.

"Okay," Jenkins's voice says. "I want you to start your taxi and take off. Cruise at one thousand feet. I'll tell you what to do next."

"Yes, sir. Flight check." I go over the flight check in my head. The routine helps to calm my breathing. Check. Check. Check.

"Taxiing," I say. The Link doesn't move. Nothing moves but the speedometer and altimeter. This is not like flying to me. The Link box just sits there. There's no wind in my hair, no sun on my skin. Not even stars or the wet feel of cloud spray. This is just mechanics.

My throat gets tight. My vision starts to dim. Suddenly, this little box is too small for me to have ever even gotten inside of it.

"Jones, are you all right?" Jenkins's voice sounds far away.

I don't know how long he has been calling my name. I try to respond, but I can't. I'm drowning. I start to bang on the hatch. The tiniest part of me, the part that says not to panic or I'll wash out, is suffocated by the screaming animal inside of me that says I am going to die if I don't leave this box.

"Jones!"

The hatch whooshes open with a burst of sweet, cool air. I throw back my head and grab the sides of the opened cockpit, gasping for breath. I can't draw it in fast enough.

A hand takes mine. I hold on to it the way I held on to my daddy's hand beneath the lake, feeling it pull me up into the light.

"Slow down, Ida. Take a deep breath and open your eyes." Walt Jenkins is there, his hand clutching mine, a look of worry in his eyes. I cling to his hand and fight to do as I'm told.

With each slow breath, my panic slides away. Embarrassment takes its place. The whole class is watching us. It feels worse than our dance at the Avengerette. Jenkins lets go of my hand, his eyes no longer worried, and squeezes my shoulder.

"Thank you, Miss Jones. That will be all."

My stomach hits the floor. I leave it and all of my big dreams behind in the Link. *That will be all.* I'm going to be sent back home. My legs tremble slightly. I go stand between Patsy and Lily, who give me worried looks but otherwise leave me be. I wonder if failure can rub off onto other people, the way Melanie Michaels must have rubbed off on me.

But that's ridiculous. In the end, I failed because I'm lying. I'm only pretending to be white. White kids never tangled in the undertow of Lake Pontchartrain. As light as I am, no matter what I do, I'm still that little colored child who almost drowned.

"And that, ladies, was a classic example of what can happen while flying under the hood," Instructor Jenkins says, using the more common term for flying instruments only under a covered hatch. "It's called a panic attack, in this case brought on by claustrophobia." Jenkins smiles at me, and I want to slap the smile off his face. How did I not hear the sarcasm in that friendly voice before? Melanie did. Now I do, too. Like the instructor at Tuskegee. It hurts to hear.

Maybe he sees the look on my face, but Jenkins stops smiling. "Don't worry, Miss Jones, it happens to the best of us." He takes a step toward me and his voice softens. "It happens to most of us. You get inside that box or a plane at night, and you don't know up from down." I feel myself flush. Fortunately, he turns back to face the rest of the class. Why does this man make me feel so flustered?

"We're creatures of the daylight, ladies," Jenkins continues. "We like the sky above us and the earth below. But under the hood, all of your natural instincts go out the window. Sometimes the stars can look like city lights and you fly too high. Sometimes tailwinds send you faster or slower than you thought and you miss your landing mark.

"But that is why you have Link training. And that is why you have me." He puts his hand fondly on the Link. "Contrary to what you've seen today, the Link is our friend. You will all get a chance to try it. You will all have your own moment of panic. And then you will listen to me. We will retrain your instincts. And every last one of you will fly out of here, day or night, as if they are one and the same."

My stomach slowly rises back to its usual spot. I am not a failure. I am like everyone else. But I need to see it to believe it. Jenkins steps back from the trainer and offers the door. "Next?"

Patsy edges forward to give it a shot. Of all of us, she ends up being the one that lasts the longest that first day. Ten whole minutes. Hardly long enough to fly halfway to Baker's Pond. But I'm not alone. I haven't failed, not really, not yet. I watch each girl's face as they climb out of the Link like they are rising out of a coffin. Then I grit my teeth and prepare to do it again.

"Ida! Ida, come up!" Lily's voice carries through the water like an old gramophone recording. Stretched, thin, and bubbly, it sounds more like she's the one underwater instead of me.

I give her a thumbs-up, then hold up all ten fingers. Ten seconds more. I've been sitting at the bottom of the town swimming pool for twenty seconds. Ten more and I'll have reached my goal. My lungs ache. I want to open my mouth and exhale. At the mere thought, bubbles escape my nose. I try to stay calm, but I'm already shoving off the rough pool bottom toward the surface. I break through the top with a gasp.

"Ida, thank goodness. You know you scare me when you stay down so long." Lily rushes toward me with a white towel. "I'm not sure I'll be able to tell if you ever get in trouble down there."

I accept the towel gratefully and dry my face before wrapping the towel around my shoulders. "Oh, believe me, you'll know, from all the thrashing and churning I'll do. I don't think anybody ever drowns peacefully."

Lily frowns. "Ophelia did, in *Hamlet*."

"No, you only hear about it afterward. They always candy-coat that stuff."

I shiver beneath the little towel. Lily frowns.

"Goodness, you must be cold. It's getting too chilly to keep doing this before spring, Ida. Maybe we should give it a rest."

I hate to admit it, but she's right. "It is only warm in the sun these days." Even in New Orleans, December was usually cause for a cold snap. And no one wants to believe how cold it can get in the South in the wintertime, even without snow.

"It'll be warm at the Beach. Let's go."

The Beach is actually the strip of sand that runs between the rows of barracks. Thanks to the metal siding of the buildings and the lack of trees, the Beach gets hot enough to suntan in year-round, according to the upperclassmen. I've avoided it until now, because, quite frankly, getting a tan is the last thing I should be doing here, and not just because of the workload. The minute I get a shade darker than I am, I'm convinced a group of MPs will descend on me and throw me into the hoosegow.

"I think I'll just take a shower," I tell Lily as we reach the barracks. She shrugs.

"I'll only be out for a little while. I burn like crazy in the sun," she says. She grabs the chair from the foot of her bed and drags it behind her into the yard. I wait for her to leave before I carefully undo my hair from its swim cap. It's become a ritual, pulling it straight and tight, braiding the ends so they tuck up neatly beneath the two swimming caps I wear, with a little towel sandwiched underneath the rim. Whatever it takes to keep my hair from getting too wet, too kinky. It's harder now that I can sit underwater for so long. Sometimes you can see the air bubbles squeeze past your ears and let the water in. That's when I came up with the towel. At least it keeps the water from the crown of my head. Now, a lot of girls wear swim and shower caps during the week—there's just not enough time in the morning to deal with shampoo. But my little getup is just strange enough that I try not to let anyone see it.

Once my hair is safely unbraided, I comb setting lotion through with my fingers and look out the door while I massage it into the damp ends. Colored or white, setting lotion is a girl's best friend. It can help a style hold all day or, in my case, keep my hair from frizzing up. The smell of the lotion reminds me of Jolene and how we'd sit together at the beauty parlor on our days off, laughing and gossiping under the big hair dryers. My stomach feels hollow from missing her. With all the studying and flying, I'm usually too busy to feel homesick. But not today. Today is a lazy day. It's hard not to think of home.

Outside the door, Lily and about seven other girls are out there, stretched out in swimsuits and nighties on the strand, their desk chairs tilted seat down on the ground so they can use the backs like lounge chairs. It's down to a fine science, the art of sunbathing at Avenger Field. Patsy waves at me from her lounge chair. I smile and turn to take my shower.

The hot water feels good running over my shoulders. I've tucked my hair into a shower cap to help the lotion soak in, and the water bounces off of it in a rapid pitter-pat. I sing little bits of "Zoot Suits and Parachutes" in my off-key voice. Halfway through, I switch to that ditty Jolene and I used to listen to while we cleaned the Wilson place. "T'aint whatcha do, it's the place that you do it! T'aint whatcha do, it's the time that you do it!"

By the time I'm out of the shower, the other girls have come in from the beach. "Almost ready, Ida?" Patsy calls. I quickly pull on a sweater and skirt. Christmas is coming to Avenger Field. We're going into town to shop for the holidays.

"Ready when you are."

Patsy and Lily have joined with some of the girls from the barracks next door to take us into town. One of the girls is from Houston. She drove to training and keeps her car at the field. I haven't spent much time in the actual town of Sweetwater. I feel more comfortable on the base, where I don't have to worry about NO COLOREDS signs or worse. Still, I'm feeling good after my successful swim lesson, and I desperately want to get Mama, Grandy, and the boys something nice for Christmas.

The ride into town is chilly, chillier than it has been in Sweetwater since we first arrived. Bad enough it's December, but the cold gets even worse at night. On the open plains, it drops twenty degrees or more when the sun sets. "I'm going to have to buy myself another sweater," I tell Lily as we climb out of the car.

"We're the same size. I've got a dozen of them in one of my trunks," she says. "You can have whatever you need."

The rest of us stop in our tracks. "You still have your steamer trunks?" Patsy asks. "I thought they made everyone ship them back home after the first day."

Lily blushes deep red. "My mother was horrified at the thought of leaving me out in the 'wilds of America' improperly dressed. She doesn't know about Urban's turbans, or the

144

zoot suits, or anything. It would kill her. So my clothes are in storage down at the train station. Don't tell anyone at the base." She shakes her head. "It really is too much."

We laugh and head off down Main Street to see what we can see. "I think I'm going to buy a new tablecloth for Mrs. Harper," Patsy says. "She was the sweetest little lady you could ever meet. Ran the boardinghouse in Florida where I lived last season with my air show. Closest thing I've got left to family, next to you girls."

"Oh, Patsy," Lily says. We squeeze her hands and she squeezes back.

"The life of a wing-walking gypsy, eh?"

"There's a linens shop just down the road," Lily offers. "I'm sure you can find something there."

"Join me?" Patsy asks us.

"Oh, no, I've got to find the drugstore and see if they have Mother's favorite perfume. It's a tradition, every Hanukkah."

"What about you, Jones? Anything on your list in the way of linens?"

I shrug. "My mother might be able to use a new towel or two."

"Or maybe an apron?" Patsy suggests with an encouraging waggle of her eyebrows. I laugh.

"Maybe. But it would be nice to get her something that didn't remind her of all the work she has to do."

"There's always perfume," Lily suggests. The thought makes me laugh again.

"You don't know my mother. She'd say, 'Ida Mae, God gave us soap to keep us clean. Why do I need to cover it up with lilacs or lilies?' Oh, no offense, Lily," I add. But Patsy and Lily are both laughing.

"Then I guess bubble bath is out of the question."

"I guess so," I admit. "I really haven't thought of anything good, except for an awl for my grandfather. There's a hardware store around here somewhere, right?"

Lily shrugs. "I suppose so, but we'll have to ask." She looks at her watch. "We'll have to hurry, too, if we want to get back to base and finish our homework before dinner."

"Well, that settles it, musketeers," Patsy announces. "One for one and all for themselves. Meet you back here in forty-five minutes, presents or no presents. I've got a table-cloth to hunt down."

We all nod and walk off in our separate directions. I haven't gone far down the sidewalk before I realize that I have no direction. Sweetwater is a small town, so I imagine I can manage to find the hardware store without any help. There just aren't that many streets to walk down. But this is the first time I've been alone in Texas since I got here and it makes me nervous. As long as Lily and Patsy are with me, I blend in and look like I belong. But the minute they disappear into their storefronts, I can't help but start seeing the WHITES ONLY signs hanging in every window.

A second look tells me it's not every store, just the nice ones where Lily and Patsy have gone. I remind myself who I'm supposed to be and head off down the street once again. I doubt there are two hardware stores on Main Street.

The street is full of strollers, window-shopping and gathering Christmas gifts. A little towheaded kid runs by me in dungarees and a camel jacket. "Hey, Tigger!" he shouts. I jump, then realize he's not talking to me. A little brindle-striped dog has just rounded the corner. The boy doesn't see him. He looks about close to tears. "Tigger, where are you?"

I swallow my fear and call to the boy. "Don't worry, he's just over there." I point to where the dog is standing in the shadow of a lamppost, his pink tongue lolling as if he is laughing at the whole adventure. The boy grins at me.

"Thanks, lady. I thought he was lost for sure."

I smile back. The boy reminds me of Abel. "You'd better go fetch him," I say.

"Hey, you're one of them army airplane ladies, aintcha? Out at the base?"

My smile gets even bigger. "That's right. I'm training to be a WASP."

The boy's eyes gleam with what I mistake for enthusiasm. Too late, I realize, it's mischief. "My mama says the WASP are easy women. Loose as a goose, she says. Is that true?"

My smile drops into a deep frown. An angry fizzle fills my chest, but there's no point taking it out on a child. I don't let my shock show on my face. "Son, your dog's getting away."

The kid turns to see Tigger disappear around the corner. Without another word to me, he takes off after the dog, shouting its name.

Half a block later, I find the hardware store. I walk in through the front door and think about how Grandy always has to use the rear entrance at the big hardware store back home or shop at the smaller Negro-owned one outside of town. I hold my head up high, so high that I almost run into a stock boy.

"Whoa, sorry, miss," the kid says. He can't be more than fifteen. I feel like a real adult compared to him, and I act like one.

"That's quite all right, young man," I say. "But maybe you can help me. I'm looking for an awl."

"An awl?" The boy's face screws up, and for a moment I think he doesn't know what I mean.

"Yes, an awl. You know, for boring holes in wood?"

"Yes, yes, I know," he says, sounding insulted. "I'm just trying to think of where I put them." He smiles self-consciously. "I've been here four weeks, and I'm still trying to get the inventory down right. You might ask Jacob, up front. He's real good at recalling the stock."

"Thank you." I squeeze down a narrow aisle of penny nail bins and make my way to the counter. A colored farmer is standing in line before me, overalls dusted with clay, rough hands holding a new length of chain out to the store clerk. The look of distaste on the clerk's face is evident. I've seen that look before, aimed at me.

"Sorry, MacIntyre, we don't have any more like that."

"I don't want to buy more. I want to return it. You sold me more than I need."

"We don't take returns on cut chain, boy, you know that."

It burns me to hear a man as old as my grandfather called "boy." But I duck my head, the way I've always done, and listen, and take it. And so does the farmer, MacIntyre.

"Can I trade for it, then? I could use some nails for the barn door."

The store clerk shakes his head. "Sorry. May I help you, miss?"

It takes a second for me to realize he is talking to me. It's as if the farmer and his complaint no longer exist.

"Uh, yes. I'd like to buy an awl. The best you have."

"Oh, those are in the stockroom. I'll be right back. Anything else before I go?"

I look at the chain in the farmer's hands. "Yes. I actually need a piece of chain like that one. How long did you say it is?"

The farmer looks startled. He takes his hat off to me and lowers his eyes. "It's two feet, ma'am. Two feet, seven inches."

I smile brightly. "Why, that's perfect. That'll chain my granddaddy's shed door perfectly!" I turn to the clerk and frown just as darkly as my smile had been bright. "Oh, but you said you're out of that chain, didn't you?"

The clerk hesitates. "That's right. But we've got other types of chain in the back."

"Oh, no. That one was the perfect size. Well, that's too bad. Maybe I'll wait and buy the awl and the chain together somewhere else."

Evidently, there is a second hardware store in town, because the clerk suddenly looks inspired.

"I tell you what. Old MacIntyre here was just about to trade in that piece of chain for some nails, weren't you, boy?"

MacIntyre has the dignity not to nod. He just stares at the store clerk, who goes a bit pale beneath the glare.

"Well, why don't we do this, then. Give me that there piece of chain, boy, and pick out the nails you need. A quarter pound. Not an ounce more, mind you, and we'll call it even. And ma'am, you can have your chain and your awl right here, easy as pie. That is, if you don't mind a chain that's been touched by a nigger."

I smile brightly again, but this time, it doesn't reach my eyes. "I guess it'll have to do."

MacIntyre shakes his head and drops the chain on the

counter. The clerk watches over him as he measures out a quarter pound of nails. It bothers me enough that I clear my throat. "I really am in a bit of a hurry," I say.

"Oh, of course." The clerk takes a last look at the farmer and hurries back to the stockroom.

MacIntyre takes his time filling the little paper sack with nails, but when he is done, it weighs exactly a quarter of a pound. He puts his hat back on and nods without looking at me. I do my best to ignore him, like a white lady should, but I can't help a little smile.

He passes close to me as he leaves the store. In a voice so quiet I barely hear him, he says, "Child, you gonna get yourself killed, or worse, doing what you're doing."

I look at him in surprise and I know that he sees me for what I am—a colored girl playing at being white. My stomach twists and I feel my cheeks start to burn. I look up and the stock boy is standing in the aisle, watching us. The old farmer takes the chain off the counter and drops it into my hands. "Get on out of here, now," he says. The door swings shut behind him, bell chiming as it closes.

My heart pounds in my ears and I drop the chain. The jangle of metal makes the stock boy jump. He rushes to pick it up, but his eyes are on me. I feel cold. And now this skinny little white boy is staring at me like an ape in the zoo.

The clerk abruptly reappears, all smiles, with my awl. His face falls when he sees the chain on the floor.

"Damn it, Henry," he says to the stock boy. "Sorry, ma'am. Watch your step there. I've got that awl for you."

I can't reply for fear that my voice will shake, and then what will this white man think? The stock boy, Henry, puts the chain on the counter.

I swallow hard. Move, Ida, before the stock boy says anything. But my legs feel weak. Killed, or worse, the farmer said. I stumble on a knot in the wooden floor and have to catch myself.

"Ma'am," the clerk says with concern, "are you all right?"

"No . . . I . . . I . . . " I fumble through my purse for my money. Calm down, Ida, I plead with myself. He's just a stock boy. Even if he did hear what the farmer said, he's a kid. I'm a woman. A white woman. Just stick with it.

It's harder than any flight maneuver I've ever peformed, but I manage to find my wallet and pay hurriedly, sweat on my brow, my hands shaking. "Thank you." My voice comes out in a dry whisper.

The clerk frowns. "I can call a doctor for you—"

"No! I'm fine, just fine." I force myself not to glance back at the stock boy as I rush past him and back outside into the cool December air. I can't hear anything over the sound of blood rushing in my ears. My face is hot. Every moment in the open street feels dangerous. It takes all of my willpower not to break into a run.

Suddenly, Patsy and Lily are there.

"There's our girl," Patsy exclaims. But one look at me brings a frown to her face.

"Oh, no! Are you sick, Ida?" Lily asks out of concern.

I shake my head. "No, no. Just tired." My voice is high with strain.

"You poor dear, you do look exhausted. Let's get her home." Patsy steers us toward the car where the other girls are waiting.

Their concern soon fades into talk of the holiday to come. I take my seat in the back and smile when necessary, but it's a false smile. Not until we reach the gates of Avenger Field do I start to breathe again. Sweetwater isn't safe for a colored girl like me. One word from that stock boy, or the farmer, or someone else who can see me for what I am and I'm finished. Texas isn't kind to coloreds. Grandy tried to tell me that. From now on, I'll stick to the base. But inside, I know even New Orleans won't be the same for me anymore. I'll only feel safe in the sky.

Chapter 16

I'm flying under the hood for real this time, a canopy pulled over my cockpit like a glove, blocking out the sky to simulate night flying. The trick, I've discovered, is concentration, just like sitting at the bottom of a swimming pool. I've got to climb into the cockpit and picture the sky outside around me. It's better than the Link, where there is no wind tugging against the wings. No, when you're under the hood in a real airplane, you can't see the sky, but you can feel it. I feel safe. My breathing is steady. I even smile sometimes, though no one can see it.

Jenkins sends me up for my first solo instrument flight. This is the last hurdle between intermediate and a long-distance senior solo flight, then graduation. Lily comes with me as my navigator. There'll be no instructors to save our skins on this trip. She sits behind me, reading the maps strapped to the leg of her zoot suit with a small flashlight. I keep both hands on the throttle and both eyes on the control panel in front of me. It is dimly lit, like starlight, but with practice, I can read it plain as day.

We're flying in broad daylight. It's eleven o'clock in the morning, civilian time. Two days before Christmas. But so far as we can tell, it's midnight outside.

"Having fun yet?" Lily asks me.

"Boy, and how," I reply. I still sweat a little when the hood first closes, but once we take off, once we're in the air, I settle back into the routine.

"We make a good team," Lily says, and feeds me the coordinates for our next maneuver. Jenkins has us flying around in a big zigzag. Other WASP are stationed here and there throughout the area with binoculars. Once they spot us, they radio back in. We radio when we think we're over them, and then Jenkins gives us the green light for the next leg of the trip.

"We do," I agree. "What are you going to sign up for after commencement?" I ask. It no longer feels like a jinx to talk about graduating. We've made it this far, we'll make it all the way.

Lily laughs through the speaking tube. "I was going to ask you the same thing."

"Hmm. Target towing sounds kind of dull," I confess. "I was hoping to sign up for ferrying detail. That way, I'd get to fly every type of plane we have."

"That's what I was thinking. Patsy says she wants to test pilot. I was sort of hoping we'd all end up at the same place."

The thought of our little trio breaking up gives me a moment's pause. "I guess I hadn't really thought that far ahead."

"Yeah."

We fly silently for a while. For the first time since leaving New Orleans, I think about life after Avenger Field. I gave up Jolene to be here. And a lot of the girls I've met at Avenger have washed out or gone home of their own accord. Melanie Michaels was not the last. Deatie Deaton was right—more than half of our original class is gone. I don't want to give up Patsy and Lily, too.

Lily announces we've reached our second target area. I radio in our location and circle while Jenkins signals back the okay. Lily directs me to the next target.

"It'd be a shame to break up a team like ours," I say finally.

"Then don't. I propose a pact. These two musketeers, at the very least, will serve through this war together. And maybe we can get Patsy to join us."

"I accept." My smile is back. "Besides, give Patsy a few days of flying old patched-up planes and she'll want back in the race with us."

"That's right," Lily says. "Test piloting isn't as experimental and exotic as she thinks it is. At least, not all the time. Right?"

"Right." I frown. "I think."

"We're here. Radio in."

I reach for the radio. Patsy will have to wait until we land.

Half an hour later we are on the ground.

"Good work, ladies," Instructor Jenkins tells us. "Right on the mark every time." He puts that infamously warm hand on my shoulder. "See, Jones, you've come a long way."

I can't help but respond whenever he compliments me. In spite of my better judgment, Walt Jenkins makes me feel happy inside. When I smile at him, my grin goes from ear to ear.

"You too, Lowenstein," he tells Lily.

"Thank you, sir," we both say.

Jenkins looks at his clipboard. "Oh, and one more thing."

We hesitate. His face is so serious, my stomach starts to sink.

"Ladies?" he calls out.

From out of nowhere, the rest of Flight One comes running, Patsy at the forefront, grinning like a maniac. They hoist us up onto their shoulders and bodily carry us to the wishing well in front of the ready room.

"Congrats, ladies. You've made it!"

They toss us unceremoniously into the water. It's the happiest moment of my life. Although the water's barely knee deep, we cause enough of a splash to make me grateful for my tightly braided pigtails and all of my time in the pool. Without hesitation, I reach down to the bottom and scoop up a few lucky coins to give to Instructor Jenkins. Even after the other girls pull us out, I can't stop laughing.

Christmas dawns cold and clear at Avenger Field. We have the day off. The cafeteria is decorated in red and green garlands that remind me of decorations in an elementary school. I've sent the awl off to Grandy, along with the chain and a new lock. Abel's got two new pairs of wool socks for the winter. For Mama, well, I know she's been praying over me and Thomas both, so I bought her a new hat for church. And for Thomas. Well, the last we heard, he was in someplace called Manila in the Philippines, south of China somewhere. I guess signing up for the WASP is the best present I can give Thomas. Anything to help him come home sooner.

Instead of joining the other girls for breakfast, I drag a chair outside to the Beach to be alone. In the soft silence between the barracks, my eyes lose focus as I try to picture my family's usual early, messy Christmas mornings, with Mama frying ham in the kitchen, me making biscuits, and Abel hopping around in a pile of wrapping paper. Thomas usually had some girl or other he'd beg Mama to let him go see that afternoon. Mama would say, "Christmas is for family," but by three o'clock, she'd be glad to have him out of the house. The house was so full of noise and people on Christmas.

But today, it's quiet as a grave out here between the bunkhouses. Too cold for the sunbathers to make an appearance. And at home, I know it's just the three of them now, with our usual pile of presents dwindled down by the war effort. There will be no new silk stockings for Jolene or bicycle tires for Abel, and no candy canes.

"Boy, you look long in the face," Patsy says. "You've been staring at the clouds all day." It's true. I've been hiding out here. Bundled up in a coat and hat, I'm not exactly worried about getting too much sun today.

"With the planes grounded for the day, it was the only place I could think of to get some peace and fresh air."

"That doesn't explain the sad face," Patsy says.

I shrug. "Been thinking about my family, I guess."

Patsy drags another chair behind her. She plunks it next to mine, sits on it backward, and joins me. "Oh, I gave that up a long time ago. But I do think about Mrs. Harper. And the boys at the air show. That was a great time for a while there. A really fun run." Patsy holds up the scarf around her neck. It's a nubby mix of purple and lilac.

"Mrs. Harper made this for me during the last cold snap in Florida. She was everybody's mother at the boardinghouse. You meet all kinds of people on the road, Ida Mae."

I nod, caught up in my own memories. It takes a moment for me to register her words. "Patsy Kake, that's the first time you've ever called me by my Christian name."

Patsy smiles at me and shrugs. "It's Christmas. When else

157

am I gonna do it if not today? So, are you gonna sit out here all day, or tell me what's on your mind, or neither? In which case we should go inside. There's cocoa and coffee in the mess."

I laugh. "Hmm. Well, I guess I should make some sort of decision here." I shake my head, at a loss for the right words. "Well. It's just, we've been here for months now and it looks like we're making it, Patsy."

My smile is wistful. She shares it with me.

"And I haven't said it until now, because being a WASP means everything to me." I hesitate. "Almost everything."

Patsy's face gets very serious, and I feel sad inside. "I miss my family," I say.

Patsy stares at me for a long time.

"Oh, honey," she says at last. "You really are green. It only hurts on major holidays. Besides, we're your family now. Let's find Lily and open presents. That always helps."

I can't help but laugh at my own moodiness. "All right. As long as I can have marshmallows, too."

We get up and drag the chairs back to the door. "Marshmallows?" Patsy says in feigned surprise. "There's a war going on, missy. We need those marshmallows to make bombs and fight the war!"

The tension in my shoulders eases as the day carries on. There are Christmas carols in the rec room and a few games. Patsy gives me a handkerchief with the name Jonesy embroidered at the edge in the WASP uniform color, Santiago blue.

"Something to remember us by," she says. "Wipe the tears away at graduation in style."

Lily gives me a small bottle of perfume. "My mother swears by it," she assures me.

As for me, I give Patsy a new red lipstick "for after the war."

"Or just after finals," she says with a wink.

And to Lily, I give a set of hairpins to help tame her curls.

"Oh, thank you, Ida. I'd be lost without at least seven bobby pins on either side. You'd think those turbans we wear eat them up, I lose so many of them."

All in all, the evening is homey and wonderful. After a big meal of roasted chicken and mashed potatoes, we wander back to our bunks, singing "God Rest Ye Merry Gentlemen," with some of the lyrics confused.

No sooner do I sit at the foot of my bed than one of the beginning trainees comes to the door.

"Is there an Ida Mae Jones here?"

"That's me." I stand up, wondering what it could be. I hope it's not something at the administration building. Post-holiday meal, my khakis are wrinkled and my clothes are simply too casual to have to take into Mrs. Deaton's office.

"There's someone at the gate for you."

"Who is it?" I don't know anyone in Sweetwater that doesn't live on base.

The girl shrugs, brown curls bouncing with the motion. "Don't know. A nigger woman. Maybe your housekeeper?"

She turns and leaves without another word. I do nothing but stare after her. Just nod and say nothing.

"Well?" Patsy says. "You gonna go see who it is, or do I have to?"

Her words shock me out of my thoughts. "No, no. I'll go. See you soon."

"I hope everything's all right," Lily calls after me. "If our maid, Dorcas, showed up at base, I'd think it was the end of the world," she whispers to Patsy. Her voice carries in my ears as I go out the door. End of the world. What would be the end of the world . . . ?

In a rush, I realize who is at the gate and what it might mean. I break into a run, trying not to worry, not to think, just to get there.

The MP points to the side of the guardhouse. I slow down, take a breath, and turn the corner.

Mama is sitting there, on the little block of concrete that serves as a bench. She stands up when she sees me, and we stand there, looking at each other like each of us has never seen another human being before.

I'd forgotten how beautiful she is. Her warm coffee-colored skin seems so dark to me after so many months away from home. I reach out and touch her arm.

"Mama," I whisper.

Something, whatever it is that's been building inside me all day, breaks in a great wave. I throw my arms around her, but she stops me. Her eyes dart over my shoulder, and I understand. The guard is watching us. I force myself to laugh and pat her on the back.

"Mama Stella, how are you?"

"Fine, fine, Miss Ida Mae," Mama says in a voice so meek, so . . . Southern, it makes me feel sick to hear it.

"What brings you to Sweetwater?" I ask, as lightly as I can. "Is my family all right?"

"Fine, fine," Mama says in a high, wavering voice. "Your granddaddy sends his best and your baby brother, too."

Aware of the guard at our backs, we fall into the pattern of mistress and maid. Watching my mother play the role of servant, I feel a sour taste in my throat. I never meant for my own role-playing to bring her such humiliation.

I don't know this guard. He gives us a suspicious once-over, the look of someone trying to earn his status. "It's all right," I tell him. "She's our housekeeper." The word burns my throat, but we can't afford his wariness. "We won't be long."

Mama and I both smile at him. At last, he nods and disappears into the booth.

"How's Thomas?" I ask quickly.

"Oh, Ida Mae," Mama says, her voice strong and warm once again. Her eyes fill with tears. She reaches into her purse and pulls out a letter.

"This came last week. From the army. They say that Thomas has gone missing. And you know, they don't go back looking for colored boys."

My heart drops to my feet. "No." I clutch Mama's hand, still holding the letter. "No." It's like Daddy dying all over again. The world shrinks and it's just me and Mama and fear and an agony of sadness. My heart stops beating. I can't breathe.

Mama shakes my hand, brings me back to her. "Ida, listen to me. They don't go looking for colored boys just because their mothers ask . . . but they might do it for you. You're a white woman now, and you work for the army. If that means something, if that means anything, then use it to help Thomas."

My head spins. Could it work? What would I say? I can't call him my brother. A family friend? The son of my maid? Would they see our shared last name and know I am passing?

Tears of shame sit heavily beneath my eyelashes. I feel like Judas to my own family.

She steps back. "Look at you. You look every inch the lady. I can't claim to understand what you are doing, but the day this letter came, I felt so helpless. Grandy went into town to see what the local recruitment office could do. All they offered was help with funeral arrangements, like he was already declared dead.

"Every day I collect bacon grease for the war, but it's useless, isn't it? We can't fight the war with rationing stamps and canned vegetables. We can't save our sons by planting gardens. No matter what they say, we can't. It's not enough. My boy could be dying overseas, and I will not sit in the kitchen waiting for them to send his body home."

She reaches into her purse again and pulls out a handkerchief. She wipes her eyes. "You do this one thing for me, baby. You help bring Thomas home."

"I will, Mama." This time, I don't care if the guard is watching. I throw my arms around my mother and hold on to her like I'll never let her go home. Tears flow down my cheeks, into her hair, onto her collar. She shushes me, like when I was little.

"It's gonna be all right, Ida Mae. Thomas is alive. I'd know otherwise. It's all right."

And I pray to God that it's true. I pray for my brother to find his way to safety. I pray for the strength to make it through this war, through this year, through this night. Hour by hour. I repeat the words.

"What's that, honey?" Mama asks.

"Hour by hour, Mama. That's how we'll win this war."

Mama smiles at me. Slowly, we let go of each other until we are standing there again, staring like it's the very first time.

"What was it, that song you and Thomas used to sing?"

I laugh, but it turns into a sob. "Shoo, fly."

Mama nods. "That's right. How's it go?"

I shake my head, smiling sadly. She knows exactly how it goes. "You're not gonna make me sing it."

Mama gives me a look, and I know better than to argue. She's trying to make me feel better. I take a deep, shuddering breath.

"Shoo, fly, don't bother me. Shoo, fly, don't bother me. Shoo, fly, don't bother me. For I belong to somebody."

Mama joins me. "I feel, I feel, I feel like a morning star. I feel, I feel, I feel like a morning star . . ."

I turn around. The guard has come back out of the guardhouse. I smile and wave, but we stop singing. He shakes his head and goes back inside.

"I'd better go," Mama says.

Suddenly, I have so much to say. She can't leave me. "Where are you staying? Are you in town?" I think of how hard it must be to find a hotel for coloreds out here.

"Oh, no," Mama says. "Don't worry. I've got my train schedule right here. I'll be heading back home in a few hours. I just needed to see you. And tell you about Thomas. This is the first Christmas we've all been apart."

"I know." I pause, feeling like anything else I say will be useless. "Did you get the hat I sent you?"

"I did. I won't wear it until you both come home again."

"Oh, Mama, I meant for you to enjoy it now. Wear it and think of me."

Mama huffs. "Girl, I don't need a hat to think of you. I never stop thinking about you or any of my babies. Now, finish up your work here and come home as soon as you can."

"Yes, ma'am." I salute her.

"Merry Christmas, Miss Ida Mae," she says.

"Merry Christmas."

I think we might stand here for hours, just to be together again, but the guard sticks his head out of the box, and Mama looks at her watch.

"I've got a train to catch."

She leaves the gate and climbs into a truck that I've only just now noticed has been waiting. Before I can even ask her who it is, I see the driver. An older, colored gentleman in overalls. It's MacIntyre, the farmer from the hardware store. The man who saw right through me and made sure I knew it. I shiver at the memory of his warning.

Mama turns and nods at me. "Grandy knows folks all over," she says. And they drive away into the night.

I stand there, bewildered, as they disappear into the deep black-blue of the nighttime grassland. It feels like a dream. And then I think of Thomas, and it becomes more of a nightmare. It's several long minutes before I willingly leave the cold air of the gate to find my bed.

✈

"Is everything all right, Jonesy?" Patsy asks in a quiet voice when I reenter the barracks. I've missed lights-out. Everyone's in bed except for Patsy and Nancy Howard, who is trying to read a book by flashlight three cots away.

Patsy sits up when I come in. The light from the bathroom casts a dim glow across the bunkroom floor.

"No," I whisper, and sit on the edge of her bed.

"Well, who was it?"

"My mother . . ."

I say it without thinking. Patsy looks at me, but I can't read her face. Across the room, I can hear Nancy Howard sit up on her cot.

"I thought that girl said there was a nigger out there," Nancy hisses. She folds away the book she was reading and starts to stand up. My skin goes cold.

"Sit down, Howard," Patsy says. Her voice is low, but still sharp enough to make Nancy hesitate. "Can't you see she's upset?" Patsy puts her hand on my arm.

"What happened, Ida?"

"My mother's maid came to tell me some bad news." I take a deep breath and hate myself more than I ever thought possible. I shrug nervously. "She wanted my help."

"I thought you were a farm girl," Nancy snipes. "Must be some farm if your mother's got her own maid."

I press my hands to my cheeks as if I can hold back my blush. I'm too rattled to lie well.

"I said leave her alone," Patsy snaps at Nancy. "So what if they have a maid?"

I don't know if Patsy really believes me, but if she doesn't, she never lets on. Nancy Howard sits back down on her cot, but I can feel her eyes boring into me.

"What did she come to tell you, sugar?"

I close my eyes and try to find the words. I will go to hell for this, I think. I should go to hell. My mother's face looks back at me in the dark, my own mother who let me treat her like a servant just so she could talk to me. When the first tear rolls down my face, I can't tell if it's for Thomas or for pure shame.

"To tell me her son is missing in the South Pacific. He . . . we grew up together."

Patsy says nothing. She looks past me at Nancy Howard. I'm glad I'm not on the receiving end of that look. Nancy sniffs and lies back down on her bed. "Didn't take you for a nigger lover. Tough luck, Jones," is all she says.

My face burns and I stifle a sob. Yeah. Tough luck.

Patsy takes my hand. Her fingers are still as cool as that first day we shook hands on the bus.

"Don't you mind her. You were raised with your mammy's son. She was raised with snakes. What kind of help did she need?"

"Finding him . . . Do you suppose I can put a request in with Mrs. Deaton tomorrow?"

"Sure, honey. If not, she'll know what to do. Now, where's that kerchief I gave you?"

"What?" I blink up at her. "Oh . . . here." I reach into my footlocker for the embroidered cloth and start to wipe my eyes.

"No, give it here. I'm gonna teach you something." Patsy takes the handkerchief and ties one of the corners into a knot. "This is a worry knot. You're a WASP now, and that's a lot like being a carney. We've got to travel light, light bags, light worries. Tie up all your cares into this knot, Ida. It'll be there for you when the war is done. You'll untie it when that boy comes home. No point in carrying it on your shoulders."

She hands me back the handkerchief and I finger the little knot. It's hard and tight, not likely to come undone anytime soon. That feels just about right.

"Thank you, Patsy." I want to say more, but Nancy Howard is listening. All I can do is squeeze Patsy's hand and hope she understands.

"Sure, kid. Good night." She kisses me on the forehead and goes back to her bed.

After a long moment, I get up again and brush my teeth, wash my face, change into my pajamas, and crawl into bed.

Thomas has to come home. And so do I. Becoming a WASP was selfish. Selfish, stupid, and dangerous. God, Nancy Howard almost had me tonight, and in Texas, that could cost me my life.

All I could think of was wanting to fly. The war was just an opportunity. It wasn't real. But it's real now. It means my brother is missing. It means my mother has lost her husband and now maybe her son. And she came all this way, letting me treat her worse than a dog, just to tell me. To tell me what? That my world will never be the same again.

I tuck my knotted handkerchief under my pillow and try to let it take away my cares. I think of Abel, lying in his little bed hundreds of miles away, without even his mother to tuck him in on Christmas night. I make a promise to him. By next Christmas, I'll be home to stay.

February 1944

Chapter 17

Walt Jenkins and Deatie Deaton helped me find Thomas's commanding officer. I wrote letters to the army and to the Department of War, but no one had answers for me. Russia has pushed into Poland and the U.S. is too busy organizing bombing raids over Berlin to look for one colored boy. Despite the organization I see every day, finding one missing soldier is like looking for a drop of water in the ocean. Weeks turn into months and, while the Allies are slowly making progress in Europe, there's less news from the Pacific and we still have no word. I write my third letter home telling my mother, for all of her faith in me, I've failed her. The only thing I can still do right is fly. And training doesn't wait. Before it seems possible, Lily, Patsy, and I are assigned our first cross-country flight. Pull this off, and we graduate when we return to Sweetwater. Then we'll be WASP for real.

The cargo plane takes off into the cold February air with a chugging sound that reminds me of a train as it transports us back east to Philadelphia, where we'll pick up a shipment of brand-new BT-13 Valiants bound for California. Patsy gives me a mock look of alarm. Despite my personal worries, we're all excited about today. This is the real thing. The twelve of us sit facing each other, strapped in to low benches, all painted that wonderful army green. I'd swear the military has something against beauty. Sergeant Middleton would say the olive drab color is for camouflage, but this is an airplane, not a jeep.

Who ever heard of an olive green sky? As we pull off the runway, I grip my seat. Those butterflies I came into training with are back, but now the worry is all for my big brother. I feel the knot in my handkerchief inside my zoot suit pocket and sigh. The sky doesn't quite feel like home, knowing Thomas is missing.

I look at my friends. Patsy is all grins. Her baby blues twinkle as she nods toward Lily. "Jonesy, look."

Lily sits across the plane from us, a dreamy look on her freckled face.

"Penny for your thoughts," I say, glad for a distraction. Lily startles.

"Oh. I was just thinking, when this war is over, Harry and I will finally be married." She leans forward excitedly, wisps of auburn hair escaping her turban. "You'll both come to the wedding, won't you? Mother's planning a gorgeous affair at the Waldorf-Astoria. The ballroom there is as big as a football field. I won't know most of the people she's inviting, I'm sure. But if you two are there, it'll be just fine."

"Wouldn't miss it for the world," Patsy says. I don't say anything. After the war, Jonesy would be welcome in any joint in America. But not Ida Mae Jones. My stomach sinks just thinking about it. Mama told me more than once—color is not a line you can cross back and forth over just as you please. I think about my dance with Walt Jenkins. When this war is over, where will I stand?

If Patsy notices my silence, she keeps her own counsel. We haven't spoken about the night my mother came to the base since it happened. Telling her the whole truth would only make her an accomplice. She deserves better than that. Besides, if she suspects at all, you wouldn't know it. If anything, we're closer than we were before.

Lily claps, caught up in her own daydreams. "Oh, good. Patsy, I can't wait to see you cut the rug in front of all those stuffy old society people my mother knows. Harry will just love you. And maybe we could go to the Palladium one night, too, and show you where we like to swing."

"Sounds swell," Patsy tells her. "Doesn't it, Jonesy?"

"Terrific." I fold my hands in my lap. They're getting cold at this high altitude. One thing at a time, Ida Mae. "First, we've got to pull this mission off."

"You worried?" Patsy asks.

"Why should she be? Ida's the best navigator in the flight," Lily says.

"Not worried," I admit. "Just ready. I want to graduate so badly I can taste it. Just to say, look at me. Look at all of us. Look at what we've done."

"Amen," Patsy says.

"Good luck to all of us." Lily shakes our hands with such solemnity that we all start to laugh. The flight to Philadelphia is a long one. We settle in and try to get as much rest as we can. No more energy spent on personal demons. The flight to California will be long and strictly solo. Just a girl and her machine.

The Valiant is an everyman plane, a basic trainer every WASP checks out on as an intermediate. Flying one of these across country will be like making the trip with an old friend. Twelve planes are lined up in the hangar at Boeing's Pennsylvania factory, just outside of Philadelphia. The City of Brotherly

Love is just a smudge in the distance across the ice-crusted river. I'd have liked a chance to see the Liberty Bell, but I'll get plenty of sightseeing from the cockpit over the next few days.

"California, here we come," Patsy says.

"I can't wait!" Lily exclaims. Neither can I. It'll be warm in California.

We've got our baggy flight suits on under fleece-lined leather coats, with our maps strapped to our right thighs. Flying in February isn't exactly a warm proposition, even with an engine-heated cockpit. A quick briefing with the commanding officer at the plant confirms our orders. These planes are due in California at the Long Beach base by Wednesday. It's Friday morning. The plan is simple—fly as fast and far as you safely can, taking whatever pit stops you need. We'll meet up at designated sleep points along the way, but this isn't a conga line. It's every woman for herself, as long as we're all there by twelve o'clock Wednesday afternoon. And if I know these ladies, we will be.

I do my flight check twice, annoying the engineer.

"Lady, just get on with it. It's a new plane," he says.

"I know that, mister. And I don't care. This is my first real ferrying job. I'm not going to mess it up just because some 4-F flyboy didn't fuel her up right."

It was the wrong thing to say. The engineer glares at me. Some of these boys wanted to be pilots and didn't cut the mustard. It must burn him up to see women behind the sticks of these planes. The colored parlor maid inside me wants to duck her head and apologize immediately, and I almost do, but the pilot part of me wins. I know I'm right. I'm following procedure. I take a deep breath. Being colored, female, or both—none of that's going to help me fly this plane safely to California. We finish the rest of the flight check in near silence. As it turns out, the plane is in perfect order. But now we both know it's true.

I take a last trip to the restroom. There won't be another bathroom break until Ohio, tonight. My mouth is dry, but a sip of water now could cost me a whole hour down the line.

"Maybe I'll see you girls at the pit stop in Cleveland," I say to everyone.

"Cleveland?" Patsy calls from her own cockpit. "I'll be in Gary, Indiana, by the time you make Cleveland."

I check my fuel gauge. It's full to the top. "You're on."

Patsy laughs. I pull my goggles on and taxi out onto the runway.

I never do get to see the Liberty Bell. Up here, above the airfield, I'm still too far away from the city to see anything properly except for my own frozen breath, let alone a bell in some building. But I don't mind the cold or missing the city sights. There's plenty enough to see from where I'm sitting. I circle the airstrip and test my wings. This bird is one sweet plane. With a last look back, I see the other WASP trainees taking off, one by one, like silver geese into the sky, and we fly west, away from the rising sun.

"BT-13 to base, BT-13 to base. Permission to land."

The Cleveland tower controller's voice crackles over my radio. "BT-13? Base to BT-13, where are you?"

I waggle my wings. "Southwest of the tower, Base. Over."

The fellow on the other end of the line sounds exasperated. "Base to BT-13. Sorry, but that's a military name and all I see is a military plane. Are you in trouble? Over."

I have to stop myself from laughing. Our squadron leader, Audrey, warned us this could happen. "No, sir. I *am* that military aircraft. WASP trainee Ida Mae Jones, requesting permission to land. I need to use the facilities."

"A dame?" The controller does nothing to hide his surprise. "We've heard about you girls. Sure, come on down! I mean . . . permission to land granted. Take runway three, just north of you."

I come into a landing smooth as ice cream and hardly wait for the wheels to stop rolling before I throw back the cockpit hood. Cleveland is my first pit stop, after all. I land with barely enough time to run to the first toilet I can find. Flying in layers of clothing to keep warm has its disadvantages.

"Excuse me. Where's the ladies' room?"

The three soldiers that greet me on the tarmac blink in astonishment. "It really is a girl," one of them says.

"Yes, a girl that needs to use the latrine. Where is it?" Funny how having to go makes you lose your manners.

"Over there," the second soldier says, pointing to a Quonset hut a few yards away. He hesitates. "But it's not a ladies' room. I mean, we don't have a place for girls."

I stare at him. "Then it will just have to do."

It turns out, except for decor and cleanliness, men's toilets work just the same as women's. I wash my hands as quickly as I can, resisting the urge to splash some water on my lips. Patsy's probably having a steak dinner in Indiana by now.

"Thanks, boys." I wave as I run past my three soldiers and climb back into my plane.

"Permission to take off," I radio to the tower.

"It's that dame again," I hear the radio controller whisper. "Yes, BT-13. Permission to taxi. Have a safe trip."

"Thank you, sir."

I take off into the blue sky again.

✈

Two days later, weather and wind have blown the twelve of us as far as Nebraska.

I look at my charts for the umpteenth time. "We fly through the night, stop once to fuel, and we can still make it on time."

The other girls stare at me.

"It's the only way we're going to make it."

"Like hell," one of the girls says. Her name is Mandy, a brunette with short curly hair and a pixie smile. She's not smiling now. "At least truckers have caffeine. We can't even risk a cup of coffee in these boats."

"And that, ladies, is how the army will get rid of us," Patsy says. "Men will always be able to fly farther than women."

"Stupid relief tubes," Lily says with a frown. Relief tubes are just what they sound like, tubes equipped for men to allow them to "relieve" themselves in mid-flight. They don't exactly work for women. And so we stretch our bladders, go thirsty, and make do the best we can. Rumor has it that somewhere around Avenger Field, there's a map of every ladies' room from sea to shining sea. Top secret, of course. Those are the first places they'll look if a WASP ever goes missing.

We all laugh, and the tension of the last few days ebbs just a little. Patsy puts her map away and salutes the group of us. "Saddle up, girls. It's time to stick it to them, right in the relief tube." She squeezes my shoulder. "Be good, Jonesy."

"You too, Pats. I'll see you in Long Beach." She smiles and waves goodbye. Steely-eyed as the dawn, we climb into our planes, ready to do our best.

177

They tell you all kinds of things about night flying when you're training in the Link. They tell you about star navigation if your instruments should fail and how to find your landmarks in the dark. They talk about the disorientation of the few minutes just before sunrise and sunset, when you don't know how the light of the sun will hit you. It can be blinding and deadly.

What they don't tell you is how to fight your body's natural urge to shut down as the day closes. They don't tell you how to keep from going stir-crazy with nothing but you and the occasional burst of radio information to keep you company. My mind drifts back to different things—our upcoming graduation, which commission to request. Thomas.

Mama risked the trip out to Sweetwater to tell me he'd gone missing. He could be dead or worse. Stories coming out of Europe tell me it can all be a lot worse than I ever imagined the world could be. I can't stand to think of it, knowing there's nothing I can do. Maybe I should have gone home with Mama right then and there. But if I finish this mission, I'll be sending Thomas one more plane to fight for him in the Pacific. I cast around the sky but see no sign of the other WASP. Even if I'm the only one on schedule, this is one plane that will get to him on time.

My thoughts turn to my mother and little Abel, Grandy and his tractor parts, Jolene and her dancing shoes. I miss them terribly when I think of them, so I try not to. It's a mistake, I know. Lily invited me to her wedding after the war. But right now the war seems like it will never end. We're losing ground overseas, and the enemy is gaining. Then again, if it all ends tomorrow, so does my reason for passing. Like Cinderella after midnight, I go back to being colored. And *that* Ida Mae Jones, the real Ida Mae Jones, could never go to Lily's wedding as anything other than a serving maid. I'll never have another dance with Walt Jenkins. I'll never know what it's like to be more than just his trainee. I won't even be able to tell people back home I was in the WASP. Or I could make the other choice and stay white. No home, no family. Simple as that.

It makes me wonder what we are fighting for. But then I have to shake my head to clear it and remember. Thomas. I am fighting to bring Thomas home.

The sun rises behind me, lighting up the California landscape as I come in over the San Gabriel Mountains. The phrase "purple mountain majesties" takes on new meaning for me. It's beautiful. As the morning grows bright and warm, I feel the cobwebs of worry clear from my mind.

"California." My voice sounds funny, my throat and tongue are too dry. But the word is sweet. "California. California. Woo!" I let out a whoop that cracks before it's over, but it is a whoop nonetheless. I've made it. I've made it. Wednesday morning dawns clear but windy. I don't care. I rub my eyes and take a closer look at my maps, pointing the way to Long Beach.

I land to little fanfare. I am the first of the WASP to arrive. The commanding officer sends for me, and we exchange the paperwork for the airplane.

"These will be camouflaged, packed up, and shipped overseas within the week," the CO tells me with the pride of a man who loves his operation.

"It's been nice doing business with you." We shake hands, and I return to the tarmac to see the arrival of the rest of the girls.

Lily and Mandy land an hour later, almost at the same time. "We both got lost over Arizona," Lily tells me. "I saw Mandy circling and caught up to her. We'd still be out there if not for each other."

Three more girls come in, then five. Eventually, everyone is accounted for, except for Patsy.

"It's almost twelve o'clock," I say. "Another few minutes and she'll be officially overdue."

"Well, that doesn't affect the rest of us, does it?" Mandy asks. "It's not a group grade. Is it?"

Lily frowns. "I'd be more worried about our classmate, if I were you," she says angrily.

I *am* worried. "Where could she be?"

"Anywhere between here and Nebraska," Lily says. She starts to pull out her map and stops.

"Remember how late she was on her flight test with Martin?"

I do remember. How worried we had been and for nothing. "You're right. She's always got a reason. We should just relax and wait." But this time, Happy Martin's not riding shotgun with Patsy, slowing her down. Anxiously, we wait on the bench outside the ready room, scanning the sky for any sign of her.

At exactly one minute to noon, a silver BT-13 appears in the sky over the control tower.

I wave up to the plane, unsure if Patsy can see us. The wind has picked up since we've been here. Patsy's Valiant buffets a little in the wind.

She waggles her wings. By the looks of it, her permission to land is granted. Patsy circles the base in her beautiful machine and comes in for a landing.

As the wheels touch down, a spray of fluid arcs out from the plane, catching the sun in a rainbow of fuel and engine oil. The plane skips back into the air, up, then down, hard. The fuselage smashes against the asphalt ground, showering sparks into the sky like angry fireflies.

"Patsy!" We shout her name and run toward the crumpled plane, still skidding full tilt down the airstrip.

A siren starts whining in the distance and a bell signals the arrival of a fire truck. I pray that it won't be needed.

Patsy never stops. Her plane skids right to the end of the runway, where it collides with a lone outbuilding and bursts into flames.

I feel the heat of the explosion on my face. This shouldn't be happening. It can't be.

The fire trucks are there. I can't run any closer. The flames are too hot, too high. Lily's hand is on my shoulder, and we stop and stare, watching Patsy's plane burn.

Chapter 18

They say grieving is a process. At least, that's what the counselors tell me here at the base. Audrey Hill recommended Lily and I talk to one of the counselors after Patsy's accident, seeing as how we were such close friends. Lily went readily enough. As if talking to a stranger might help. Mama taught me a long time ago that colored folks deal with their sorrow in their own way. My way has always been to hide it, turn it into something else. That's how it was after Daddy died, when all I wanted to do was hate everyone I loved so they couldn't leave me hurting the way Daddy did. I never exactly ran away, but I was gone in my head, up in the clouds, flying away from everything. I was gonna soar straight up to heaven to meet him one day. That was the plan of a sixteen-year-old girl.

I'm not sixteen anymore.

In the end, it took Walt Jenkins telling me he couldn't let me back in a plane without a psych evaluation that made me go see Doctor Monserud. He's a medical doctor, but he also deals with head problems. I didn't want Walt to worry about me or, worse, to think there was something wrong with me—so I went.

"It's natural," he tells me. "It's natural to feel angry. And scared, and sad."

I don't say anything, but I nod and get through it. Doc Monserud's a nice fella, but he doesn't know a thing about me being sad. I can't tell him how hard it is to deny my own brother so I look like I belong here, how scared I feel knowing Thomas is missing and maybe dead. What it was like to leave Mama, Grandy, Abel, and Jolene way behind, not just miles, but color lines away. Or what it's like to lose Patsy. The only girl here who might have accepted me, no questions asked, if I'd had the guts to really tell her the truth.

So, I sit there, and I nod, and I let enough of my sadness show that the doctor thinks I'm healing the right way. And I leave his office and go back to the barracks to take a shower so hot it's like to peel my skin away. And after the hot water's run cold, I get out, get dressed in my Santiago blues, and take a minute to tie a second knot in my handkerchief, hard and fast for Patsy. Time enough to grieve later. For now, I'll travel light, because today is graduation day. I am going to be a full-fledged WASP.

Even the death of a comrade can't dampen the mood of most of the girls lined up here. Row upon row of cadets, in deep blue pantsuits, just waiting for silver wings to be attached to their crisp white blouses, over their hearts. We look like the airplanes do, lined up and waiting in the yards in Delaware to be picked up and flown across the land. Lily squeezes my hand quickly. It feels small and cold in mine.

"Patsy's smiling at us," she says, nodding toward the perfect blue sky.

"So is Jackie Cochran."

Lily blinks and drops my hand. "Where?"

"Over at the grandstand." Even I feel my spirits lifting a little. After Bessie Coleman and Amelia Earhart, Jackie Cochran is my hero. It was Jackie Cochran who convinced Uncle Sam to form the WASP in the first place.

"Why, she's so small," Lily says. I laugh.

"So are we."

"I know, but . . ." I know what she means. Jackie Cochran is a living legend, but she can't be much taller than I am. She's beautiful, of course. With a cosmetics company of her own, she should be. What you can't tell from looking at her, though, is that she came from nothing and made more than something of herself. She's the bee's knees.

Jackie Cochran was born to poor folks in Florida. She came from the dirt and grew up to run her own company. She also married a man smart enough to let her fly. Jackie holds more flying trophies than any woman alive today. And I'm going to shake her hand.

Tears suddenly spring to my eyes. I don't know who I miss more right now, Patsy or Daddy. They both have that same fiery spirit as Mrs. Cochran. If Patsy had known she'd be here . . .

She'd what? Have checked her plane twice before the last leg of our flight? She would have somehow known that the fuel line had a leak? She did know. That's what they've been saying. That's why it took her so long to come in. She was low on fuel and flying safe, lower to the ground in case she needed to land. She should have flown the way she used to. Maybe she'd have made it. Maybe she could've wing-walked her way out of the plane before it burned.

But I know it's not true. When she landed, the spray of oil must have blinded her, made her bounce the landing, sparking the fuel line. Nothing can outmaneuver a fire that fast. Not even Patsy Kake.

Lily clears her throat, and we all sing "Silver Wings and Santiago Blue." Jackie Cochran tells us she is proud of all of us, all of "her girls," as she puts it. She mentions Patsy, not by name, but as a "sacrifice," one we are all willing to risk.

I wish she had just said her name.

One by one, we all file up to the stage, and Deatie Deaton hands our silver wings to Mrs. Cochran, who pins them on us. It's an honor for her to be here at all. She's been busy fighting for military status for the WASP back in Washington. If she wins, girls like Patsy will be sent home with military honors, on the military dime. Instead, Lily is paying for Patsy's funeral. She wired her mother the day after the accident and made arrangements. Mrs. Emily Harper down in Florida was the closest thing Patsy had to a family. Lily and I will attend the funeral after graduation, and then we have a week at home before reporting to duty at our new assignments.

"Congratulations, Miss Jones," Jackie Cochran says to me. She shakes my hand, and hers is warm and firm, like Patsy's. I can't help but wonder if she'd shake it if she knew I was a Negro.

"Thank you," I say, cool as November. Inside, I'm all mixed up. I want to shout, I want to cry. I want to be happy, but it's as bitter as it is sweet. I descend the steps from the stage, my silver wings glinting at my collar. I've done what I came to do. Abel won't believe it. I know I hardly believe it myself.

"That's it, girls. Introducing class 44-W-3. Congratulations, ladies. You're WASP now!" Mrs. Deaton announces. The place erupts in cheers, applause, and a few unladylike whistles.

"All we need are mortarboards to toss in the air," Lily says, reminding me of my high school graduation.

"My mother wouldn't let me throw my cap," I tell her. "She was afraid it would get dirty, and she wanted to save it."

"Well, we'd better keep our hats on now, too, then," Lily

says. "Mother knows best." Judging from the hats tossed into the air around us, not everyone would agree.

✈

That afternoon, we leave Avenger Field behind with a dusty kind of sorrow. I know the minute our bus passes through the gates that it will never be the same place for me again. Other WASP used to come through on ferrying missions now and again, and they always had the same sadly bemused look when they saw the place. I didn't understand it until now. It's like that saying "You can never go home again." Only I am going home, as soon as we bury Patsy. And I hope it will be the way it was before I left.

✈

Florida is as green and lush as it is back home in Louisiana; the air is thick and slow here. You can even hear it in the drawls of the people at the bus station. Mrs. Emily Harper is no exception. She sounds like the Southern belles you hear in the movies, not in the real South. All the same, she is kindly. She greets Lily and me at the station. She's dressed in an ocean green skirt suit. We shake hands and make pleasantries like we're at a church social when all I want to do is hug this woman that Patsy thought of as a mother and a friend. But not now. There's business to attend to.

Two station workers, little colored boys that can hardly be called men, struggle with the box that now holds Patsy's remains. I am reminded that all the able-bodied men are overseas. Or closed up in coffins, like Patsy. The thought makes me shiver, even though the day is hot. Please, God, don't let there be a coffin for Thomas.

The streaming sunlight makes everything feel like swimming in slow motion. The sounds of farewells, greetings, and baggage being hauled fade away and grow tinny as we follow Patsy's casket from the station platform to the borrowed truck outside.

"Undertaker couldn't make it today. Too many funerals," Mrs. Harper explains. She introduces us to the driver of the truck, a worn-looking little man with a too-large face and ruddy cheeks.

"Mr. Evanston here is on his way through from Mississippi. He's staying the weekend in town, offered the ride."

"Thank you kindly, Mr. Evanston," I say, and shake his hand.

"Miss." He nods in that polite way you don't get from Northern men.

We pile in and ride straight to the funeral parlor. Evidently, the undertaker can spare just enough time to take Patsy inside. We give him her best dress and Mrs. Harper offers her own earrings for her to be buried in.

"Please," Mrs. Harper says, and hands the undertaker's men a small cloth bag. "I wore these on my wedding day. Pearls. She always fancied them on me."

The undertaker clears his throat. "I'm sorry, ladies, but this is a closed casket funeral. Please, keep your jewelry."

Mrs. Harper hesitates until Lily rests a hand on her arm. "It's all right, Mrs. Harper. Patsy wouldn't want you to give them up."

The older woman nods, even though she doesn't quite understand, but I do. Lily and I saw the flames that devoured Patsy's plane. There's nothing left of her to dress up. Still, the undertaker takes the dress we gave him to make us feel better.

I close my eyes for a moment so I don't cry in front of everyone, especially Mrs. Harper.

Lily and I both fall silent for the rest of the ride to the boardinghouse. Some things just can't be said.

When we arrive, Mrs. Harper shows us upstairs to Patsy's old room. "We had a fella staying in here, but he was more than glad to move when I told him you were on your way. Now, make yourselves at home. I've got supper to fix. We sit down at five thirty. I hope you'll join us."

"Of course," Lily says, the first words she's spoken since we left the undertaker's. Mrs. Harper shuts the door behind her just as softly as if we'd been sleeping babies. The room is comfortable and larger than I would have expected a boardinghouse room to be. The walls are papered in a powder blue with tiny pink rosebuds here and there. Two beds fill the room, one a full, the other a tiny single pressed up against the wall of the front of the house. A window over the single bed looks down to the street below. No one is out in the yard. Lily drops down onto the little bed as if the life's gone plumb out of her. I know how she feels.

"Ida?"

"Yes, dear." I sit across from her on the bigger bed. Every ounce of me feels tired, as if the heat and sorrow are more than a soul can bear.

"I want my mother," Lily says.

I go sit next to her and put an arm around her. "So do I."

She rests her head against mine and quietly, I start to sing. "Amazing Grace." Daddy's funeral song. The song Mama was humming when I decided to join the WASP. I sing it softly, and then the words just turn to a hum. Lily sighs and I stop feeling so numb, a little at a time. And somehow we are able to make it through the sit-down dinner at five thirty, and through the rest of the night, and through watching our best friend lowered six feet into the ground the next afternoon, when the only place she ever wanted to be was in the sky.

Chapter 19

It takes two different railways to get from Florida to Louisiana. The trains look different in wartime from when we're at peace. Most of the men at the stations and even here on the train are in uniform. Or old, or only boys. And the women, they travel in groups, some with children, eyes wide and eager for reunions or red with saying goodbye. After Patsy's funeral, I kept on my dress blues; the pantsuit makes for easier traveling than a skirt. My silver graduation wings are still on the lapel. I'll take it all off soon enough. Mama, Grandy, and Abel are waiting for me on the other end of this track. It's been five months, and I'm finally going home.

A smile tugs at my lips, but my stomach drops. Thomas is still missing in action. My daydream of a family reunion has an empty spot where my big brother should be. Mama will be angry with me. I promised I would find him, but those promises led nowhere.

"First seating for lunch, ma'am." The porter bows politely. I rouse myself and follow a handful of other passengers to the narrow whites-only dining car. Coloreds don't get dining cars on most Southern trains.

The porter gives me my own booth, with red velveteen upholstery and scratched china plates. I order a bowl of tomato soup, then rest my cheek on the cool glass of the window and close my eyes. How can I eat when Thomas is missing? And Patsy . . . I shake my head. I don't want to think about Patsy.

Three months Thomas has been missing, lost somewhere in the Pacific. I say a little prayer over my lunch. Please help my brother stay alive. After a few minutes, I give up on my soup and return to my seat two cars away.

Through the window, Georgia gives way to Alabama in a haze of thick green trees. The air is heavy down here. Even with the windows open, I feel the humidity, like the sky is trying hard not to cry.

Or maybe that's just me.

The woman across from me glances at my uniform. She has green eyes set in a face so pink, she looks like a baby doll. She sees me looking back at her and smiles, a pinched smile. Maybe I remind her of someone. Or, more likely, she's thinking of the stories she's heard about the kind of girl that would join a man's army. I shrug. I'll change out of uniform tomorrow and go back to being Ida Mae Jones. In the meantime, I'm proud of what I am, a Women Airforce Service Pilot. A WASP.

I smile at the thought and stick my nose out the window. The wind rushes by and lifts my hair off my face. It feels good. Almost like flying. For a moment, I can forget the sore spot in my heart. I need every moment like this I can get.

I sleep sitting up through Alabama. In the morning, as the train leaves Mississippi, I take my duffel and walk the length of the cars until I come to the door marked COLOREDS at the back end of the train. I find the ladies' room between the two cars and slip inside. I'll leave the train as a colored girl— Grandy will be waiting for me.

The room is more of a broom closet, with a small sink, a short metal toilet, and a mirror on the wall. I straighten my blue uniform in the mirror, wipe away a bit of lint, and touch the cool silver metal of the wings on my lapel. It looks right on me, against my pale skin and soft brown hair. It makes me feel older than just twenty years. But only white women can wear them, and New Orleans is just an hour away. Time to turn back into a pumpkin.

With a sigh, I open my bag and pull out my civilian clothes, a travel suit of soft brown-and-cream-flecked summer wool. The next time I look in the mirror, I'm no longer a WASP, young and white, able to fly. Same pale skin, same soft hair. But now I can pass for colored, just another light-skinned girl.

Someone knocks at the door. I let them knock. I wait in the toilet until I feel the train come to a stop and the conductor announces we've arrived in New Orleans.

Only when I hear other people moving from both cars do I close my bag and unlock the bathroom door. I exit the train in a crowd of both coloreds and whites. If anyone recognizes me, they won't know me for the white woman I was when I boarded the train.

Grandy is waiting for me outside the train station, away from the segregated platform. The old yellow pickup truck with its deep, rusting bed and slumped seats is a welcome sight. But not as welcome as my grandfather's coffee brown face. I grin at him and walk over. He nods at me and grabs my bag.

"Didn't know what color you'd be when I saw you, so I thought it best to let you decide," he says seriously.

"Grandy!" I scold him with a swat on the arm. "Where's

Mama and Abel?" I ask. "I thought they'd be here." I can't hide my disappointment. Maybe Mama hasn't made peace with my new life, the way I hoped she would.

Grandy shakes his head. "Your mother's back at the farm," is all he says. It worries me.

"Any news about Thomas?"

Grandy shakes his head again and I can feel my heart sinking. It's not a real homecoming without all of us there.

The rest of the ride back to Slidell, Grandy tells me small news, stories of the folks about town, how the farm is doing, and the like. I tell him what fun training has been, what the graduation was like. I'm careful to say nothing about Patsy. As much as I want to talk about my friend, I know what happened to her will only scare Mama. And from the looks of it, that's the last thing I can afford to do.

We pull off the main highway, down our old dusty road, and my shoulders relax. It'll be harvesttime in a couple of months. The strawberry fields are getting thick with fruit, and the shutters on our old yellow house still need painting. The porch is empty, but the windows have been thrown wide open to catch the breeze. I put my hand on Grandy's arm as he shifts the truck into park.

"Lord, it's good to be home."

Grandy smiles at me, that strong, white-toothed smile. After a minute, I follow him out of the truck.

"Leave it for later," he tells me when I go to get my bag from the truck bed. It makes me hesitate.

"What's going on, Grandy?"

"What do you mean, baby girl?"

I stop, and my hands go to my hips, just like Mama's do. "I mean, I have never in all my livelong days heard you say 'leave' anything for later. In fact, I've been switched for saying as much myself."

Grandy frowns at me, and I think I've gone too far. "Young lady, I am still your grandfather. If you know what's good for you, you'll get inside."

He shakes his calloused hand at me, a sweeping motion that gets my feet moving again, even though my luggage is left behind. Up the front steps that echo hollow as a good mush melon, through the screen and wooden front doors, and into the foyer I go.

"Mama? Abel? I'm home," I call. I'm disappointed that they aren't waiting for me, but I'm so glad to be home, I try to be patient.

"I'm home," I say again, more quietly.

"About time, too," says a voice. A man's voice.

"Thomas?" I run into the parlor. Plain as day, there is my big brother, laid up in Abel's narrow little bed. It must've taken two men to bring it downstairs. Thomas grins at me, and his face, half Mama's, half Daddy's, is so beautiful, so perfect, I almost don't see the wince of pain when he waves or the bandages on his arm and chest.

"Tommy!" I run toward him to throw my arms around his neck and hug him tightly.

"Easy, girl. Your brother's got enough broken on him without you breaking anything else," Mama says. The words are stern, but she's laughing.

Suddenly, I see the whole room clear as day. Mama is there, right next to the bed, and a gangly kid stands on the other side of him. A gangly kid, whom I recognize as my not-so-little brother Abel.

"Oh my God!" Instantly, I gasp. You don't take the Lord's

name in vain in Mama's house. But this time, no one seems to notice.

"Thomas, Abel! Look at you!" Five months can change a little boy almost as much as two years can change a man.

I turn to Mama and laugh. "I must be Rip Van Winkle! How long have I been gone?"

Grandy comes in from the hallway, his hat in his hands. "Long enough for the military to do their dern jobs and find your brother."

"And long enough for Abel to have a growth spurt or two," Mama adds with a grin.

It's too much. I want to hug everyone, I want to laugh, and I want to hear everything. Instead, I burst into tears.

"It's all right, Clayfoot," Thomas says, patting my arm with his good hand. "We're home now. Everybody's home."

After dinner, when Abel's gone off to catch fireflies with the neighbor boys and Grandy's gone to bed, Thomas shows off his broken hip, the pin in his ankle, and tells me the story of his tour of duty.

"The Philippines are something else, Clayfoot. Hotter than a down-home July, most of the time. My first night, the mosquitoes were so thick, it was a wonder we all didn't come down with malaria. We were at the back of a platoon of colored soldiers, not really going anywhere, just holding our ground, keeping this particular island away from the Japanese. We were treating dysentery and fevers; jungle diseases, not war wounds. And then, one night, bang! Like a bolt of lightning hit the place. Next thing I know, I'm hearing Japanese."

Thomas laughs and points to himself, lying on Abel's bed in the living room in his pale blue striped cotton pajamas, the buttons winking pearly and bright. "They caught me with my pants down, Ida. Too hot to sleep in pj's, I was in my boxers when the Nips came. And I was lucky. Of all the personnel at the hospital, only two of us survived."

In the kitchen, I can hear Mama humming as she puts the dishes away.

"Tommy." I put my hand on his leg. It's just like it used to be, me sitting on the foot of his bed, a big cup of warm milk in my hands, listening to stories when I couldn't sleep. Only now, I've got stories of my own to tell when the time comes.

"They tortured us, Ida, something fierce. Didn't even want information. Just wanted to listen to us scream, I think." He looks at me with hooded eyes. "They'd never seen Negroes before. We were a novelty, like damn circus elephants. They didn't believe I was a doctor. Didn't believe I could be." He looks off in the distance. The night is soft around us. "Who knows, Ida? Maybe it saved my life.

"Then one day, American planes started flying overhead. We were in the jungle pretty deep, but they found us. Some of the other boys I was with were killed in the rescue. But the guys who pulled us out didn't know they were rescuing anybody. They were just hunting Japanese. Said the Japs blew up our hospital when they took us. It was such a mess, they thought everybody was dead."

Thomas rests his head back on the goose down pillows Mama's plumped up all around him.

"I came home just as soon as I knew the trip wouldn't kill me. Don't know if I'll ever run again . . ." He trails off and pats his hip. We're both thinking about him running to save Daddy. *Look at Thomas fly.* I put my hand over his and he sighs. "Looks like I've got about a month's worth of healing left." He grins at me. "My own prognosis. But that'll probably be down to two weeks with Mama on duty."

I grin back. "She was so worried about you. She'll fix you up right and then love you to death, but she'll take good care of you."

Thomas shakes his head. "Don't I know it. Remember that time I fell off the barn trying to catch swallows?"

"Yeah. And you call *me* Clayfoot."

Thomas laughs. It makes him suck in a little air. "Ribs are still bruised. And broken," he explains. "Just like when I fell off that roof. Mama sat up with me around the clock until I could breathe without flinching. The only reason she's not in here right now is because you are."

"Good," I tell him. "She could use the break. And so could you."

"Don't say 'break.'" He groans.

We both laugh. I take a sip of my milk and am reminded of Lily trying to calm herself before our flight test.

Thomas reads something in my face. "Now, what's this about you joining the army?" he asks. "I thought you were going to stay here on the farm."

Like I asked you to. He doesn't say it, but I hear it just the same. The wind leaves my lungs. I denied Thomas was my brother so I could stay in the WASP. He's watching me, but I can't meet his eyes.

"Don't think I don't remember what you said," I tell him. "I tried to stay, I really did. But the news coming back from overseas was worse and worse, and it was just so hard, sitting on my hands, waiting for you to come home. So I joined the fight the only way I could."

"By pretending to be white?"

My stomach aches. It sounds so outlandish to hear him say it.

"Abel showed me this article one day, about Uncle Sam looking for women who could fly. Suddenly, it was like everything Daddy taught me about flying was for a reason. A good reason, too."

Thomas is quiet, but I've found my footing again. "I've flown from Philadelphia to California. I even learned to swim."

"You? Swim?" Thomas looks impressed in spite of himself. Then he shakes his head. "That's great, Clayfoot. But Mama needed you on the farm."

"No, she wanted me at home, but she didn't need me, Thomas. She doesn't need much of anything. Between her and Grandy, this place runs like a Swiss clock. And Abel's got more friends all the time. No, it was just me and Jolene cleaning the Wilson house, collecting cans and panty hose." I twist my fingers together, as twisted as my tongue feels. "You just wouldn't understand."

Thomas smiles. "Sure I would, Clayfoot. It's like standing in that field out there, too small to pick the tractor off Daddy and too slow to get help in time."

My breath catches in my throat. I look at my brother, and old tears rise to the surface of my eyes. Thomas has always blamed himself for not being able to save our father. That's why he wants to become a doctor. Kind of like me becoming a WASP when I couldn't save Thomas. But I still couldn't save him.

"Yeah," I agree. "Like that."

"And you wish you could do more," he says quietly.

"Yeah."

Thomas sighs. "The only difference is, you *can*. And you are. But it's a dangerous thing you're doing, Ida Mae, playing white. I've been in this man's army. I hate to think what'll happen if they figure out you're colored." He shakes his head, and I think of what I've already done in the name of passing.

"Tommy, I'm so sorry." I grit my teeth to keep from crying. God help me, I've lied so many times over to join the WASP, and I know I'll keep doing it, as long as they let me fly.

Thomas shrugs. "Still, I'm proud of you, Clayfoot. I think about the sight of those planes flying over that prison camp, and I know that they were there because of girls like you. And I couldn't be prouder."

I laugh, a choking sound, and feel like I can breathe again. "Stop messing with me, Thomas."

"Oh, I know better than to mess with a WASP."

I swat him, and he swats back. Maybe he understands. Maybe this is his forgiveness.

Mama comes into the room. "Ida Mae, don't make me tell you again. You'll break that boy beyond repair."

"He started it."

"I don't care who started it." Mama gives us her best "there'll be trouble in this house" look, hands on her hips, dish towel still in her hand. "It's finished now." And then she smiles. "Lord, it's good to have you home. Now you can both be home to stay."

Thomas and I look at each other. "I've been honorably discharged," he explains apologetically.

"Oh. Well. I'm just getting started."

Thomas nods, as if to say, "I know." But Mama doesn't look happy.

"Mama, I—" She leaves the room without a word.

Thomas and I sit there in silence. I know better than to go after her now. If I do, I'll be asking for permission to leave, and she didn't really give it to me the first time. She certainly won't now. But I have to go back. I have to report for duty.

Thomas squeezes my hand.

"Don't worry, Clayfoot. You know she's proud of you, don't you? All she could talk about once she was done talking about me was you." He laughs and shakes his head. "I must admit, I didn't know you had it in you."

I raise an eyebrow. "Well, Brother Thomas, there's more where that came from."

Now Thomas laughs even harder. "Boy, we're in trouble now."

I find myself laughing, too. I've got six days at home. I won't ruin them by arguing with Mama now. It can wait. It will have to.

"Well, it's past my bedtime." I stand up and stifle a yawn.

"You're kidding?" Thomas says. "It's six A.M. in Manila right now."

"Well, it's bedtime in Slidell. I'll see you at breakfast. Good night."

He pulls me in for a one-armed hug. "Good night."

I mount the stairs, hearing the familiar sounds of the house creaking around me. Abel is asleep in his room on a cot Mama used to keep in the attic but deemed too springy for Thomas to convalesce in. I tiptoe into Abel's room and kiss my bean-pole little brother good night.

Back in my own bed, the ceiling is too low. I miss the bar-racks, believe it or not, and the open cockpits of our trainer planes. I close my eyes and pretend I'm simply flying at night, with the glowing instrument panel my only guide. It helps.

My thoughts drift to Lily in her apartment, ten stories above Manhattan's Fifth Avenue, and Patsy in Florida, unable to wear her landlady's wedding pearls. Patsy Kake. I sit up and dig around in my suitcase for my knotted handkerchief. I undo a knot for Thomas and feel lighter for it. Patsy was right. It helps to travel light, but some things you just can't leave behind. Those are my last thoughts, and then I fall asleep.

Chapter 20

"Girl! Look at you, look at you!"

Jolene hollers from down the block. I wave and she rushes down the street toward me, still in her cleaning clothes, a satchel in one hand and sweater in the other.

We're outside of Miss Mary's three-chair beauty parlor, built into the side of her house. The long white wooden building has merliton vines growing in the side yard. Jolene drops her bag when she reaches me and I sweep her into a hug.

"I've missed you so much," I tell her, breathing in the familiar smell of pine cleaner and Cashmere Bouquet soap. Her scent is a sudden anchor to my old life.

"I'll say." Jolene pulls back. "You've put on some weight." She pinches my arm. "But it's solid."

"Calisthenics," I say.

"But you look pale as a ghost, Ida Mae. Don't they let you see the sun out there?"

I smile weakly. I don't want to talk about skin color. "Come on, Miss Mary's waiting."

Jolene and I are going to the picture show on Canal tonight. It seems plenty of sailor boys are making their way through New Orleans while heading toward the Gulf of Mexico, and Jolene wants us both looking good.

Miss Mary is a smiling woman with round glasses and a flair for the latest hairdos. She waves at us as we come in and rises from the card table where she's been doing a crossword puzzle. I breathe in the sharp smells of straightening lye, newly pressed hair, and memories. Miss Mary gave Abel his first haircut when he was three.

The shady room is a welcome change from the sun-bright street outside. We settle into the pink hair-washing chairs, with their neck rests low against the black sinks.

"How you been, Ida Mae?" Miss Mary asks me as she rinses down my hair. Miss Mary loves doing my hair. "Smooth as silk and easy to press," she says. Today, she runs her fingers through it, smiling at me.

"Haven't seen you in a while. People've been talking."

I look at Jolene. She shakes her head and rolls her eyes. Of course there would be rumors, and Mama's not one to bother with gossipers. She'll just say, "None of your business," which only leads to more speculation. "What kind of talk?" I ask.

Miss Mary shrugs and her young assistant, Eliza, turns her head to hide a smirk. "It's just that good girls don't disappear from home for months at a time."

Jolene starts to say something, but I beat her to it. "Good girls, Miss Mary?" I tilt my head to look up at her. "You think I'm not?" I can feel the heat rise in my face. "Do I look like I've been off having babies?"

At the next sink, Eliza shrugs. "Or not having them."

"Eliza Brown, that is enough," Miss Mary says sharply. "Now, I'm sorry, Ida Mae. I think the world of your mama, so I think the world of you, too, but you should know that people are talking, and a lot of that mess is said right here. So, what should I be telling them?"

I'm too angry to speak. Jolene didn't tell me there was gossip to worry about. From her chair, she gives me an apologetic shrug. Miss Mary sighs. "Listen, child, I'm trying to help. Anything I say, they'll believe. For a while, at least."

I take a breath. Mama did try to warn me. Jolene did, too. "Tell them I'm in the army."

"You enlisted?" Eliza whirls around to look at me, eyes wide with something like respect. "I didn't know that, Ida Mae. Good for you. They got a lot of colored nurses in the army now. Some of them even working on white men."

Jolene catches my eye and raises an eyebrow enough to let me know that any rumors were moved along by Eliza here. So, let her fill in the blanks any way she sees fit.

I shake my head and change the subject. "Thomas is home."

"Thank the Lord for that." Miss Mary relaxes visibly. She ties on her apron and soaps up my hair. "We've lost too many good boys," she says. "Glad to see one of them come home alive."

At the next sink, Eliza gets to work on Jolene. "Danny Taylor came home last month," she says in her high, young voice. I brighten to hear Danny's name. I remember his strong bright smile that day Jolene and I saw him doing roadwork. The day before we went to war.

"He came back in so many pieces, they said they'd have to have two funerals to fit them all." Eliza chuckles nervously. I gasp.

"What happened?"

"Lord, whatever happens," Miss Mary said. "One of them minefields or airplane bombs. His mama's lucky to have any piece of him back."

My heart sinks to my feet. "Jolene, did you know?"

Jolene stays quiet for a long time. "Yeah," she says at last. "I went to the funeral."

The sunny mood of our afternoon is dampened, and we sit through the rest of our hair washing in silence. It's not until we are under the dryers that Jolene perks up again.

"So, tell me everything. Starting with height."

Her hair is a nest of combed-out curls and mine still in curlers. She's only halfway through her styling process, and I'm practically done with mine. The two of us are completely alone in the back of the salon. Even shouting over the hair dryers, no one can overhear us. Not even Eliza with her big old gossip-hearing ears.

"What do you mean, height?"

"Well, how tall the men are, of course! A man in uniform always looks taller to me, like all that extra starch Uncle Sam's been using in the laundry gets into their backbones."

I shake my head. Jolene is as boy crazy as ever. Not even a war could change that.

"It's not like that," I tell her. "There aren't any men stationed at the field anymore, outside of instructors, and it's strictly forbidden to mix it up with them." I don't tell her about my dance with Walt Jenkins. That would scandalize even Jolene. I wish I *could* talk to her about him, though. I wonder what she'd think of him if he wasn't white. My face flushes just thinking about it. Ida Mae, you have to watch your step, I remind myself. I didn't join the WASP to find a white man.

Fortunately, Jolene's not looking at me. She frowns and flips through her copy of *Woman's Day* magazine. "Girl, I thought you'd been having yourself some fun. Just marching around and flying airplanes sounds dull, dull, dull, dull, dull."

"Well, it's not. I like it."

"Mm-hmm. And how are the girls? Are white army girls as snooty as civilians?"

"No. Well, not all of them. I've made some really good friends."

"Right," Jolene says, and I know what she's thinking. Good friends as long as I'm white. But a real friend would accept me even if they knew the truth. Or would they? I frown. It's a question I haven't got an answer to. But I do know that I won't tell Lily the truth while we're still in the service. If I got found out, we'd both be in trouble. But maybe afterward, when all of this is over . . .

I sigh. We'll just have to see.

"They really are good people, Jolene. You would have liked my friend Patsy. She's . . . well, she was a lot like you."

"What do you mean 'was'?"

My face gets hot, but it's killing me not to talk about it. "Oh, Jolene. She died on our last flight. Mechanical failure."

Jolene drops her magazine and throws her hood of the dryer up.

"I thought you was flying planes. You never said anything about dying."

I close my eyes. I shouldn't have said anything, but Jolene is my best friend. I wanted her to know. "Please don't tell my mother. It's not anyone's fault if it happens. I'm careful, as careful as anyone can be."

Jolene shakes her head. "You're a fool, Ida Mae. At least when a girl passes for white down here, it's to have a better life. Not to end up dead. You are a colored girl, no matter how high yellow you look or how white you act. The army don't even know who your family is. If something happens to you,

you think they'll write a letter to some colored folk so we can collect the body?"

"Seems like everybody around here is so busy telling me I can't that they won't spare a minute to say I can, and did, do what I said I would," I snap. "You can't take it away from me, Jolene. Even if you're jealous. Even if your skin's so dark all you'll ever be is a housemaid. No, don't worry about me. I'll be just fine."

The ladies up front are watching us now. Apparently they *can* hear something. Eliza is leaning forward to listen better, and Miss Mary looks worried. My cheeks are burning with anger and embarrassment. I lift up my hair dryer and feel my curls. They're dry enough. "I'm done here." I stand up. Jolene watches me with hurt in her deep brown eyes.

Well, I'm hurt, too.

Jolene shakes her head again and goes back under the dryer. I pick up my own magazine and walk to the front of the shop, where Miss Mary sets me down to style my hair.

"Everything all right, baby?" she asks.

"Everything's just fine." The angry lava inside me is already cooling down, turning into a lump of cold pride. And regret. But all I want to do is go home.

It feels like a lifetime before Miss Mary tells me my hair is done. Jolene is still under her dryer, her face hidden by a magazine. "Please tell Jolene I've gone home," I ask Miss Mary.

"Of course, darling." She lets me out of the chair and grabs a handful of my curls. "Such good hair," she says, smiling. "Such good hair."

When I get home, I find Mama in the kitchen, making drop biscuits to go with the chicken she's roasting. There's a pile of mustard greens on the table. I wash my hands in the kitchen sink and sit down in front of the greens without a word, glad to stop using my head for a while. Jolene's got me so turned around, I don't know which way is up. I wish the army had taught us how to navigate feelings as easily as they did a starless night sky.

Mama's new Fiestaware bowl, the one that looks so much like jade in the afternoon light, fills slowly as I sift through the greens, sliding my fingers down the spines, breaking off the tough, soil-heavy stems. Greens should go down smooth, not rough and hard to chew. The sharp, spicy smell of the leaves sprays the air. Mama just keeps mixing her biscuit dough. We fall into the rhythms of the kitchen so easily it's a wonder I've ever been away.

Mama hasn't said much to me since my first night back. If things were different, she'd know something was wrong now and ask me about it. She'd give me advice on what to say to Jolene, tell me how friendship is more important than pride. But her silence is stubborn and I don't know if she'd take her own good advice right now. Not when she's set her mind otherwise. That's something I guess I learned from her.

I remember how she was when Daddy left her, still pregnant with Abel, and went off to Chicago to learn to fly. Mama wore black that whole five months and acted like she'd been widowed. Daddy hated knowing she was dressed that way. Said it was like a flower putting on a hat, covering everything pretty. Daddy was back before Abel was born, but Mama never really forgave him.

I shake my head at the memory. Funny to realize that when she actually became a widow, Mama only wore black once, at the funeral, and then never again. Maybe she thinks Daddy's watching his flower from heaven now.

"Hey, Ida." Abel comes bounding into the kitchen, his arms full of strawberries. "Found these at the far end of the field," he says with a grin. "Mama, can I have a bowl?"

"You know where they are," she says, shaking her head. Mama's back is turned to us, but I know she's smiling just the same.

Abel pulls out his shirt from the bottom with one finger, making a hammock, and dumps the berries from his arms into the cloth.

"Abel," I warn him.

"Young man, if that stains, you'll be bleaching it out yourself," Mama says, turning around from her biscuit dough for the first time. The white batter clings to her fingers in little peaks. Abel giggles and reaches over the counter for a bowl.

"You said get a bowl," he insists. Lucky for him, there's nothing but a little dirt left on his shirt. He shakes it off into the garbage pail and rinses the berries under the faucet.

"Can we save some biscuits for shortcakes?" he asks.

"Now, where do you think I'm going to come up with cream just so you can have shortcake?" Mama asks him, moving to the sink herself to wash her hands.

Abel shrugs. "I thought it'd be nice. Ida's home."

Mama glances over at me for the first time. Her face softens. "That's a fine idea, Abel," she says to him. "We'll see what we can do."

"Thanks, Mama." Abel smiles at both of us and tears out of the kitchen just as fast as he came, in the way that only young boys do.

"I can't believe how big he's gotten," I say, watching those long, jackrabbit legs carry him out of the room.

"Three children, and I never get used to how fast you all have grown up," Mama says. She towels her hands dry on her apron and opens the oven to baste the chicken.

"Another hour on dinner," Mama says. She puts her biscuit dough in the icebox. Nice thing about drop biscuits. You don't have to worry about them rising.

"Now, let's see about that cream." Mama reaches for a coffee can on top of the icebox, where she keeps her rationing coupons, and sits at the table.

"I've got some snap beans in the icebox that could use some cleaning, if you got the time," she says.

I've got the time, all right. Jolene isn't going to want to see a movie with me now, or ever. Maybe even if I had the words to apologize. "We having snap beans or greens tonight?"

"Put the mustard greens on," Mama says. "There's salt meat in the icebox to season them with. The beans are for tomorrow."

I find the big pot Mama uses for greens and drop a few pieces of the pink-and-white salt meat into the bottom with the greens. Mama's cooking up a storm, but today I've lost my appetite.

"I've missed you, Ida Mae," Mama says out of the blue.

I join her at the table with the bag of green beans. "I've missed you, too, Mama."

We work in silence for a while, me with my green beans and Mama shuffling through her stamps looking for a coupon for a pint of cream.

"Aren't you going downtown with Jolene tonight?"

"No, ma'am." I swallow around the lump in my throat. "Not tonight."

Mama stops her shuffling and looks up at me. "What did you girls get up to?"

I shrug, but Mama knows how to get an answer out of me. She sets her elbows on the table and gives me a stare that says she's got all the time in the world.

"We got into it over nothing," I say. But it isn't nothing, really. It's everything. "She's mad at me because I'm passing and she can't."

Mama raises an eyebrow. "Is that what she said?"

I think about it and shake my head, getting angry all over again. "No. What she said was I'm a fool, a fool for thinking I can be a WASP. But I'm not, Mama. I'm doing it, no matter what anyone says. I know you think I should come home, but I can't. They need me to fly just as much as any of you need me here."

Mama laughs sharply. "Baby girl, Uncle Sam doesn't need you. Uncle Sam doesn't need anyone in particular. He just takes whoever he can get and tosses them up to the slaughter."

"Mama, don't start." I drop the snap bean in my hand into the bowl.

"Somebody needs to. Somebody needs to talk some sense to you."

I stand up from the table. "I thought you understood, Mama. When you came to see me at the base, when you risked everything to tell me that Thomas was missing, you said you were proud of me. I thought you finally understood why I wanted to be a WASP. Are you saying that's all over now that Thomas is back home? Now we can let the country fend for itself, let all of those other sons and brothers find their own way back home because we've got ours?"

Mama is standing now, too, and for the first time I realize we are both exactly the same height. She stares me down with those brown eyes, nostrils flaring, as if to say, "Girl, don't you take that tone with me."

But she doesn't say it.

Instead, she looks at me hard and says, "Ida Mae, people are dying. Women are dying. You think I don't read the paper? Every time there is an airplane crash reported, I think of you. Do you think I don't wonder if maybe, on this or that stormy night, you're up there flying in the lightning and the hail? Just the way I worried about Thomas overseas, trying to save those boys from dying in the swamps and the heat." She comes toward me, grasping my hand in both of hers.

"Baby, I don't care if you come home and clean houses or even if you run off like your daddy's people and pass for white in some town I've never seen. But I want you to be safe. Safer than I can keep you if you go back and fly for the army, your country, or any other reason. I want my little girl to live."

I stare at my mother for a long time, and suddenly, I can't keep the truth from her. "My best friend died last month, Mama. It was awful. Worse than I can say. She knew something was wrong with her plane, but there wasn't a thing she could do about it. I watched her come in for a landing, all wrong, but there wasn't anything else that could be done. And when her wheels hit the ground, it sparked the fuel tank and . . . I've never seen such a ball of fire."

Mama pulls me into the hug that I've been wanting ever

since that awful day. "Her name was Patsy, Mama. Patsy." I cry on my mother's shoulder, and she holds me the way she used to. I don't feel so tall anymore, standing in the kitchen with her arms around me.

"Mama, I get so scared sometimes. But then I feel so free when I'm up there, like nothing can go wrong. I know it does sometimes. I know it does. It's dangerous, but life is dangerous, isn't it? You've heard the news, the same as me, Mama. This war is bad. If it reaches our shores, who knows what will happen? I can't let fear stop me. Not when there's so much in this world to be afraid of."

Mama pulls away from me and holds me at arm's length. "Baby girl, I'm sorry about your friend. But I don't know what I'll do if it happens to you. Thomas being back home is a miracle. I don't know if God will give me another one."

I feel such misery, I can only look at my mother and think again about the high cost of war. Why should she have to pay?

Just then, Abel comes running back into the room. "Grandy got some cream from Mr. Brandy's cow. Mr. Brandy said we could have it if we bring him a shortcake." He's excited, out of breath, and so carefree he seems to float across the linoleum toward us. Mama wipes her eyes with her apron and turns to him.

"Well, isn't that nice?"

"Can I have a pitcher?" he asks.

"Of course. Now, thank Mr. Brandy for me." She moves to the cabinet and pulls down a small jug.

I sigh and pick my bowl of snap beans off the table.

Abel passes me on his way out. "Your hair looks pretty, Ida Mae."

"Thanks, Abel."

He grins and is gone.

"Supper's in half an hour, Abel," Mama calls after him. Just like that, we fall back into the kitchen rhythms and stop all talk of war.

Coming home isn't what I thought it would be. I come down to help with lunch on my last day and the tension that had broken between Mama and me is back. She moves slowly through the kitchen, making sandwiches, not quite looking at me. She knows I'm leaving, but she's more sad than angry about it now. Rather than sit with that sorrow, I tell her I'm not hungry and head outside to be alone. Jolene isn't talking to me ever since that day at the hairdresser's. My face grows warm with shame just thinking about the things I said to her. But I don't know how to take them back. I'm not even sure if I want to. Maybe both of us were wrong.

No, home isn't what I thought it would be. I don't know what I was expecting. A parade, a party, or a reception like those people sitting on the hoods of their trucks out at Baker's Pond gave us. But not this.

I walk out into the strawberry fields. When I was young, I would lie on my back at the edge of the field and look at the clouds. Today, I just keep walking. On the other side of the field, past the tree line, is a little stream. More of a ditch, really. We used to fish for crawdads in the mud there, when Daddy was still alive. I go there now and find a good rock to sit on. The clouds skid by overhead on the spring breeze.

God, I wish Daddy was here. He understood me. At least, I like to think he did. We grow up into people our families don't always recognize. Like little Abel, whose growth spurts make him look like a basketball player now, and Thomas, who used to be so big and strong, suddenly bedridden and weak. And me, I don't even know if I'm colored or white anymore. Ida Mae Jones or Jonesy. I want to be them both.

"Ida, Ida Mae!" Somebody's hollering after me. I slide off my rock and rest my back up against it. If I'm lucky, they won't see me from the other side.

"Girl, don't be hiding from me. I can see you just the same!"

Shoot. I peek over the rock. Grandy's coming toward me, an oily rag in one hand, a tractor engine part in the other. I don't know if that old thing's actually ever broken or if he just likes taking it apart.

"Sorry, Grandy. Just looking to be alone for a little while."

Grandy comes up to me, sweat on his brow, his overalls a patchwork of dirt and grass stains. Aside from his hands and his work clothes, Grandy is the cleanest man I've ever seen.

"Plenty of time to be alone on the way back to Sweetwater," he tells me.

I smile at him, but it's a sad smile. "I don't know if I'm going back."

Grandy looks at me like I'm the fine print on a city lawyer's contract. "Of course you're going back."

He turns and walks back through the trees, toward our strawberry fields. I have to jump up to catch up with him.

"I want to, but Mama's against it."

Grandy shakes his head. "The two of you are more like sisters than mother and daughter. Twins, at that."

He turns around to face me. "Ida, you've been hardheaded for far too long to stop now. That's your daddy in you, and your mama, too. And if there's one thing I know, you can't fight blood. That's why your mama had to let your daddy fly. And that's why she had to pretend she didn't love every minute of it when she was up in that damn plane with him.

"You see, we all have our nature at the core of everything we do. There's no changing it, no matter how we try. That's why I'm a farming man. Have been, ever since Lincoln gave my granddaddy an acre and no mule to work it with. And why your mother is the head of the household, man or no man around the house. And why you have to fly, no matter what it takes."

I blink, astonished. Sudden tears fill my eyes. "But it's dangerous, Grandy." I think of Patsy's tiny funeral, with only me, Lily, and Emily Harper present. At least we knew about Patsy's landlady. But I can't risk telling anyone about my family. Jolene was right. If something happens, who will tell them about me?

"A tractor killed your daddy, Ida Mae, but we still use tractors. An airplane is no different. It's just a tool, if you know how to use it right."

It's the same argument I gave Mama, but I shake my head. "Everything I'm doing is based on a lie. I've turned my back on where I come from, Grandy, on being who we are."

We've reached the tractor, resting in the field like an ailing cow. Grandy reaches under the shiny red hood and yanks out a rubber tube. "Baby girl, haven't you heard a thing I've said? You are who you are, Ida Mae. Black or white, red or brown, you can't change it."

He hands me the hose and the engine part. I stand by dutifully while he dives in with both hands.

"If . . ." He grunts, pulling at another hose. "If some white

216

folks want to buy what you're selling, let 'em. In the end, the goods are delivered. Right?"

"Right." The tears are coming now, but I'm smiling, too.

"They get their planes, don't they? You ain't selling them to the secret Negro army, are you?"

"No, Grandy. I'm not." He's trying to make me laugh. It's almost working.

"Well, then. Give me that hose back." I hand it to him. "This damn tractor's useless."

"Then why do you keep giving it a new paint job every year?"

Grandy frowns at me. "Don't sass me, girl. Besides, a man's got to have something to do with his hands."

For the first time, I look at Grandy's tractor engine. "You know, at the base, we learned to fix our own airplanes. I bet I could take a look at this for you."

Grandy finishes reassembling the last piece. He turns to me with a disapproving glare and slowly wipes the grease from his hands onto his faded red rag.

"Ida Mae Jones, you truly haven't heard a thing I've said. I told you, a man's got to have something to do with his hands. This tractor is mine. You go find something else to occupy your time."

I stand there in front of my grandfather and think he's the next-best thing to having Daddy here. Grandy keeps that stern face up, even though he's got me smiling from ear to ear. I throw my arms around his neck and pull his head down so I can kiss his bald spot.

"I think I know where I can find a few airplanes," I tell him.

Now Grandy smiles, pink gums and white teeth. He laughs, a low chuckle that sounds like he's heard a dirty joke. "Now, that's my girl. Finally got her ears open. Tell your mama you've got a job to do. She'll come around. Even if she says she won't. That's the way it was with your daddy."

"Thanks, Grandy." I hug him again. This hug is going to have to last me a long time. Because tomorrow morning, I head to California to start my first day on the job as a full-fledged WASP.

Chapter 21

"Ladies, welcome to March Field."

The lieutenant addressing us introduces himself as Charlie Washington. "Like the president," he says with a little laugh. Charlie Washington is young, probably my age. But I don't feel like a kid anymore. Something about the training, maybe, or all of the hours in the air, but in the past two years, it feels like I've gotten twice as old as I was when I showed up in Sweetwater. It's the first time Lily and I have been back to California since Patsy died. I'm glad it's not the same base. I'm not sure how I'd handle that.

"I thought Roosevelt was president," one of the girls says. Lily and I laugh. There are four of us new WASP assigned to March. The other two are from another class, half a year our senior. They've been reassigned from Delaware.

Charlie Washington's happy grin falters. "Uh . . . I'm supposed to show you to your barracks. They're new, just finished last month. Before that, all the girls on base had to stay in town."

We nod. It's a familiar story. Two years into the program and still half the army isn't prepared to house women. It's all part of what the WASP are lobbying for in Washington.

"Anything's better than the bunks we had in Delaware," the taller of the two girls tells us. Her name is Lucille. She's a big-shouldered gal from Tennessee, with hair the same color as a cup of black coffee, no cream. "That little state's as cold as a brass bra in winter." Her partner, Delilah, is from Massachusetts. I guess the cold weather didn't bother her half as much.

"It'll all be changing soon everywhere," Lily says. "Once we get full military status, the WASP will have real barracks like the rest of the army. Heated, too."

"A girl can dream," I say. Sure, Jackie Cochran and Nancy Love have both been fighting for the WASP in D.C., trying to get us full soldier's rights, but it doesn't look like Washington is going for it. For one thing, if they make us military, then we get to stay, even when the war ends. It's a nice thought for some, but a lot of WASP have a life not easily left behind. Some of the women have kids. Or mothers like mine, who want their daughters to have a normal life. And friends like Jolene, who just don't understand. It's a real mixed bag. And then there are all those men who'll want their jobs back when they get home from the war.

"Well, never say never," Lily replies.

I shrug. "If anyone can make it happen, Jackie Cochran can."

Charlie Washington leads us to a low cinder-block building at the edge of a cluster of other cinder-block squares. "Home sweet home, ladies," he says, with another teenaged grin.

"Thank you, Lieutenant," I say, and we salute him before checking out our new home.

March is the third base Lily and I have been stationed at since going on active duty a month and a half ago. It's much the same as the others, except here the WASP have their own barracks. At our first assignment, in Arizona, we had to bunk on the floor of the base nurses' rooms. Sleeping bags are a hard way to live for weeks at a time. Especially after having just slept in your own bed at home. The run-down boarding-house outside our second base was no picnic, either. We were both more than glad to pull down target-towing duty out here in California.

The officer in charge shows up at our barracks after lunch and tells us his boys are on night practice. We'll be taking off as soon as it's full dark, at about twenty hundred hours.

I drop down onto my cot. It's the second to last one, at the far end of the room, just like my old bunk at Avenger Field. It's my own little superstition, and I'm sticking with it. Lily has taken up the bunk next to mine against the wall, where Patsy used to sleep. I'm glad of it, and I try not to think of it as a bad omen. I may have lost Patsy and Jolene, but Lily's become the sister I never had. I'd die before I lost her, too.

"Did I tell you I got another letter from Harry?" Lily asks me. Her eyes are as bright as her voice. I smile. Only a hand-ful of letters have come for me since Jolene and I had our fight. I keep writing to Grandy and Thomas, who tells me Mama's still mad I didn't stay, but she heard what I had to say before I left, about having a job to do. She understands what that means, and she's willing to forgive. When it comes to Jolene, though, I don't know what to say. Lily's better at long-distance relationships than I am.

"What's lover boy up to now?" I ask her.

Lily rummages through her duffel bag and pulls out an envelope. Draped across her bed on her stomach, red curls shining in the afternoon light coming through the window, she looks for all the world like a love-struck teenager mooning over some movie star in a magazine.

"Here, he says he's been keeping up on all the latest field medicine and the latest swing dances at the officers' club. Oh, but he promises he never asks the girls their first names. Keeps it very polite."

Lily frowns at me. "That doesn't seem right, does it? I ask people's first names. I'll have to write him and tell him to do it, too."

"That's right," I say. "Call them miss, or missus, or Mary Jane. Just don't call them sweetheart."

Lily throws a sock at me. "Oh, he'd never do that. I don't know why you make me worry so, Ida. What we need to do is find you a fellow, too, and then you'll have plenty to keep you occupied when we aren't in the air."

I roll over onto my stomach and try not to think of Walt Jenkins. "Oh, I don't need a man to keep me occupied. I just wish we could get into another plane. Being a WASP sounded more glamorous before I became one."

"Well, that's the way everything is," Lily says. "I mean, look at me. I'm giddy as a schoolgirl about marrying Harry, but when was the last time you saw an old married lady get giddy over anything?"

I sigh. "Nothing lasts, I guess."

"Nope," Lily says happily. "Not a thing." She flips onto her back and smiles up at Harry's letter. "Including this horrid war. When it's over, you're going to be my maid of honor."

I smile. "Sounds great."

"It will be." She hugs the letter to her chest, and we while away the rest of the afternoon until the sun goes down and it's time to go to work.

The Curtiss A-25, or Shrike, is a single-prop attack plane with a dark body, white belly, and stars set in a circle of blue on either wing. The Shrike's a dive-bomber, with room for a pilot, a gunner, and a couple thousand pounds of bombs. Not that we get to do dives on towing duty. Target towing sounds simple, and it is. We go up, two of us together, Lily and me in one plane, Lucille and Delilah in the other, pulling giant target flags attached to the tails of our A-25s. That's all the skill there is to it. Then we circle over the gunnery range in long slow lines. Down on the ground is where all the action is. Tonight the boys will be using 90-mm antiaircraft guns, big, long-nosed guns that can shoot twenty or more rounds a minute. Two soldiers man a searchlight, scanning the sky for the target, and the rest of the crew cranks that gun around as fast as they can, aiming to shoot a bull's-eye on our flag.

"La de dee, la dee da," Lily hums as we take off. All systems are go and everything is smooth as silk. It's a beautiful night for flying, too. All of that Link training has paid off. I feel just as peachy flying under the starry sky now as I do under the noontime sun.

We do our first pass, and the deep thocking sound of the guns echoes from below. Lily looks out the window as I circle around. If you do it right, the target takes its time catching up to you, and you can see if it's been hit or not.

"One hit, not exactly a bull's-eye," Lily says with a chuckle. "They took the tail corner off."

"Not good enough." I grin. We swing around for our second pass. It's too loud inside the plane for us to hear the silk flag rippling in our wake, but I imagine I can hear it. It sounds just like the snapping silk scarf Bessie Coleman used to wear when she flew. I like the sound of that.

"Holy Moses!" Lily shrieks. I see it, too. The cauliflower burst of a shell *in front* of the plane. Not behind us, where it's supposed to be.

"What the heck are they doing down there?" I ask. Lily is on the radio in nothing flat. "Target One to Gunner One, Target One to Gunner One. Adjust your aim. You're targeting our plane."

I'm proud to say it, but Lily is calm as can be on the radio. You never want to sound hysterical, talking to the men on the ground. They get a kick out of scaring little girls, as they put it.

"Gunner One to Target One, we copy."

"Good," Lily says, exasperated. She hangs up the radio mouthpiece and scans the sky. I keep us steady and right on course.

When the bullets hit us, they come right through the left wing.

"Jesus, Lily, they're shooting us!" I adjust the wings and speed up the plane. The faster we get out of range, the better. If we get killed by friendly fire, Mama would never forgive me or Uncle Sam.

Lily grabs the radio again. "Mayday, Gunner One, mayday. We've been hit."

"Not possible, ma'am," the voice on the other end of the radio says.

"Damn right it's possible. You stop shooting right now. We're coming down!"

I've already got my headset open to the control tower. "Target One to tower. Emergency landing. We've been hit by Gunner One."

"You've been what?"

"Hit by Gunner One. They're all over the place down there."

"Are you safe to land?"

I scan the instruments in front of me. Oil pressure is fine; I'm holding altitude. "Roger that. Mostly cosmetic damage, I think. But don't hold me to that, and don't leave us up here long enough for it to change."

"Copy." The traffic controller clears a path for us to land. The base fire truck and a medical jeep are at the far end of the tarmac when we come in.

The second we roll to a stop, Lily jumps to her feet. "I'm gonna kill someone," she says. Her cheeks are almost as red as her hair.

I unstrap myself from my chair. "You'll have to wait in line."

"Is that really all we are to them, Ida? Guinea pigs? Disposable targets?"

I think of the way Patsy died, the way the engineer tried to rush me through my flight check that day. Testing new planes and guns on WASP, like any other scientific experiment. "You might be right, Lily. God, I hope you're not right."

The line of holes punched through the left wing makes my heart sink. I run a finger lightly over the edges of torn metal. For someone who wasn't targeting us, Gunner One sure did a bang-up job. A few inches to the left and we might not even be standing here.

This time, we don't go through channels. We commandeer

225

the med jeep and drive out onto the gunnery range. The poor driver barely brings the jeep to a stop before we jump out.

I storm up to the first soldier I see who isn't still manning one of the guns. His back is to me and his head is in his hand. I grab his arm. "Who the hell's your CO?"

He turns around, startled. It's Lieutenant Charlie Washington, our guide from this morning. "It's me, ma'am. I . . ." He looks lost. His eyes are big as a cow's.

"It's my . . . my first commission as gunnery command. I . . . these guns are . . . I'm awful sorry. Are you and the other lady hurt?"

"You son of a—" Lily stops in her tracks when she sees Charlie. I turn in time to see recognition dawn on her face.

She pats Charlie on the back. "You poor kid. You poor, stupid kids."

She points, and I see that Charlie Washington is the oldest of the lot.

"Holy moly. Is this what we're down to?"

Lily nods. "Uncle Sam'll be issuing diapers next."

"Sorry, Lieutenant," I tell him. "This is going to be in our report. Do better next time."

"Yes, ma'am," he says, taking off his flack helmet.

"Helmet on, soldier!" a man shouts from another jeep that's just pulled up. By his uniform, he's a captain, and Charlie's in a world of trouble.

"This is an active gunnery range. Ladies, I'll have to ask you to leave. We'll discuss this in the morning."

"Yes, sir, Captain, sir!" Lily and I shout, and salute him.

Later that night, Lily and I sit up in our cots playing Old Maid by moonlight.

"How did this happen?" I ask her.

"What happen?"

I look at her face. The freckles are still just as fresh on her nose as they were the day we met. "How did we get to be so old? I mean, you saw those kids out there tonight. They were babies."

Lily sighs. "I know what you mean. Do you know what my mother said when she heard about Hitler invading Poland? She said, 'These are the things that make us old.'" She shuffles through her cards and then stops, frowning. When she looks up again, her eyes are damp with unshed tears.

"Ever since Patsy died, I've been thinking, what if this is it? What if this is it for all of us? There's another accident, like there could have been tonight, or I don't know, what if Hitler wins?"

I stretch my arms and sigh. Sometimes I miss Jolene and my family so much that it wears me out inside. At least my family is talking to me, though. Jolene is like a hole in my heart that just won't heal. "This war will make old maids out of all of us."

"I hope not," Lily says. "Harry might not want to marry me if I'm an old maid."

I chuckle and drop my cards, my heart no longer in the game. We sit there on my cot beneath the window, watching the moon float in the sky like a bar of Ivory soap in a bath.

"Now," Lily says. "If only we could get our hands on a real plane. I feel like a bus driver up there in that Shrike."

I laugh and throw a pillow at her. "Amen, sister. Amen! They don't call it the 'Big-Tailed Beast' for nothing," I say, referring to one of the A-25's nicknames. Inwardly, I shrug. Why worry about tomorrow when you can worry about today?

Less than a week later, our prayers are answered. A letter straight from Deatie Deaton herself says Jackie Cochran has reviewed our records, and there's something special she wants us to fly. Two days later, Lily and I say goodbye to Lucille and Delilah and take the train back east to Birmingham, Alabama, to see what the first lady of aviation's got in mind.

Chapter 22

"Ladies, have you ever heard of the B-29 bomber?"

Lily and I exchange glances. We're in a briefing room at Birmingham Army Air Base. We arrived last night with no further instructions than to see the commanding officer. Colonel Leland Griffith is a kind-faced man with graying temples and a gruff voice. He made sure we had a hot breakfast at the officers' mess before our meeting. It's 7 A.M. Lily and I are in our dress blues. I clear my throat.

"Yes, sir. It's experimental, isn't it?"

Colonel Griffith looks uneasy, but he nods. "Do you know what the flyboys call it?"

"The Superfortress, sir."

It's the right answer. Colonel Griffith relaxes back into his chair. I feel a flash of pride. I've done my homework well.

"Did you ever wonder why the army'd design a plane big enough to fit a platoon of elephants?"

Lily answers first. "No, sir. But the army must have its reasons."

Griffith actually smiles this time. "Good answer, Miss Lowenstein." He pauses, takes a glance at a file on his desk, and frowns.

"Ever see one?"

"No, sir," we reply.

There is an honest-to-God twinkle in the colonel's eye when he asks, "Would you like to?"

"Sir, yes, sir!"

I break into a face-splitting grin before I can stop myself. I look at Lily, and she's grinning, too, so I guess it's okay.

With another nod, Colonel Griffith rises from behind his desk and leads us out to a hangar at the back of the airfield. In those few moments, with the crisp blue Alabama sky above us and the comfortable sound of transport planes overhead, I feel as if I could float away on a cloud. Or worse, wake up and miss all the excitement.

The B-29 is the largest plane I've ever seen. It's a mastodon compared to the little ATs and P-50s we've been flying. Daddy's little Jenny would fit in the belly of this plane three times over. This is the real deal. Flying her will take skill, strength, and a little bit of luck. My fingers tingle just thinking about it.

Lily claps once in delight.

I can't help but ask. "What kind of bombs are they carrying in this thing?"

At last, the wrong question. Griffith frowns at me. "None, as of yet. Damn thing's harder than a mule train to fly." He stops in the shadow of the starboard wing and turns to face us.

"Let's get down to brass tacks, ladies. I've been reading your records. So have a few other folks up top. You've got three days to learn how to fly this thing."

Lily and I blink at him. "And then what?"

The colonel glances up at the wing soaring over his head. He looks small compared to the big bird. And if he looks small, I know I look like next to nothing.

"And then," he says, "we'll see."

For one whole day, Lily and I sit in a private office in the officers' compound, poring over the specs of the plane. Nobody bothers us. Just a few flyboys who haven't seen girls in a while "accidentally" knocking on the wrong door. The way we figure it, the B-29 must be experimental. It wouldn't be the first time a WASP had flown something new or difficult. Planes like the PT-19 were considered too powerful until a WASP showed she could handle it. Lily and I are determined not to let the WASP down. We study every inch of that plane, and when our eyes get crossed and start seeing double, we have dinner with the colonel in his private dining room and get a ride back to the boardinghouse off base where women visitors have to sleep.

On the second day, Lily and I head back to the hangar to visit the B-29 in the flesh, so to say. With a work light in one hand and the manual in another, we explore every detail. It's a big plane, like I've said. It takes all day. But by the end of it, we're both pretty sure of ourselves, sitting in that giant cockpit. Colonel Griffith joins us to explain the next day's procedures.

Normally, there'd be a crew of eleven that goes up in these birds—pilot, co-pilot, three gunners, and a crew to handle targeting and dropping the bombs. Since tomorrow is just a lap around the airfield, Colonel Griffith wants us to take three of his men up with us.

"So you get the real feel of her," he says. We both know it's so the men can take over if the girls choke.

✈

"This is fine," Lily says from her piloting chair. We've both strapped in and are getting comfortable with the reach of the controls.

"Oh, yes, it is," I agree. This is a big plane, and she's going to be heavy as a sack of wet sand to pull off the runway, but it's a treat just sitting here. No sirree, these two girls won't fail.

So far, our stay at Birmingham has been pretty quiet. There's all sorts of activity on the base when we drive on in the morning and when we leave at night. But nothing that involves us. That's why it's a surprise on the morning of the third day when there's a crowd out to greet us on the tarmac. It looks like just about every doughboy this side of the Mississippi has shown up. Colonel Griffith rides out to the hangar with us in a jeep. He's in full dress uniform, so you'd think he had planned the whole thing, but he sure looks upset at the sight of all those soldier boys.

"Aw, hell. Who called them here?"

"Sir?" Lily and I are in our zoot suits and pigtails—one of the privileges of being full-fledged WASP, no more turbans for us. I've got butterflies the size of eagles this morning, and facing the masses when I'm in my flying jammies doesn't help.

Griffith drops down in his seat. "Keep going." The driver takes us past the crowd of soldiers and into the hangar with the B-29. He drives fast, but not fast enough for Lily and I to miss one of the men shouting, "Another Widowmaker."

"Excuse me, sir, but what's going on?" Lily asks.

"Begging your pardon," I add. "But what did he mean by 'Widowmaker'?" Every WASP knew about the first "Widowmaker"—the B-26 Marauder, a plane that tended to crash on takeoff. I look the colonel in the eye and wait for an answer.

Colonel Griffith actually blushes. He takes off his hat and steps out of the jeep. A full thirty seconds pass before he turns to us.

"Ladies, you have twenty minutes to get in that plane and get it down that runway. We've got a crowd out there, and we might as well use it."

Lily and I exchange glances. I don't like not knowing what's going on, but this is the army. We don't have to like it. We just have to do what we're told.

Lily frowns at me, then shrugs. We both take a deep breath and start our flight check. While we're going over the wings, the rest of our flight crew shows up. Colonel Griffith, who has been pacing by the jeep like a daddy-to-be in a hospital waiting room, introduces them to us.

"Ladies, this here is Captain Hank Rhodes, Lieutenant Davis Warner, and Lieutenant Daniel Sparks."

We shake hands down the line. Captain Hank is a square-jawed, dark-haired man, about Thomas's age. Davis Warner and Daniel Sparks could be twins, except Warner has brown hair and Sparks is a redhead. They both have freckles, blue eyes, and wide grins. They can't be much more than eighteen or nineteen. But then again, I'm only twenty-one.

"We're the bombardiers," Sparks says once the colonel has returned to his pacing. "We'll be flying navigation and radio today in case . . . well. You can call me Sparky."

I know what the "in case" is. The bombardier's seat is in the nose of the plane. If we can't fly this thing, it's the worst spot to be in for an emergency landing. I guess I can't hold that against him.

"Thanks, Sparky. You can call me Jonesy," I say.

"I'm afraid I'm just Lily, but that'll do, too." Lily shakes Sparky's hand.

"Sparks, let the ladies finish their flight check. Everything's got to go perfect if we're gonna pull this off," Hank says. His voice is surprisingly high for someone with such a square jaw. He looks like Clark Gable without the mustache, but he sounds like Mickey Rooney.

"Thank you, Captain," I say, and Lily and I double-check the wing before moving on to the fuel line.

"Ready, Eddy," Lily finally says, checking off the last of our list.

I nod and open the door to the plane. Lily wheels up a stepladder. "Gentlemen first," we say. Sparks seems to like that. He chuckles, shakes his head, and climbs aboard.

The men settle into their stations in the compartment behind the pilot and co-pilot seats and we head out of the hangar and onto the runway with little fanfare. I'm surprised the colonel didn't have us leave under cover of darkness, he seems so displeased by the crowd outside. Then again, maybe this is what he really wants.

"I just had an idea, Lily."

"What's that? Fly us all to Acapulco for supper?"

"No. I mean, it seems to me the colonel is using us as an example. You and I both know that the army can keep a secret when it wants to."

"That's for sure," Lily agrees.

"Well, then, why do you suppose there just happen to be sixty soldiers with nothing better to do than watch us this morning?"

Lily frowns, then smiles. "Because they want to see what a girl can do."

I nod. "With the 'Widowmaker.'"

Lily grins. "Oh, boy. This should be a hoot."

"What are you ladies talking about up there?" Captain Hank has stuck his head into the cockpit. Lily and I put on our best innocent faces.

"Just the weather, sir. Now, go buckle in; we're about to take off."

We taxi into position and run an engine check, firing each engine separately from left to right. At full throttle, a B-29 engine will rattle your teeth. Lily and I grin at each other. This plane beats a Jenny any day. The engines work just fine, so I power all four of them up to a deafening roar. The plane jostles and shakes like a wild horse trying to throw a rider.

The green flag waves and I release the brakes to start off our long takeoff roll. B-29s take twice as much runway as smaller planes to get off the ground. We roll forward, gaining speed as the runway rushes beneath us.

"Ready, Lily?"

"Ready, steady," she says with a nod. I flex my arms, preparing for liftoff.

The end of the runway looms before us. I grab the stick and pull. My muscles go tight, but the nose of this thing is barely budging. I grit my teeth. It's harder to lift than even I thought it would be.

"Ida?" Lily sounds worried. She's got her hands full with levers for the landing gear, but she sees me struggling.

"Got it, got it," I say. But I don't. Not yet, anyway.

And then, I do. The nose of the plane lifts so quickly, you'd think it was apologizing for reacting so late. We bob up into the air, a little wobbly, but in the air all the same. From there, we climb steadily and the engines smooth out from a bone-shaking roar to a sweet, steady hum. Turns out the B-29 is like a seagull, awkward and ungainly on land, but boy, it sure can fly.

Lily gives a little cheer. I hear it echoed from the navigation station by Sparky. When we reach our cruising altitude, I loosen up my arms. My biceps are sore, but in a good way. I guess all those years of picking up Otis Wilson's laundry finally paid off.

"Would you look at that?" Lily points out the window. The entire airfield is looking up at us.

"I bet their mouths are hanging wide open."

"I certainly hope so." We veer off on a wide loop of the air base. That's all Colonel Griffith wanted. A victory lap, so to speak. We circle the airfield two times for good measure. If only my daddy could see me. They used to say that colored folk couldn't fly, but look at us now.

Lily is in her own private world of smiles, too. It's a good feeling. All the hard work and training it took to get into the WASP is paying off in a lump sum.

"Smooth flying, ladies," Sparky says from the back. Without even turning around, I can hear he's all grins. I am, too.

"Thank you, Lieutenant Sparks," Lily says for me. I'm too busy lining up for the final approach. I take a deep breath.

"And now, for the tricky part."

"Landing gear, ready," Lily says. We've studied it every which way, and in the end it's the same. The B-29 has trouble landing. She tends to stall out and just drop. Some planes are too big to glide to a stop comfortably. That's why the army doesn't have more of them around. That's probably why they're calling it the "Widowmaker" on the ground. And that's exactly why we're here to fly it.

"Here we go," I say.

Suddenly, the plane lurches like an old drunk. The steady drone of the engines stops. When it starts again, it's too quiet.

"We've lost an engine," I say, trying not to panic. The plane wobbles. I grip the stick with both hands to correct it.

Lily says nothing, but the knuckles gripping the sides of her seat are white.

From the compartment behind us, somebody shouts. Someone else swears.

"Status, boys?" I call out. My voice is getting too high. I belatedly pull up from the final approach. We can't land. Not just yet.

"Davis is hurt. Got his hand smashed climbing through to the gunnery. What happened?"

I shake my head. "What the B-29's probably famous for. One of the engines stalled. We're running on three now."

"Number four's on fire," Lily adds. My eyes go wide, and I spare a quick look. Oily black smoke streams away from the right wing. I can't see any flames, but that doesn't mean they aren't there.

"That's just peachy," I mutter, and try to figure out what to do.

There's a shuffle, and Captain Hank appears between Lily and me.

"I think it's time I take over," he says. His eyes are on the airfield. The B-29 shudders around us. Limping in. It's only a matter of time before we lose another engine. Or the fire spreads.

"No." I stay in my seat. "No, sir. We've trained on stalled planes before. I know how to handle it."

237

For the first time, the look Captain Hank gives me isn't friendly. "Well, you may have noticed that the B-29 isn't just any old plane. I'm surprised your arms didn't give out just getting us into the air. I'll be hanged if I'm going to get caught in a crack-up just because some dame wants to prove a point."

"It's not our point, sir, it's Colonel Griffith's." Lily's finally found her voice. I'm glad because whether I like it or not, this plane is heavy and keeping her steady is like wrestling an angry gator. Any energy spent trying to convince the captain makes flying even harder.

Lily's right. It's enough to make Captain Hank hesitate. Before he can think of anything else to say, Lily picks up the radio and asks the tower for Colonel Griffith. I make a full circuit of the airstrip while they connect us to the radio in his jeep. With any luck, the engine fire will burn itself out. Or we'll land first.

"Captain Hank," I say, trying not to grit my teeth. "Please strap yourself in. We don't want any more injuries, do we?"

Captain Hank looks at me, then at Lily. He shakes his head, crosses himself, and returns to his seat.

"What should I tell the colonel?" Lily asks.

I shrug as much as my grip on the stick will allow. "Tell him the truth."

Lily looks at me, and her brown eyes are wide with worry. "What is the truth, Ida? I've seen you land a pursuit plane in a stall before, but this? We're burning."

For an instant, we both see it, Patsy's Valiant blooming into flames, like some terrible flower.

I take my eyes off the view in front of me just long enough to read the look in Lily's eyes.

"Don't be stubborn, Jonesy," she says. "Be safe."

"Right." I don't say anything for what feels like forever. It's funny how danger can make time stand dead still. I think about the plane I'm holding up by sheer force of will and the four souls on board with me. For some reason, I think about Thomas, running up that country road, trying to get to a doctor before Death could get to Daddy. I think of Mama trying to keep me at home. Of Jolene trying not to tap her toes to the radio when Mrs. Wilson was in the house. Of Patsy never letting old Unhappy Martin tell her how to fly.

I take a deep breath and look at Lily. She's my last friend on earth right now. I'd never do a thing to hurt her.

"I can do this," I tell her. And as I say it, I know that it's true. "We can do this."

Lily looks at me a moment longer. The radio crackles.

"Griffith here."

Lily hesitates. She takes a deep breath.

"Colonel Griffith, this is Lily Lowenstein. We have a slight problem up here. Engine three's stalled out and number four's on fire. It's procedure to have emergency services waiting on the ground. If you want them. This is your show, Colonel. We'll do our job. We're coming in on the next circuit. Lowenstein out."

The radio lies silent.

"It'd be nice to have those fire trucks out there," I admit. "Just for comfort's sake."

Lily blanches. "You said you could do this, Ida."

I nod. "I can, I can. Still . . ."

I shake my head. "Aw, hell. Say a prayer, rabbi. We're coming in."

I don't know if Griffith has gotten the fire trucks out on the tarmac. I don't know if he's trusting we can land. My eyes are on the horizon as it lines up with the white lines down the runway. The plane is shuddering now as we drop lower. The men are silent in the bombing bay, probably straining their ears to catch what happens next.

What happens next is like nothing I've ever done in training. We drop from the sky and another engine fails.

"That was number one. But you're clear. No smoke," Lily says. One engine fire we can handle. I throw in the towel at two.

"Lily, I need your help," I say through clenched teeth. It's just too much. The plane is nose heavy and unwieldy. Lily undoes her straps, wraps one around her shoulder, and leans over the chair to help me. We groan with the straining of the wings. We pull for all we are worth. Silently, I swear, I scream, I pray.

And then we are level, and then we are landing. Too fast, too damned heavy and fast. All the weight in the nose of the plane smacks the ground with force. The tail of the plane almost spins, we're so top heavy and off balance.

"Hold it, hold it!" I grab Lily by the arm. She slips but keeps her hands on the stick. I stand on the brakes with both legs. Not too fast, not too fast, or we could roll.

The muscles in my legs burn. My fingers ache from holding the stick.

And then, we stop. We are on the ground, safe and sound.

"Look," I say to Lily. At the end of the tarmac, a single fire truck, lights off, trundles toward us, out of sight of our audience by the hangars.

Lily starts to laugh. I join her. We laugh until there are tears streaming from our eyes, down our cheeks. Captain Hank and his boys are on us in a second.

"They're hysterical, sir," Sparky says. That makes us laugh even harder. Captain Hank, who's had more experience with the hazards of flying and with the hazards of women, merely shakes his head and follows us out of the plane.

"Dames are crazy, Sparky. Don't you ever forget it."

"No, sir," Sparky says seriously. "I won't."

Chapter 23

Lily and I don't step off that plane until our knees stop shaking. Then we undo our pigtails. She fluffs out her hair and I smooth down my frizzy braids. We put on our reddest Cochran Cosmetics lipstick and walk down the steps just as cool as cucumbers. Captain Hank and Sparky follow, with poor Davis and his banged-up hand in between them. I notice he keeps his hand out of sight of the crowd.

Colonel Griffith is waiting for us. He shakes our hands with a grin almost as big as the B-29's wingspan and helps us into his jeep. Without a word to any of the men standing around, we head back to the colonel's office.

"They'll be talking about this for weeks," Griffith says. He's pleased as punch, I can tell. "The day two girls tamed the B-29. Corporal, get Dulles on the horn for me."

The jeep driver grabs the radio, squawks into it, then passes it to the colonel.

"Dulles, Griffith here. They did it. Damned if they didn't, with a bum engine, too. No. I'll give Cochran a call when we get to my office. But spread the word. We'll have no trouble finding pilots now."

Lily and I exchange glances. I shake my head. How can I be so proud at succeeding and feel so insulted at the same time?

"WASP aren't going to be delivering these bombers, are they, sir?"

Griffith looks at me. "Of course not, Miss Jones. This was

strictly to prove a point. You girls are a lot braver than most of the men we've got out there. They hear 'Widowmaker' and run the other way. But I got word the WASP had something to prove. And you did it, by gum, you didn't back down, even when the engines crapped out. Why, I'd buy you a drink if I didn't think you look too young. But the B-29 is back in business. Now maybe we can get this war over with."

Lily and I take the next jeep available back to our boardinghouse.

"How do you like that," Lily fumes. "Good enough to risk our necks for his stupid demonstration but not good enough to fly full-time."

I drop down to my bed and strip off my boots. "It's nothing new, Lily. They've been using the WASP to do dirty work since the program started. Testing planes that aren't fit to fly. 'If a girl can do it, so can a man.' That should be the army's new motto."

Lily paces the floor, hands on her hips.

"I wish there was something we could do. I don't know, write a letter to the president. Better yet, his wife. Anything. We can do so much more than they'll ever let us do."

I don't say anything for a long time. Lily's just finding out what I've been living with my whole life. She's never known what it was like to be hobbled by somebody else's rules. Suddenly, I've got a sorrow so deep inside of me, it hurts to breathe.

"Sacrifice," I say finally.

"What?" Lily stops in her tracks.

"I said, sacrifice. My grandfather told me that war is about sacrifice. We don't get any medals for the things we do. We don't get a parade when we go home. That's for the boys. And

I'm sure they'll deserve it. My brother deserves it and then some. But what my granddad didn't know is that women sacrifice all the time." I look up at Lily.

"You know what I mean. My mama's back home right now saving up bacon fat and counting ration stamps so her family can live another day. My girlfriend Jolene works her fingers to the bone cleaning houses so one day she can wear a proper dress at her wedding.

"My mama gave up her son to fight the war. And let her only daughter go, too. And your mother, too, Lily. That's a sacrifice that gets no reward. So why should we be any different? We're WASP, not military, not soldiers. They won't let us be. But you heard Griffith the same as I did. He thinks the B-29's gonna end this war. And that's all the reward either one of us will ever get. It's all the reward we need."

Lily sinks down on the bed beside me. Our khaki zoot suits look coarse against the fine crocheted bedspread. Our hands are rough, grease under the nails; our hair is still pinched and mussed from our flight helmets. We are not the girls we were a year ago. It's no wonder Jolene and I have nothing left in common. I'm a different person now, inside and out.

"Harry will come home," Lily says quietly. She laughs. "And we can get married. Oh, Ida, it all seems so unreal, so far away."

"It might be." I take her greasy hand in my own, the hand of my new best friend. "But when it gets here, you'll have earned every second of happiness you get."

"Both of us." Lily grins then, and the world is okay again.

"Wash up," she says. "We're going out for a steak dinner. Sky's the limit!"

We do what we can to look like pretty girls for the night.

Lily puts her hair in a bun, and I tie mine back with a ribbon. Our best dresses have survived being rolled up tight in a duffel bag for so long. Within the hour, we're presentable enough. Lily tosses her hair.

"Patsy would be proud," I say.

Lily grins. "Come on, war hero. Let's eat."

Our marching orders are waiting for us when we get back to the hotel. I kick off my shoes and lie back on my bed to open the envelope that was waiting for me down in the lobby.

"Hmm, I'm supposed to go to Delaware. They've got a shipment of Helldivers to fly out here."

"Mmm," Lily mumbles, but she isn't listening. She had two envelopes waiting for her on the lobby table. The thick white envelope with her orders lies untouched on the other bed. She sits with her back to me, reading the second letter.

"What is it?" I sit up to get a better look, but no luck.

"It's a telegram," she says at last. She looks at me, and her eyes are bright. "From Harry! He's back in the States, Ida, but only for a short time. Stationed in Pennsylvania. That's on the way to Delaware, right?"

"Sure, if you want to cut north early, I suppose."

"Oh, good!" She jumps up and runs a little circle between the beds, like she literally doesn't know which way to turn. Finally, she just runs to me and gives me a hug.

"Ida, we're getting married!"

I pat her on the back. "I know, honey, you've talked about it since the day we met."

Lily pulls back, shaking her head. "No, no. I mean now! In Pennsylvania. It's all arranged with the base chaplain. He's even got a copy of the Torah! Now, I know it's not the same

245

as a rabbi or a real wedding at temple, but I'll take it, Ida, I will! I'm going to be Mrs. Harold Cohen. I can't wait!"

Fortunately, Lily's orders have her flying with me to Delaware. We make things difficult for the travel dispatcher, taking the long way up to Pennsylvania to get to Delaware, but it's worth it. The roundabout trip puts us in Chicago for a day, long enough to buy a proper veil and an easy-to-fly-with white satin dress.

"Is it all right, Ida?" Lily asks me in the dressing room of Marshall Field's.

"You look like a million bucks, Lily. Trust me. You'll knock Harry's eyes right out of their sockets."

"I wish I could," Lily says. "Then they'd have to Section 8 him and he could stay home with me."

"Right, and blame you for ruining his career as a surgeon." I grin.

She smiles back at me in the mirror. "I just wish Mother was here. But she wouldn't approve of this. Running off to join the WASP was bad enough, but coming home married? What a scandal! Never mind that she approved of the engagement, threw a big party and everything."

She turns to me and sighs. "Mother always used to say, there's nothing a good girl can do after midnight that she can't do just as well beforehand. Only, instead of midnight, it's this war. I suppose we should wait until the war's over, but I don't want to anymore, Ida. The longer I wait, the more I think the war will never end."

I shrug. "In that case, you'd better grab your coat."

+

We arrive at the base in Pennsylvania early on a Tuesday morning. Just before breakfast, I get my first look at Harry Cohen.

246

Harry is exactly Lily's height, with wavy dark brown hair trimmed neatly above the ears and neck and a way of making his stiff army officer uniform look casual. I like him instantly. He meets us on the tarmac as we come off our transport. Lily flies into his arms faster than a pursuit plane.

"Yes, Harry, yes, Harry, yes!" Lily exclaims, kissing him all over his happy little face. I stand by our duffel bags and try to give the lovebirds a little privacy. It's a long time before they take their eyes off of each other long enough to introduce me.

"Ida Mae Jones," Harry says, pumping my arm like he's jumping a car engine. "I've heard a lot about you from Lily's letters. What a pleasure!"

"The pleasure's all mine, Harry. If I can call you Harry."

"Better yet, call me brother. Lily says you're like a sister to her. So that makes us all family. Or it will in a few minutes. Let me scare up the chaplain and we can get this show on the road!"

The base chapel is nothing more than a clapboard room off the side of the administrative building. I help Lily get dressed in the lavatory. Someone's donated a handful of daisies picked from the officers' club lawn to serve as a bouquet. Twenty minutes after landing, we walk down the aisle.

There's an altar with a cross on it, but a Star of David has been placed alongside it for the ceremony. One of Harry's friends, another doctor named Mike, stands next to me as a second witness. The chaplain is a young fellow going prematurely bald. He mops his brow and stumbles through some of the Hebrew wording.

"This is my first wedding," he explains. "I'm a base chaplain. I . . . well, it's an honor to perform this service today."

No matter how the chaplain does, it doesn't seem to matter. Lily looks like she's hearing angels sing, and Harry's got the same stars in his eyes. It's the look Mama used to give Daddy before he died. A look no one's ever given me, but I suppose I'll recognize it now if they do, and I'll marry them straightaway.

"You may kiss the bride."

Harry pulls Lily into a clench that would do Clark Gable proud. We clap when the chaplain introduces them as Mr. and Mrs. Harry Cohen.

"What now?" Lily asks.

"Now it's time for the reception, of course!" Harry takes us over to the officers' club for an early lunch. We toast the happy couple and feast on salmon and boiled potatoes.

"And now I've booked us the bridal suite at the best hotel in town," Harry says when we've finished polishing off the plate of cookies that served as a wedding cake.

"Harry, that's impossible! We've got a plane to catch in less than an hour," Lily says.

Harry blushes. "Actually, I've had a look at your pilot. He seems a little flushed. Mikey here's going to give him a thorough examination before he can take off. We might even prescribe a night's bed rest."

"Is that so, Harold Cohen? You wouldn't be abusing your Hippocratic oath, would you?"

"My dear lady, I've sworn to do no harm. And what could cause more pain than missing out on my own wedding night?"

"Ida, do you mind?"

"Of course not. A night in a fancy hotel sounds swell. Enjoy it, Lily."

"Oh, that's the other thing," Harry says, blushing red again. "It's not so much a hotel as one of the officers' houses on base. He owes me a favor and he's out of town, so I have the key."

"A real home?" Lily asks, sounding more excited than she did about the hotel room.

Harry grins wide. "Only the best for my baby."

It looks like Delaware will have to wait.

Chapter 24

The honeymoon lasts all of eighteen hours and then the new Mrs. Cohen and I head to Delaware, where they have us testing newly repaired planes and running the occasional VIP from base to base. Not as glamorous as the B-29, but testing the planes can be a challenge, especially when the repairs don't take. By the end of the eighth week, we've used our parachutes so much that we've both joined the Caterpillar Club ten times over. And then we get our new marching orders—report to officers' training school in Florida.

"What does it mean?" Lily asks. She's just washed her hair, a once-a-week luxury for someone with curls like hers. It takes more time to comb them out than we usually have in a day. I've been plotting our next mission. The map lies forgotten on the bed.

"It means Uncle Sam is finally making honest women out of us." I slap the letter against my thigh. "Hot dog! This is it, Lily, the whole kit and caboodle. Officers' pay, officers' honors. Maybe we can even get them to go back and give Patsy a proper commendation."

"And a military burial," Lily adds. She squeezes her hair dry in a thick white towel. "Now Mother will have to take me seriously. I'm not only a married woman, but I'll also be an officer in the United States Army Air Forces." Her eyes sparkle at the thought, and I know mine must be sparkling, too.

What will Mama say when she finds out? Or Thomas, for that matter? They'll be so proud. At least, I hope they will. I'm not saying that it's permanent, but until the end of the war, this is a whole new life for me. One I've earned. I feel a grin take up residence on my face, and it looks like it's there to stay.

"Ida?"

"Yes?"

"Harry and I got married almost two months ago."

I roll my eyes and collapse back onto the bed. I cover my face with a pillow. "I know, Lily, it's been one month and twenty-four days. You said so yourself this morning. You'll count off every day for a year if someone doesn't stop you soon."

Lily frowns at me. "That's not what I mean. Do you remember how they used to keep track of our monthlies back at Avenger Field?"

"Boy, do I." It was something we all hated, having to tell Doc Monserud when we had our periods. Patsy said it was to make sure none of us was pregnant, but the Doc claimed it was to see if women with cramps could still fly. I'd never been so embarrassed in my whole life as I was that first month.

"Once a month," Lily says absently, pinning her hair up off her face.

Suddenly, I get a funny feeling. "Why, Lily? What's going on?"

Lily says nothing. Just keeps pinning up her hair into a bun. When she's finished, she comes and sits next to me. Her hands fumble in her lap.

"Ida, it's been two months and three days since my last period."

We both sit there, staring at each other. My travel clock ticks loudly on the dresser across the room. We both speak at once.

"I think I'm pregnant."

"Congratulations!"

"Oh!" Lily gasps, her hands flying into the air. "Congratulations? Ida, you're not mad? I thought you'd be angry with me."

"Of course not, silly. You're married. That's what married women do, have babies."

Lily throws her arms around me and hugs so tight that her terry-cloth robe leaves little damp impressions on my khakis. Tears fill my eyes. "I'm so happy for both of you. Harry's gonna be thrilled."

"He will be, won't he?" Lily claps. "Oh, I can't wait to tell him. But it's got to be in person."

"Well, is he still stateside? We could swing by on the way to Florida."

Lily pauses, her shirt pulled over only one arm. "Ida, I can't go to Florida. They'll make me take a physical. They'll send me home."

I close my eyes for just a second, to let it really sink in. "I know." I realized it before she said it. She looks so happy. Otherwise, I could never let her go. "Well, I guess I'm flying the rest of this war without you."

Lily smiles at me and touches my cheek. It's an odd gesture, coming from her. "You looked like my mother when you did that," I tell her.

Lily smiles even wider. "You know, Ida Mae Jones, you were born to be a WASP. You'll do just fine without me."

Dear Jolene . . .

I stop with my pen above the paper. I don't know what comes next. All I do know is that I've never felt so alone in all my life since Lily left.

"Do you think you'll ever go home, too?" she asked me when I dropped her off at the train station this morning in a borrowed jeep. "Your family would love to have you back."

"Yeah, I suppose they would," I told her. "But . . ." There were so many things I couldn't say, so I said nothing. Lily shook her head.

"Like I said, born to be a WASP. Well, stay safe, Jonesy. And good luck."

"To you, too, Lil." We hugged for a long time. I promised to come visit, and then she was gone.

Chapter 25

I'm not a drinking person, but if I were, I'd have a drink right now. I leave my letter to Jolene unwritten and head across base to the officers' club, where I can get a cold Coca-Cola and enough warm bodies around me not to feel quite so alone.

This is Delaware. The air is damp and cool here. It smells like a summer rain might be on its way. I put my hands in my pockets and walk faster.

The door to the OC swings shut behind me.

"Well, if it isn't Jones."

"Leave it open, we could use the breeze."

I peer into the afternoon gloom and see a blond head turned my way. It's Audrey Hill, my old squadron leader from Avenger Field.

"Audrey!" I rush toward her and our vigorous handshake becomes a hug.

"Hey, it's just like the old days at the Avengerette," Audrey says. She's smoking a cigarette and looks tired around the eyes, but I almost believe her.

"You remember Randi?" She nods to the sultry redhead on the next bar stool, the same one she introduced me to that first night out on the town during training.

"Sure, I do. Men are the enemy, prepare to do battle," I say echoing our last conversation.

Randi gives me a big smile. "Those were the days, weren't they?" She shakes my hand.

"Say, where's the little gal you used to fly with . . . Lori, was it?"

"Lily." I feel the temporary ban on my blues vanish. "Well, believe it or not, she got married and she's having a baby."

"That's a one-way ticket home for sure," Randi says.

"Good for her," Audrey exclaims. "See, Randi, that's the way to do it. Find yourself a good man and settle down."

Randi snorts and I realize there's rum in the Cokes they've been drinking.

"That's what I've been trying to do," Randi replies.

I fidget with my shirt buttons. "So, what sorrow are you girls drowning today?"

"Sorrow?" Audrey laughs. "No, we're celebrating. You should join us." She offers me the empty stool beside her. I sit down, glad of the company, even if it is tipsy.

"Barkeep, a drink for the lady," Audrey says, sounding more than a little like Patsy.

"Coca-Cola, please," I add.

When the drink comes, I hold it with both hands. I don't seem to know what to do with them otherwise.

"So, what are we celebrating?" I ask again.

"Operation Overlord, of course!" Audrey says, waving her glass in the air. "Don't tell me you don't listen to the news."

"Or the scuttlebutt," Randi adds.

"Well, sure," I reply. "But—"

Audrey interrupts me. "Nine hundred thousand men storming the beaches of France. We've broken the Nazi line, Jones."

"The war will be over in a week," Randi exclaims.

"Hear, hear!" Audrey salutes her. "Bloody messy, though," she adds more quietly. "We lost as many as we took."

"So I hear," I say. It's an understatement. Six thousand dead, and they've not finished counting the wounded. I take a sip of my cola. It's gone flat. Quite a celebration.

"I ferried some of the fighters they used in the cover mission," I tell them. It was an Allied gamble that had worked. Eisenhower faked an attack up the coast of France with phony tanks and a few real planes. Hitler had his eyes on the northern town of Calais when the Allies stormed Normandy to the south.

"Congratulations, Ida." Audrey clinks her glass against mine. "Consider yourself a toe in the boot that kicked Hitler's arse."

For the first time, I smile. "I'll drink to that."

"Now, what else should we celebrate?" Randi asks. She looks like she's celebrated plenty enough to me. But I remember my good news.

"Oh, I know. I'm off to Florida for officers' training. It looks like Jackie Cochran's going to get us militarized after all," I announce.

I raise my glass, but the other two girls just laugh.

"Aw, Jones, don't you know it's just a show?" Audrey asks. "Like Eisenhower's fake attack over Dover. Jackie thinks if she gets us into planes, the army will keep letting us fly."

"Well, they have, haven't they?"

"Sure, but not without a lot of complaints. Besides, you heard Randi. Scuttlebutt says if all goes well in France, this war will be over soon. The minute those soldiers come home, it's all over for us WASP."

"It's not," I insist. "The men will come back, sure. But we've proven ourselves. We're some of the best pilots they have. We fly safer than any of those flyboys."

"Sister, you're preaching to the choir," Audrey says.

Randi nods, her face pressed up against her glass. "What a world, what a world."

"We've *been* to officer school, Ida," Audrey explains. "And look at us . . ." She waves her glass around the sad little room. "We're lower than a couple of first-years. It's enough to make you wonder why we ever even signed on in the first place."

I think of my handkerchief, back in my room, and wonder if I'll be tying on another worry knot soon, but I say nothing. I sip my flat Coke. It tastes like metal on my tongue.

"Go to Florida, have a good time," Audrey suggests with a pat on my shoulder. "Get a tan. It's fun. But if you wake up one day and you're not an officer in this man's army, remember that's not why you signed on originally. It might take some of the sting out of it."

Randi rouses herself from where she's slumped against the bar.

"I did it for love." She burps softly. "For the love of my daddy. Dear old Dad. He always wanted a boy."

Audrey nods. It's like I'm back at Slidell Methodist, listening to the women testify. "I did it for a fella," Audrey confesses. "My ex-fiancé, who said I didn't 'have the head or the heart' to fly."

"You showed him," Randi says, slapping her pal on the back.

"What about you, Ida Mae Jones? Whatever made a pretty little thing like you want to go to Sweetwater?"

I blink. It seems so obvious. "I wanted to fly, and my country needed me."

Audrey smiles and shakes her head, like I've missed the punch line to some huge joke.

"Really? Did the army ask for you? Did President Roosevelt send you a letter requesting your help?"

I shake my head and look at my glass. Once upon a time, I thought that's how it would be, but it wasn't.

"They did for the Originals, you know," Randi offers.

"Nancy Love's girls, the WAFS." I nod. "So I've been told."

"Well, then, Jones, why'd you come?"

I frown at the glass in my lap. It's getting warmer by the second, ice cubes melting away to nothing.

"I came because I knew I could do it, and it beat sitting at home collecting silk stockings while my big brother was getting shot to bits in the Philippines."

"Aha! *Cherchez l'homme,*" Randi cries triumphantly.

"Yes, indeed." Audrey salutes me this time. "Isn't it funny, ladies, how there's always a man at the bottom of everything we do? Why, I bet men do all kinds of things that don't involve women."

"Like fight wars." Randi hiccups.

My head aches now, almost as much as my heart did when I came in. What Randi says used to be true, but not this time. Men are not the only soldiers in this fight. Whether they like it or not, whether the army wants it or not, we're WASP. And we're helping to end this war.

I finish my Coke and stand up. "The way I see it, ladies, we're still in this one. Now, if you'll excuse me, I've got to go see about a flight to Florida."

"To Florida!" Audrey and Randi clink their glasses together.

"All right, Jones," Audrey says to me. "Safe journey. But don't forget, we came to fight a war. When it's over, go home like a good little girl. Uncle Sam promises he'll call us in the morning."

I leave them laughing at each other in the officers' club. It's colder outside than early June should be, and it leaves me feeling uneasy. That feeling doesn't go away until the next morning, as I board my plane to Florida.

Chapter 26

It's just like Avenger Field all over again, only this time, the buses are real Army regulation unit and the air is thick and humid instead of bone dry. Patsy and Lily aren't with me, either. There are other WASP here, of course, even a few faces I recognize from Sweetwater and the places in between, but the most familiar face is one I least expect.

"Ida! Ida Mae Jones!"

Not many men know my name in Florida, especially since it's only the first day of training. But a man is calling it out, clear as day, across the green paths between administrative buildings. I glance at my watch. I'm early for class, so I turn around and look for the source of the voice.

Walt Jenkins comes jogging across the quad toward me, a warm grin splitting his handsome face. I feel a flush rise in my cheeks. It's good to see him. I'm just surprised at how good.

"Instructor Jenkins!"

"Ida," he says, falling into step beside me. "Please, it's Walt now."

"Of course . . . Walt." I blush again just saying it to his face. I clear my throat. "What brings you to Florida?"

"Same thing as you, I'm guessing. Officers' training?"

I blink. "But you're a civilian. And you already work for the army. Why would you enlist?"

"Drafted is more like it. We're full to the top with flight

instructors, thanks to you girls being so damn good at your jobs. So, it was officers' school or the infantry. They still need men there."

My blood goes a little cold. Being a foot soldier is as good as being dead in Europe or the Pacific. "You're a smart man, Walter Jenkins."

"Why, thank you, Miss Jones."

Unlike flight school, officers' training is coed. Simply not enough women to set up a whole new school, I guess. Walt Jenkins and I are in the same class. We reach our classroom and still have a few minutes, so we sit on a low brick wall and enjoy the warm breeze that is only slightly cooler than the hot still air. His shoulder brushes against mine and I want to lean against him. Somehow, it feels right to be by his side.

"I'm glad to see you made it down here," Walt says. "And I was proud of the work you did on the B-29."

I feel a little tingle of pride. "You heard about that, did you? Lily Lowenstein was my co-pilot. Couldn't have done it without her."

We nod and wave as more classmates arrive. One of them is Nancy Howard, from Sweetwater, the troublemaker from my barracks that Patsy was so very good at staring down. I haven't seen Nancy since graduation, but she still looks like she's trying to be Bette Davis. She smiles wide and bats her eyes at Instructor Jenkins before sitting on the other side of him. I feel a little territorial twinge in spite of myself. Nancy Howard strikes me as something of a man-eater.

"Well, Walter Jenkins. I heard you'd be around here."

"You ladies can't have all the fun," he says.

Nancy laughs loudly. "Fun, right. The WASP bill is gonna

get killed in Congress next week. I'd rather spend my last days as a WASP in the air."

I lean forward to look at her. "So what if the bill doesn't pass? I mean, we won't be officers, but we'll still be WASP. They need us." Or, more likely, I need them. Without the WASP, this life, my life, is over. It's back to Slidell and Jim Crow for me.

Nancy smiles, and it reminds me of the sand sharks Grandy used to pull from the Gulf of Mexico. I don't smile back.

Walt shrugs. "This is war, ladies. Anything can happen."

Anything can happen, he says. I make it through my first week of officers' training easily enough, but I wish it felt as good as I thought it would.

"Why so thoughtful?" Walt asks me one day after class.

I shrug. It's another beautiful Florida day, and all I can think about is how the fields must look back home, stripped of their early summer berries. I wrote a couple of letters to Mama and finally some to Jolene, but all I got back from her was silence. Too much was said for a few letters to wash away. Inside my pocket I absently finger the knots in my handkerchief, one for Patsy, one for Jolene. I'd miss the WASP if they were gone, but right now, I miss my family.

"Just feeling worn down, I guess."

"What? War's not much fun anymore?" he asks with an impish grin. I can't help but laugh. It turns out Walt Jenkins is very easy to be with when he's not an instructor.

"Yes, you could say that."

Walt gets a serious look on his face. "Well, what happens after this is all over for you? Do you have someone overseas you're waiting for?"

"No, nothing like that. My brother was fighting, but he's home now, injured but alive."

"That's good." We keep walking, and I realize we're not really going anywhere. After so many charted courses and timed flights, it's pleasant to be aimless for a little while. Walt smells like sunshine and Ivory soap. It reminds me of laundry drying on the line at home.

"What about you? You must've left a family behind when you started teaching in Sweetwater."

Walt shrugs. "That would be Mrs. Jenkins, my mother. We were already living in Texas. I took her in when my dad passed away. She's the reason I didn't enlist in the first place. Teaching at Avenger was just as patriotic, and safer, too."

"Will you go back to Texas, then?" We sit down under a eucalyptus tree, its fat green leaves filtering the light into a dappled blanket overhead, scenting the air with their sharp menthol smell. Walt sits close to me; our arms brush against each other as we lean back in the shade.

"Not likely. Life down south starts to chafe after a while. I flew charter planes out west before the war. There's a chance I might get to start my own business there."

"That's swell, Walt." I smile at him. "Imagine, flying for a living. What a dream."

It's Walt's turn to smile. "I'll need a few pilots, you know."

I laugh. "And here I thought we had more pilots than we could use."

Walt shakes his head. "I'm serious, Ida. You're a damn good pilot. Why not come fly for me?"

I blink, surprised and pleased, but mostly surprised. "Well, for one thing, I'm a woman. You might be fine with that, but will your customers be? And then, of course, there's . . ." I fall silent. There's the fact that I'm colored, and I never quite planned beyond the day I got into the WASP. Not once did I really think this charade of mine would outlast the war, let alone last a lifetime.

Walt Jenkins is looking at me, and his eyes are the same blue as the sky above. He's a handsome man; I've said it before. But now I'm really seeing it. I remember our one awkward dance at the Avengerette last year and the whispering it caused. And I remember the rough warmth of his hand in mine, pulling me out of the Link that first day, making me feel safe. He's leaning toward me, so close I can smell the warm, sharp scent of his aftershave. Close enough to kiss me . . . A part of me wakes up a little and says, Mrs. Walter Jenkins, co-owner of Jenkins Air.

I blush furiously, and Walt notices it.

"What was that?"

"Nothing. I . . . I have to go. But thanks for the walk . . ." I stand up and brush off my slacks. "And the talk . . . and . . . bye."

I walk back to my dorm as fast as I can, but not so fast that I don't hear him call after me, "Think about what I said."

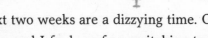

The next two weeks are a dizzying time. Officer training fills my days, and I find my fingers itching to climb into a plane every night. I remember what Nancy Howard said. If these are our last weeks as WASP, she'd rather spend them flying. And so would I. But instead, I sit behind a little desk and look more and more the way Deatie Deaton did the first time I saw her at Avenger Field. Like a woman who got chained to the ground when she should be in the sky. At first, I try to avoid Walt. There's no future for me in his world, no matter how much I'd like there to be. But it's impossible in a class our size. I get butterflies every time I see him, worse than any preflight jitters. The name Mrs. Walt Jenkins continues to float through my mind, but not seriously. No, it could never be thought of seriously.

On June 21, the WASP bill gets put to the vote. We lose. With one week left in officer training, I'm being sent back to Delaware to continue my ferrying duties. I show up at my last day of class to say goodbye to Walt. I'm not the only WASP being sent home.

"Call me, Ida Mae." Walt pushes a slip of paper into my hand. "Or write. Just promise me you'll get in touch after the war."

I smile at him a little weakly. Maybe all he's interested in is my flying after all.

"Sure, Walt. Just stay in one piece, okay?"

We're in front of the administration building where our classes are held. All around us, the other girls are saying good-bye to each other. It's like a scene from a train station. I reach out and shake Walt's hand. It's as warm as I remember from our dance.

"Ida," he says, his voice so low I almost don't hear him. "Promise me."

When he kisses me, it's so quick, so brief I don't know how to react. Just a brush of his lips against my cheek. Then he lets go of my hand and walks away. I stare after him until the crowd is all I see. I can still feel his hand in mine. This is what Jolene was talking about. What Lily felt about Harry.

For the first time in my life, I feel like I'm flying with both of my feet firmly on the ground.

✈

My transport doesn't leave until nightfall, so I have the afternoon to myself. I borrow a car and make the drive to visit Patsy's grave. The entire way, I think of Walt and of Grandmère Boudreaux, and I finally understand why she never came down our driveway. In New Orleans, maybe in the rest of the world, too, white women don't have brown-skinned grandchildren any more than colored women get to have white husbands in Texas. Life isn't black and white. It's black *or* white. Anything else is just a mess.

I reach the orange orchards that lie south of Patsy's cemetery. The trees are sweet with fruit that hangs like bright little suns beneath the shining leaves. I breathe in through the open window. It tastes surprisingly sweet and bitter at the same time. It's a familiar feeling.

I park at the base of the small knoll that marks the beginning of the graveyard and walk the rest of the way through the thick St. Augustine grass. It feels like a spongy carpet beneath my feet.

A simple headstone marks the grave of my friend. Seeing it makes my eyes sting. PATSY "CAKEWALK" KAKE. THE SKY IS HER HOME. I sit down next to her grave and rest my forehead on the cool, cool stone.

"Hiya, Patsy. It's me, Ida Mae. I mean, Jonesy. Gee, no one calls me that anymore. I'm just plain old Ida or Jones. Lily's left us. She and Harry got married on the fly, and she's gonna have a baby. If it's a girl, I'm guessing she'll name her after you. Don't tell Harry, though. He wants it to be Hannah, after

266

his grandmother." I smile, remembering how worried Lily was over this prospect.

"Oh, you'd be jealous, though. Lily and I got to fly the B-29. Boy, was that a devil to lift off. And it lost two engines on the way down, but we flew her all right just the same."

I fold my arms beneath my head to make a pillow against the stone. "More news about the WASP, too. They won't make us military. There's a good chance they won't make us anything at all soon, from what everybody's saying. And I don't know what I'm going to do, Patsy. Lily has Harry, but my best friend from back home isn't even speaking to me. And then there's Walt Jenkins. Don't laugh, but I think he likes me. Maybe even more than a little. But I don't think it will work . . ."

I can feel the tears streaming down my face, blurring the sunny sky above me. "The thing is, Patsy, I'm not who I've said I am. Not what I said I was. I mean . . ." I can't say it. I don't want to say it.

Because I don't feel Negro any more than I feel white. I'm just me. Ida Mae Jones, and I'm blue. Santiago blue. Take away the uniform and I really am nothing at all. Take away the wings and I'm someone else's. Someone's maid, someone's daughter, someone's sister, and maybe even someone's wife one day. But I can't have one life without giving up the other. I can fly and be with Walt or be with my family and never fly again. It's not fair. Mama and Jolene tried to warn me. Lies breed lies. If I go with Walt, I'll have to keep on lying. But I can't imagine going home again, cleaning the Wilsons' house for the rest of my days. That feels like a lie, too.

I cry for a long time over Patsy's grave, but she is not the only one I'm mourning. I miss the three of us, Patsy, Lily, and me, and I miss Jolene and Mama. I cry for Thomas and his shattered leg, for Abel, who's still got to grow up in this kind of world. I cry for my daddy and for Walt, for lying to my new friends and leaving my old ones behind. I cry for everything I've ever known and loved.

And then, somewhere at the end of all that crying, I fall asleep. And I dream of a deep blue sky. And when I wake up, I remember what Audrey said to me at the officers' club three weeks ago. When this is all over, remember why you signed on in the first place. And I do remember, exactly what I told Patsy when she asked me why I was there. I came to fly.

I take my handkerchief out of my pocket and gently pull apart all of the knots. It's a wrinkled mess now, like a topo-graphical map of sorrowful mountains, not even clear enough to navigate by. I smooth it out, trace my fingers along the blue threads that spell out my name. I wipe my eyes, stand up, dust myself off, and walk back down through the spongy grass to the car.

I've promised Walt a letter, and he'll get one when this war is over. I'll tell him the truth. He'll have to decide what to make of it for himself, what to make of me. Lily was right—I was born to be a WASP, and that is part of who I am. But I was also born to be Ida Mae Jones, that skinny little colored girl who learned to fly her father's airplane over the fields of her hometown. That old Jenny is still waiting for me, under a sheet in a dusty barn. And Mama, and Grandy, and my broth-ers are waiting, too. Maybe even Jolene. I just have to find the right words to say to everyone. But there will be time enough for reckonings when this day's work is done. For now, I'm traveling light.

The drive doesn't take as long on the way back, which is good. Because no matter how much of it seems like it's over, I've got my duty, and this is still a war. Whatever the future may bring, for the time being, I still get to fly.

Epilogue

In August 1945, a crew of American flyboys piloted the B-29 Superfortress over Hiroshima, Japan. A plane that, until Lily and I flew it, they were too scared to fly. The payload was something new, something called an atom bomb. Thomas heard from a friend that it blew down half the city like paper, men, women, children and all. Hitler dead in his bunker, and Japan brought to its knees like that . . . How something so awful can bring about peace, I'll never know. Any more than I'll ever figure out how the army disbanded the WASP. But here we are.

I dropped a letter in the mail today, a letter to Walter Jenkins, formerly of the U.S. Army. The war is over. All of our boys can finally come home. Their girls are waiting. Right where they left us, with a whole lot of sky in between.

Author's Note

Flygirl is a fictionalized account based on the true story of the Women Airforce Service Pilots and their heroic feats. While I took great license with events and names, here are a few factual notes.

First of all, the acronym *WASP* is both singular and plural. Since it stands for "Women Airforce Service Pilots" with an *s*, to add another would be redundant!

The WASP program was part of the United States Army, as was all other military aviation during the first two world wars. The United States Air Force, as we know it today, was not established as a separate branch of the military until 1947.

The two WASP actually assigned to learn how to fly the B-29 were Dora Dougherty Strother and Dorothea Johnson Moorman. The plane they flew was dubbed *Ladybird* and they flew several trips, from Alabama to New Mexico, before the army put a stop to the "stunt." In the story, when Lily and Ida overhear a soldier dub the B-29 "another Widowmaker," he is referring to the accident-prone B-26 Marauder—another plane the WASP proved they could successfully fly.

In 1941, Russian women began flying military missions for their country. By the end of the war, they had earned the name "Night Witches" for their nighttime bombing runs against the Nazis. The United States Air Force did not allow women to fly combat missions until the mid-1990s.

Bessie Coleman, Jackie Cochran, Deatie Deaton, General

Hap Arnold, Doc Monserud, and Nancy Love are all real people. Read more about them in Amy Nathan's wonderful book, *Yankee Doodle Girls,* Marianne Verges's *On Silver Wings*—to which I owe the wonderful WASP song the girls sing on the way to the airstrip—and many of the other reference books listed on my website, www.sherrilsmith.com. For more information on the true WASP, visit the WASP website, www.wingsacrossamerica.org, and the National WASP WWII Museum at www.waspmuseum.org.

Hazel Ah Ying, the Chinese WASP who inspires Ida Mae to join, was one of two Asians accepted into the WASP program, Maggie Gee being the other. Hazel was killed in the line of duty. There is rumored to have been one Latina in the program as well, but I have found no name to put to the rumor. There is no evidence that any African-American women were a part of the WASP program, either by "passing" or being accepted regardless of their race.

Janet Harmon Bragg is an African-American pilot who was rejected by the WASP program solely on the basis of race. She is the inspiration for the woman Ida Mae sees at the recruitment office. Mrs. Bragg learned to fly at Coffey School of Aeronautics in Chicago, where Ida Mae's father attended. She went on to teach aviation to schoolchildren, but it was not her primary career.

Of the women who flew in the WASP program, most went back to their lives on the ground—housewives, secretaries. A few found work as flight instructors, and some moved to Alaska, where the new frontier had room for female bush pilots.

The WASP bill was finally passed in 1977, under President Jimmy Carter's administration, officially militarizing the

WASP. The women who had served their country more than thirty years before, who had been forced to pay for their own funerals when denied military benefits, were finally given honorable discharges and full veterans' rights. At long last, the passing of the WASP bill paved the road the women of the WASP had forged years before, making way for the hundreds of female pilots of all races in the United States military today.